Elizabeth

Book One in the Set Free Series

Corina Yoder

D1502712

Elizabeth by Corina Yoder

Publishing Support by: Fistbump Media, LLC
Cover Photo/Design by: Regina Yoder
Editing by: Heather Lindenmeyer

ISBN: 978-1515356813

First Edition

Dedication

This book is dedicated to my husband, Wayne,
who is my best friend and favorite person to spend time with.

It's fun doing life with you.

Chapter 1

Elizabeth let out a deep sigh that sounded as if it went all the way to her bones. She stood on the covered bridge and looked around the sprawling Essenhaus grounds. She absolutely loved this June weather. It was a warm 80-degree day with no humidity. As a gentle breeze blew big fluffy clouds across the sky, Elizabeth could hear a small engine airplane flying overhead somewhere in the distance. She took in a deep breath and practically inhaled the sunshine. She was thankful that she had an extra hour before the Essenhaus workers' van would be leaving to take the Amish employees home.

Elizabeth Miller loved her job working as a waitress at the Das Dutchman Essenhaus restaurant in the small town of Middlebury, Indiana. She enjoyed serving food and getting to know her customers. She had worked at the Essenhaus for the past three years. She was originally hired to bus tables and had cleared and cleaned hundreds of tables before her promotion to waitress. At first, she was unsure if she could wait tables. However, though a shy girl by nature, Elizabeth became more confident over time. By exercising her skills of speaking to total strangers, she had transformed from a timid teen into an eighteen year old who looked forward to meeting new people. She loved collecting the tips. She realized that the friendlier she was and the better job she did at serving, the more money she would make. She loved the challenge.

The name *Das Dutchman Essenhaus* (the Dutchman's eating house) fit the restaurant perfectly. Delicious Amish home cooking was served there. Most of the people who came there to eat knew some facts about the Amish. However, today, more customers than usual had asked Elizabeth if she "dressed up like this for work" and what her prayer cap was. She explained to them that she belonged to an Amish church. She told them that wearing the cap is something the Amish practice daily because of the verses in the Bible, more specifically 1 Corinthians 11, which discusses women covering their heads to pray.

1

She understood that they were just curious and was happy to answer their questions.

The waitress who was scheduled to work the evening shift had accidentally come in to work an hour too early. Elizabeth was relieved that she did not need to start a new round of customers. She had worked hard that day, and her feet were tired. The restaurant has an area called "The Front," where customers can order off the menu; but today, she had worked in "the Barn" area and served family-style meals. For this meal choice, the waitresses would bring their diners all they could eat. Elizabeth thought it was fun to watch the eyes of new customers when she set the big trays of food on the table. The broasted chicken was always served, and the second meat choice was between roast beef, baked steak, or ham. The meal also included big heaping bowls of dressing, green beans, noodles, mashed potatoes and gravy. To top it all off, for dessert, each diner also got to choose a piece of pie from a list of over twenty kinds of pies made from scratch in the bakery. People just couldn't stop raving about the food. Almost every time she worked, she was asked one question: what's your favorite kind of pie? Without hesitation, she always answered in the same way: peanut butter pie. In her opinion, there wasn't another pie that even compared, and this answer helped her to sell a lot of these pies. Her customers often stopped in the bakery to purchase a whole pie before they headed for home.

It had been a good day at work, but as it came closer to the time that she had to go home, she started feeling very overwhelmed with grief. She decided this would be a good time to go on a walk out to the covered bridge. She stopped in the bakery to tell her friend Martha where she was going and to ask Martha if she could make sure the van driver knew that Elizabeth needed a ride home today. Martha understood that Elizabeth just needed to get some fresh air and time alone.

Elizabeth walked as fast as she could without drawing attention to herself. She did have to pass a few people sitting on the benches beside the sidewalk, but she just looked down to avoid making eye contact.

She didn't feel like talking to anyone. She bypassed the gift shops and walked across the yard in front of the Essenhaus Inn. The weeping willow tree was swaying in the breeze, and the windmill was turning with the wind. Up ahead she could see the covered bridge, and once she finally got away from the strangers' gazes, tears just gushed out of her big blue eyes. At first, she tried to hold them back. Finally, though, she just let them run down her cheeks. She put both hands across her heart and just let her body sob it out. No one could see her; but by now, she really wouldn't have cared if anyone did.

Today she really missed her parents and wished she could rewind the clock to last February, before the tragic buggy accident. It was almost four months ago, but it felt like yesterday. In the blink of an eye, she lost four members of her family.

The day of the accident, her dad had gone to the horse sale at the Sale Barn in Shipshewana. Her mom and two younger sisters had gone along to do some shopping in town. According to the police report and a few people who had witnessed the accident, a driver had run a red light at the 5 and 20 intersection and hit their buggy, instantly killing all four. The Miller family of seven became a family of four in Heaven and three left behind on Earth. At the time of the accident, her dad, Dan, was 42; her mom, Sarah, 41; Elizabeth was 18, her brother Karl was 15; Willy was 13; and her two youngest sisters were 12 (Barbara) and 10 (Katie).

The tragedy was so shocking that at times, she struggled to believe that it was actually real. But today, she believed it to the point that the pain could have almost knocked her on the ground. She had found a bookmark that her mom had created with the verse "Be strong in the Lord, and in the power of His might." She read the verse often, and she knew it was only on His strength that she was making it through the hard days. She wished she could go home and eat supper with the whole family tonight; that was the thing she missed the most. The supper table was where they always all talked about their day, and no one ever got out of the meal unless one was away from the home or sick. It was a habit and a non-negotiable practice in their home, as well as most Amish homes.

She had never imagined at eighteen years old that she would be left without parents and would be raising her two younger brothers on her own. After the accident had happened, the Amish church was very supportive and immediately came to help her in any way possible. None of them could, however, replace her family, and she counted herself thankful for all the good memories of her childhood that remained. Thank God memories live on. She wished she would have more pictures of her family, but she only had a few that she had taken with a camera she had bought after she turned sixteen. A lot of Amish would prefer to not be photographed because they believe the Bible teaches in the Ten Commandments that photography would fall under worshipping graven images.

Elizabeth was allowed to have a camera as long as she wasn't a member of the church, and she was respectful to not take a lot of pictures of her family. But now she was glad she had a few and cherished them deeply. One day, her two younger sisters got ahold of her camera, and Elizabeth still laughed at the hilarious pictures they had taken of each other with their kittens. She didn't feel like having the pictures constituted worship, so she didn't feel guilty for having them. Especially since they were gone, she saw the pictures as the most precious thing she had left of them. Second place to the memories, of course.

Life had been so full of good memories: camping, horse sales, and traveling. The last trip the family went on had been to Niagara Falls, and Elizabeth grew to treasure that final trip they had all been on together.

It seemed surreal that she and the boys were orphans. She had never known anyone Amish at her age who became an orphan, so she wasn't even sure what would happen to the three of them. She had told her Uncle Mose that she would rather take care of the boys herself than to move in with another family. It wasn't that Mose wouldn't have been happy to have them move in with his family. But Elizabeth just didn't want to be a bother. Time would tell what would happen to them. In the meantime, she knew a lot of friends and family were praying for them and cared deeply. All of them would be glad to help out in any way they could.

Dan Miller, Elizabeth's father, was a classy business man who always looked on the bright side of life. He tended to see the best in people and situations and was also very smart. He could very simply figure out what to do in any given situation. He had worked for years in the RV factories and raised horses on the side. But before his passing, Dan had been raising horses full time for a few years and had become very successful in this endeavor. For recreation, in the summertime, he enjoyed planning weekends to go camping at Twin Mills with the family.

Dan was a big believer in family time. His all-time favorite topic to talk about with his younger friends was how they raced ponies. He had stopped racing ponies himself when he joined the Amish church; but he was still intrigued with horse racing and loved to follow the big events in the newspaper. One could say his interest in horse racing was in his blood the way some people follow sports. Out of respect for the Amish church, he had laid that down and dedicated more time to spend with his family. He loved God and always led family prayer after a long day. It was something he made a priority and practiced regularly.

Sarah Miller, Elizabeth's mother, was a sweet, kind woman who kept the family running smoothly. She had a gift of hospitality and enjoyed having guests over for dinner. There was normally a plate of cookies ready to take to someone. She never wasted her words, and the things she said carried a good amount of weight. She was highly respected in the community, as women often asked her advice about anything from gardening to teething babies. She loved to garden and tended to several of her own flower gardens. She had started planting her flower gardens into quilt patterns and found great enjoyment in that activity. In the wintertime, when she didn't have garden work, she pieced quilts together. She loved choosing the designs and colors and coming up with new and creative quilts but did not actually enjoy the quilting as much as sewing the quilt together, so she often had quilting parties and invited other Amish ladies in to help her. Every year, she would make one to give away to some kind of benefit.

Elizabeth was glad her mom had taught her so much about cooking and canning because she was much better prepared to be in charge of those responsibilities when she compared herself to some of her English friends, as some of them talked about watching TV late into the evening and then sleeping until noon. The thing she wasn't prepared for, however, was to be in charge of raising two teenage boys. If her two sisters had survived the accident instead, she might have better known how to raise them.

She really missed her sisters and thought about them often. Over the years, Barbara and Katie never wanted to be separated. People often talked about how they were like two peas in a pod. They had such carefree spirits. In the summertime, when they were out of school, the girls used to help their mom with garden work and housework, but at least they always had each other. They would giggle and laugh and have fun. They soon figured out that if they goofed off too much, their mom would split them up and make them work separately. They had learned to stay focused and work hard to get time off to play together. If they knew they would be allowed to bike to the neighbor's pond to swim, the work got completed in a hurry. Elizabeth often wished the girls would have been born closer to her age, but she was happy the girls had each other. Barbara and Katie used to love coming into Elizabeth's bedroom and looking at her belongings. She didn't mind it unless she was trying to read a good book. She remembered shooing them out of her room at times, and now she'd give anything to have them pester her.

Elizabeth held her hand up to her heart and wiped the tears again and again. She just kept saying...."it's too much, it's too much, it's just too much."

She felt intense pain in her heart for the loss of the family members who had died, but the two who really brought out the deepest heart wrenching concern was for her brothers. She felt like part of all of their hearts had died, yet they were very much alive.

The boys were staying busy since the funeral, so she was not sure how they were actually feeling about everything. Karl spent a lot of time with a few neighbor men and Uncle Mose taking care of the animals. He often talked to Elizabeth about the farm and the chores but didn't say much about his feelings. Sometimes she caught Willy deep in thought and wished she could know what he was thinking about. At age 13, he still needed parents around, and it was more than her heart could take.

She reached up to wipe more tears and realized how hot her tears were. She thought to herself...*these tears don't come from a cold heart. They are coming from a broken heart.*

At least I'm not cold hearted. She actually chuckled a bit. She felt better after she had just let herself have a good cry.

She decided she'd better start walking back to the restaurant since she didn't have a watch and was not sure of the time. She smiled at the ducks swimming around the pond with their little baby ducklings. She again breathed in a deep breath of fresh country air and thought about how grateful she was for the opportunity to work at the restaurant. It was a blessing to have the Essenhaus job to go back to after the funeral because at least at work, one area of her life felt the same. The workers were like a second family and the restaurant a home away from home, so it felt like she had a bit of a normal routine in her otherwise upside down World. When she was at work, she would sometimes forget about everything and just get caught up in her customers and the food orders. A few times she had actually caught herself thinking...*I wonder if there was anything Mom wanted me to pick up in the bakery today.* Her mom loved the crème-filled long johns and sometimes would ask Elizabeth to bring a dozen home. It was hard to believe that her mom was no longer at home.

All of a sudden, Elizabeth looked up and saw Martha walking briskly toward her. "There you are! I was just coming to get you," Martha said. "The van is ready to go."

They hurried back to where the driver was parked as the last three workers boarded the van. Martha didn't say anything about the still-visible tears and gave her a compassionate smile. Some of the others noticed Elizabeth's tear-stained face as she got into van. She quickly looked away but could tell what they were thinking....*poor thing.* She didn't like to be thought of in that way and much preferred the compassion she had seen in Martha's eyes. She knew Martha was not pitying her but rather praying for her.

She couldn't get home soon enough.

Chapter 2

The minute Elizabeth opened the door when she got home from work, she was met with a pleasant surprise. The boys told her to shower and change as soon as possible because they wanted to ride their bikes to Mose and Carrie's house for supper. How could Elizabeth say no? Mose, their dad's brother and the uncle whom they were all the closest to, made for such good company. Elizabeth, in all honesty, felt pretty tired from work and letting her emotions get the best of her just a bit earlier. But as soon as she heard about the supper invitation from Carrie, she found herself re-energized and thought, *God knew that I just wanted to eat as a family tonight.* She was also relieved that she didn't have to cook. So off they went.

The two-mile bike ride went quickly, and soon they were sitting around the table eating Hay stacks, laughing at the stories Mose was telling about a raccoon that he had caught in one of his traps. Mose told such outlandish stories, and his wife Carrie always laughed the most at his escapades. Sure, some of the adventures seemed exaggerated, but they sure were entertaining. It felt wonderful to be at their house for the evening. When Mose and Carrie's younger children started getting fussy, signaling it was their bedtime, Elizabeth and the boys thanked Carrie for the supper and said goodbye to their cousins. They didn't have any main roads that they needed to bike home on, but as the sky grew darker, they were still cautious and watched for cars. They had always been careful when they rode their bikes on the roads; but the accident just reaffirmed the need to also be aware of the drivers who might not be paying attention.

The three made it back home safely, but they still had to enter a dark house and light the gas lights. It was something they were accustomed to doing over the years, but it was not as easy as flipping on electric switches.

Elizabeth told the boys she was tired and was going to go to bed. They had no idea that she had emotionally fallen apart at the covered bridge earlier in the day. They normally saw her as strong and level-headed, and she preferred they didn't realize how weak she felt at times. As Elizabeth nestled down under her big quilt, she took in a deep breath and let an equally deep breath out. It had been a hard day but a good day. She could hear horses' hooves click against the pavement and buggy wheels grind out on the road. A breeze blew the curtains gently into the room. She just loved this Northern Indiana June weather. She wished she could capture it like a firefly and keep it bottled up. *If only the weather could stay like this all summer*, Elizabeth thought. She shuddered at the thought of winter time and thought back to the day of the accident.

February 15th started like any other day, the only unusual part being the girls having a day off school and wanting to go along to Shipshewana with Dad and Mom. Dad needed to go to the horse sale, or at least he wanted to. He didn't always need anything at the sale, but he sure loved to socialize there. It was also normal for him to walk out having made a new friend or two. He was a very outgoing talker who loved people.

Mom told Barbara and Katie that she would take them to the fabric store to get some new dress material for their spring program. The last conversation Elizabeth heard the girls having was over the big decision of purchasing the same fabric (for matching dresses) or getting different colored fabrics. She never got to find out what they had decided because the Essenhaus work van drove in the lane to pick her up. *Have a good day!* Those would be the last words she would hear her mom and sisters speak.

"You too!" Elizabeth replied as she hurried to grab her coat and walk out to the van. Her dad had just finished hitching up the horse and was tying it up at the hitching rack so he could go inside to get Mom and the girls.

As he passed Elizabeth on the sidewalk, he gave her a big smile. "See ya! Have a good day."

She knew the twinkle in his eye came from knowing he was going to get to spend the day at the horse sale.

As she lay in bed, she thought about those last words. *Have a good day!* It was just something the family always said to each other. She found it kind of interesting that those four words would echo their way into her memory. In the solitude of her bed, she thought, *I hope I can live in that thought for the rest of my life. It seems like those words give me a choice.*

Though it started out like a normal day in the Miller household, February 15th ended in chaos and devastation. Elizabeth arrived home from work around 3:30 in the afternoon and was sitting at the kitchen table looking through the mail when she noticed a red truck driving extremely fast down the lane. She quickly jumped up and looked out toward the barn wondering what the maniac driver was trying to prove. *Nobody should drive in anyone's lane like that, much less a total stranger,* she thought. The truck doors both flew open, and two men jumped out. She saw that the person getting out of the passenger's seat was her Uncle Mose. She saw the men both run inside the barn, and as she looked out, she saw her brothers, Karl and Willy, coming out of the barn.

What is going on? she thought. *What would Mose need during the day and in such a rush?* So she grabbed a coat and scarf and headed outside to find out.

As she got closer to the boys and men, she quickly discerned that something was *very* wrong. The man who had been driving the red truck was wearing a paramedic shirt, and he looked at Mose to see if he was supposed to tell the children or if Mose would. They both hesitated.

Mose looked at each of their faces and then looked down at the ground. He finally spoke, though very softly: "I don't know how to tell you this, but your dad and mom and the girls were in an accident on their way home today."

He paused for a second, though what he said next hit all three Miller children like a strike of lightening.

"None of them made it."

No one moved. Time just stood still. No one knew what to say. This could not be real.

The paramedic cleared his throat: "There was no suffering for any of them. A man had run a red light and broadsided the buggy. They were all killed instantly."

He went on, attempting to reassure, attempting to soften the life-changing blow. "They would not have even had time to be scared." He paused again. "I'm so sorry for your loss."

Elizabeth and the boys were in such shock that they couldn't even cry. They just numbly looked at Mose in disbelief.

Mose mustered up strength to continue, "I know one of the EMTs and so did your dad, so he came and got me. I had to identify all four of them, and I do not want any of you to go to the accident site."

Karl looked up with a challenging *why not?* written all over his face. He didn't say it out loud, but Mose knew what his fifteen-year-old nephew was thinking. Mose just shook his head and said, "No, Karl, I'm not going to let you go there."

The next few hours were a whirlwind. Van drivers galore started transporting people, neighbors biked over, and the house filled up with family and friends in no time. Amish people sure know how to be there for each other when hard times hit. Elizabeth's body went into autopilot mode, shrugging off any grief-related fatigue for the time being. Somehow her brain told her feet when to move.

The next three days were busy. The bishop and deacons helped Mose and the children make the funeral arrangements. The bishop asked John Plank if they could have the viewing and funeral at his place. John was asked to host since Amish people do not have church buildings. They have church in their houses or sheds, and they take turns "having church." They only congregate for church every other Sunday, and they sit on backless benches. The benches are hauled from one house to the next in a big wagon called the *bench wagon.* They all decided since John's farm was next door to Dan's farm that it would be convenient for the family. John had a big woodworking shed that would hold a lot of people, but that also meant his business, Plank's Cabinet Shop, and all his employees would all be off work for the next three days. It was a big undertaking to say yes because not only would they need to prepare for it, they would also need to host two nights of viewings (funeral wakes). After the viewings, on the third day, John would also have to host the funeral services and serve a meal for everyone who attended the funeral after the burial. The neighbors and friends all helped as much as possible. All did their part, but the main burden was still on John and his wife. They had dearly loved Dan and Sarah, so they were glad to help their children. At the same time, however, it would be difficult for them to focus on all of the big tasks at hand. It was as if a big knife had been stuck into their hearts, so they almost had to just shut off all emotion to the death of their friends in order to make it through the next three days.

An Amish man from Nappanee who heard about the tragedy hired a driver to bring him to Mose's house. He presented Mose with a check to pay for the four caskets that a local Amish man had built. The caskets, though basic and simple, were not cheap, and Elizabeth could not have been more grateful for the man who picked up this entire expense.

As was custom among the Amish, the viewing hours were from 3 to 5 P.M. Then everyone stopped to eat and had viewing again from 6 o'clock to whenever the last people went through the visiting line. Elizabeth, Karl, and Willy dreaded this time so much, as they had to sit for hours shaking hands with people. The relatives sat with them to make it easier, but that also made it take longer because there were more hands to shake. Some of the big strong men shook their hands really forcefully, almost in a harsh jerking motion, and some of the women just lightly touched hands. The children knew a lot of faces that came through the line, but many were total strangers. The majority of the people were Amish people, and they would often whisper something about extending their sympathy. Most English people would say they would be praying for them. As anyone would expect, a sad, serious atmosphere permeated the room. There was no laughing or smiling. Most of the women and girls were dressed in black or dark colors. The men had on black suit coats and white shirts.

On the last night of the viewing, the color arrived, one could say.

Two of the teachers from the public school that the girls attended showed up with about seven young girls and a few of their moms. When they stepped inside the shed, the teachers and moms weren't sure where to go or what to do. An Amish man explained to them where to sit until it was their turn to view and go through the line to shake hands with family. They looked uncomfortable and out of place, but they were also intrigued to see into the life of some of their students. They all gave Elizabeth a big hug and whispered how much they were going to miss the girls. One of the little girls said, "Katie was my best friend. She was always nice to me."

The girls reached into the caskets and patted their friends' hands, whispering how they looked like sleeping princesses. A couple of the girls had brought little gifts, so the teacher told them to give them to the Amish man who was standing by the caskets instead of placing the gifts into the caskets. He gave them a smile and put the gifts on a nearby table. *This is the first time I've ever seen anyone bring gifts to a deceased person,* he thought to himself.

Mose had known that his brother had a lot of English horse and pony racing friends, but he was not prepared for the number of them who had obviously been deeply impacted by Dan's life. The first group of them came in wearing cowboy boots and jeans. When they stepped inside the shed, they took off their cowboy hats and carried them. Mose couldn't believe how they all just unashamedly let the tears run down their faces. These were tough, strong, chiseled cowboys. As they reached Karl and Willy, a few of the cowboys actually started sobbing pretty loudly since the boys and the cowboys knew each other very well. It was the first time in the few days that Elizabeth saw Karl and Willy let themselves cry. They had been holding it in and were truthfully still in shock. None of this seemed real or truthful, even though they knew it was.

The second group of horse friends was made up of important-looking business men with expensive suits, ties, and flashy rings. They didn't sob out loud like the cowboys had, but they all had tears that kept streaming down their faces like artesian wells. Mose realized that these men must have all loved Dan deeply, so Mose stepped outside to talk to them before they left.

Some of the men said they had flown up from Kentucky. They handed Mose their business cards and told him to feel free to call them, night or day, if he needed anything with the horses. Dan was the most gifted horse enthusiast they had ever met, and he had helped them with their most expensive racing horses. He made them a lot of money, and if there was anything the children needed money for, these men wanted to help. Before they left, Mose extended his hand in a formal gesture, but two of the men pulled him into a big hug and said again how sad they were.

Mose felt a sense of relief to know he had men he could call once he was ready to sell some of Dan's horses. For the first time since the accident, he felt a bit of his burden lightened. He had known he would need to make a lot of decisions about Dan's animals, and now he had some people willing to help instead of just taking advantage of the tragedy.

The day of the funeral was a bright, sunshine-filled day. The temperature was a bit chilly but uncommonly mild for February. The three children only had a few brief moments alone before they had to meet with the preachers and relatives to pray together before the service started.

Karl spoke up first and said in Dutch, "Let's get this over with." Both Willy and Elizabeth nodded their heads in agreement. It was high time that they be alone. Everyone's eyes had been on the three of them for three days. Everyone meant well, but it felt like they were fish in a fish bowl with everyone's eyes on them, analyzing their gestures, their facial expressions, wondering how they were doing. They just weren't accustomed to being the center of attention.

Elizabeth managed to smile at the boys when she said," I wish we could just go to the gravesite alone to say goodbye, but I know that's not how it will be."

For the first time in three days, Willy spoke up with frustration in his voice. "Why couldn't that driver have been paying attention?"

Karl added a few choice cuss words of his own in agreement with Willy. Elizabeth replied calmly..."I don't know, but I sure wish he would have been paying attention. He's in critical care at a hospital in Fort Wayne, but it looks like he will make it."

The rest of the funeral day was one big blur in Elizabeth's memory. The buggies were lined up as far as her eyes could see, carrying friends and family, as well as vanloads of Amish coming to pay their last respects. The main preacher delivered the sermon and discussed the free gift of salvation that we can have through Jesus; he spoke of Heaven and Hell, and the choice that each of us get to make on where we spend eternity. He made it easy to understand that the only way to Heaven was by believing in God's son, Jesus. When the service was over, everyone filed past the four caskets one last time; there were a lot of tears shed and looks of compassion directed at the three surviving Miller children.

That was exactly where Elizabeth stopped her thoughts for the night. She had not allowed herself to go to the memory of the burial yet, and she was not about to tonight, either.

Chapter 3

The first sound Elizabeth heard as she woke up the next morning was the wind chimes blowing gently in the breeze. It seemed as if God himself was playing music for her. It made her feel calm and like everything was going to somehow work out just fine. In fact, her mom had a collection of wind chimes and had always claimed they soothed her soul.

When Karl was fourteen, he worked part time at Lambright's Country Chimes and had created a wind chime to give his mother for her birthday. Every single wind chime that Lambright's created had a special name and a unique sound, like *Grandfather Clock*, *Big Ben*, *King David's Harp*, and *Sun Setter*. The newest series at that time, called *Enchanting Flower*, was advertised as "having captivating tones that would take you on a peaceful walk through a garden of flowers."

The chime that Karl had designed and assembled for his mom's birthday was a one-of-a-kind creation. He had chosen all the tubes himself and even had her name engraved on the wind chime catcher. She had been so surprised and loved it. The engraving read *Spread the Sunshine, Sarah*. That quote could not have described Sarah more perfectly. The whole family was pretty impressed with the fact that Karl had taken the time to design it and create it. And to top it off, like icing on a cake, was the fact he personalized it, too. Sarah had not realized that Karl viewed her in this special way, and needless to say, Karl's creation became Sarah's favorite wind chime.

Elizabeth lay in bed a few extra minutes, listening to the wind chimes before getting out of bed and getting dressed for the day. Karl and Willy had some extra chores to do before breakfast. Once the two boys had those completed, Elizabeth made them some biscuits and gravy. They were extremely hungry and both ate two extra helpings. As the Miller children ate breakfast, they talked a bit about their upcoming sale, which was only a week away. A big work day of preparation for the sale still awaited them. A lot of their relatives and neighbors would come to help with the sale.

After the accident, it had not taken her Uncle Mose long to get the bishop and deacons together to decide which five men would help organize the sale of the 20-acre farm and liquidation of the horse and pony business. Mose was grateful that Dan and Sarah had been good bookkeepers and that the records were all in order – every single pony and horse record, all the vet records, detailed shot schedules. It was all there and well kept. It would make the men's job a lot easier.

Mose and the men divided up the responsibility by the land and farm, the horse and pony business, the barn and house, the bills, and most importantly the children.

Initially, the children weren't sure if they wanted to move away from the home place, but as a few months had passed, they realized the enormous work load that it would take for them to stay. They also had to take into consideration that the farm wasn't quite paid off. Dan had been making good money and was wise in how he spent it, but he still had about seven years left on a loan to the Amish Bank. It wasn't a real bank, but it was a group of Amish investors who loaned money to their fellow Amish. After Dan's passing, the investors had met to discuss allowing the children to stay on the farm until one of the boys would be old enough to afford taking the mortgage on, but the investors felt that would not happen for at least four years and decided against it. It was a hard decision to come to because they knew the children wanted to stay on the farm if they could, but the men also remembered how Dan Miller's goal in life was to live debt free. Dan didn't even like to ask the investors for this loan for the farm, so they felt certain that Dan would not want a financial load like this placed on the children. So that was the final answer. The investors decided that there was only one thing that would make them reconsider, and only the investors in the meeting knew what that was. They decided if Elizabeth would get married in the next half year, they would consider letting Elizabeth and her husband take on the mortgage.

Elizabeth had no idea what the investors had said, but it wouldn't have mattered to her. A wedding was the last thing on Elizabeth's mind. She was not dating anyone and was not interested in anyone at this time of her life. Plenty of young men thought she was a gorgeous young lady, with her blond hair and blue eyes. She could tell these men thought she was cute, but she just pretended not to notice. Elizabeth was never rude to them but was far from the flirty type. Her dad always told her, "When it's the right guy for you, you'll know him when you see him." She didn't need to have a constant boyfriend like some of her friends. She wasn't going to date just to date.

Mose decided to temporarily honor the children's wishes and let them stay at the farm alone because he knew it would be healing for them. Quite frankly, it also helped the children realize it would be impossible to take care of it on their own. Mose could add extra work to his life for a season, but he had his own farm to take care of, not to mention that his own children missed him if he went over to Dan's too many nights in a row. In many ways, Mose was looking forward to having the sale over with. He never complained, but he wasn't joking around and telling as many funny stories as he normally would.

Joe & Amanda Kaufman, a young Amish couple, had come to the five men and asked if the children would consider trading properties with them. They had built a new house on a 5-acre plot of land only five years before. Along with the house being pretty new, the property also included a small barn to park the buggies in and a pasture for the horses. The home had three bedrooms and had been perfect to have as a starter home, but the Kaufmans had five little children and were quickly outgrowing the house. So one evening after work, the children took the buggy and went to see Joe and Amanda's house. As they got closer to it, they all scooted to the front of the buggy seats in anticipation. It gave a really good first impression, warm and inviting. Elizabeth immediately noticed the front porch, all the pretty flowers, two big hanging ferns, and − best of all − a porch swing. The boys weren't looking at the porch or the flowers but rather out toward the barn area. They were soon smiling from ear to ear. The barn and pasture were considerably smaller and would take a lot less work to keep up. Best of all, they saw a deer target set up out toward the woods. Both were big deer hunters and needed to practice their aim to be ready for deer season.

The children all had good feelings about the place, and Joe and Amanda showed them around the property. The inside of the house was bright and cheerful with a lot of windows. Elizabeth could tell that Amanda was a very particular cleaner. The entire house was impeccably clean, even though it housed seven people. The five little children were playing, but somehow their play area, full of toys, was still orderly and organized. Elizabeth loved the kitchen and could picture herself cooking in it. Everything looked brand new, even though she knew it had been built five years ago.

Joe showed them the wash house, which he had set up for his wife's convenience. He had even installed a wall mount heater and strung a wash line inside for her so that in the winter months, Amanda didn't need to hang the wash outside. A small kitchenette area with a stove occupied one side of the wash house so Amanda could do her freezing and canning without making her main kitchen all dirty. Joe had really thought of everything.

He did the same with the barn. It was built so the Kaufmans could hitch and unhitch the horses inside the barn, which proved to be so handy in the middle of a harsh winter season. The last thing he showed the boys was a custom built gun safe. On the outside it looked like a regular wall cabinet. No one could tell what it was until he slid a door forward, and inside the hidden safe was Joe's personal collection of shot guns. The boys were so impressed. Joe laughed and said, "I wish I could move this along with us, but I'm going to have to leave it with this place."

Both boys teasingly asked, "How about you just leave the guns, too?"

Joe just chuckled and replied, "You wouldn't *believe* how much I spent on these guns. I took this one to Montana a few years back."

Joe and the boys could have talked guns, hunting, and deer for hours, so Elizabeth had to be the one to interrupt their conversation to tell the boys they needed to get going. On the way home that night, they all were 100 percent in agreement that this move was a good idea. This new place had everything they needed. Actually, they all knew it had *more* than they needed and were so excited about the extra surprises, like the gun safe and the convenient wash house. They decided to drive over to Mose's house and make him aware of their decision.

Mose saw the Miller children's buggy coming in his lane. He held his breath. He hoped they would say they liked Joe's house and would give him the green light to move forward on the trading process. He whispered a short prayer. *God, please let this work out . . .* and that was as far as his prayer got when the boys burst in the door. Normally, they knew to knock and wait until someone answered the door, but tonight, they were just too excited. Mose was relieved to hear and feel their excitement. After all three left 45 minutes later, Mose retreated to his bedroom and knelt beside the bed. He soon began sobbing. All he could muster in Dutch was *thank you, God. Thank you, God.* His load was going to be lighter in a few weeks. He could now see the light at the end of the tunnel.

The day of the sale came before Elizabeth and the boys were mentally ready for it. But they were also tired of dreading it. The farm land was going to be traded with Joe and Amanda, but a lot of farm equipment, Dan's horse supplies, some household items, and a lot of tools were going to be sold on the auction.

On the morning of the sale, Elizabeth woke up before her alarm went off, so she took a long walk around the farm. She was going to miss the familiarity. These were her stomping grounds. She had lived here most of her life and had played for hours upon hours in the yard and barn. She could remember many hours spent in the garden with her mom and laughed at the memories she made playing with her friends. Time with her friends had recently been hard to come by since she had been so busy taking care of so much. She hoped a few of her friends would come to the sale.

Lyle Chupp, the Amish auctioneer, told Karl and Willy that he was impressed with how organized everything was and that he predicted the sale would be a real success. He appeared calm as if it was business as usual, but Lyle's calm demeanor sure didn't match what Elizabeth had overheard Lyle saying to Roger Miller in the wash house earlier that morning. Elizabeth had been getting something in the wash house when she heard the two men outside the window. She heard Lyle say, "I will need to really keep my head in the game today. It's hard to not just want to sit down and cry."

Lyle and Dan had been close friends for years, and she could remember evenings around campfires that the two families had shared at Twin Mills, talking and laughing late into those summer and early autumn nights. Lyle was more than likely remembering times that he had spent hours in the barn with Dan. The two would talk about horses and whatever came to mind at the time. Friends since their teenage years, Lyle and Dan would laugh hysterically at old stories that were not so funny to anyone else.

As soon as the sale started, Lyle knew he was there to make as much money as possible, so he whispered a silent prayer in Dutch, *God, I need your help today.* He was at the top of his game. The sale results were excellent. People seemed to spend extra because they knew the proceeds were helping out the children. But truth be told, buyers were purchasing quality items from the Millers. Dan and Sarah were known to be overly diligent in their care of their farm and property because they viewed all of their possessions as really belonging to God. They were just his stewards and always treated their belongings with respect.

Elizabeth was surprised to see the Essenhaus van workers drive in the lane on the morning of the sale. At first, she thought there had been a misunderstanding about her schedule. She soon saw that one of the van drivers had actually driven around the community on his day off to bring some of the Essenhaus cooks and their husbands to volunteer for the day. Those working at the food stand stayed busy the entire day and sold hamburgers and hot dogs until the last item on the sale bill was sold at around three in the afternoon. It had been a long and emotionally draining day, but somehow God had helped all of them through it.

As people started leaving for the day and gathering up their items, Elizabeth realized that she had not seen Uncle Mose all day long. That was strange because he had been working non-stop to prepare for the big sale. She had talked to Aunt Carrie a few times while Carrie was helping in the kitchen, so Elizabeth decided to ask her where Mose was at.

Carrie hesitated. "What do you need him for?"

Elizabeth stared at her aunt and then responded, "I didn't need anything. . . I just wondered why I didn't see him all day."

Carrie sighed. "He was here for about an hour this morning, and he just couldn't handle watching Dan's things being sold away to people like this. He said he was going to the gravesite, and I did not see him for the rest of the day. I really wish we would have cell phones at times like this. I would love to call him and check on him, just to know if he's OK."

"You wonder if who's OK?" Mose asked.

Carrie and Elizabeth turned to see Mose standing in the kitchen. They both looked surprised to see him and asked in unison, "Where'd you come from?"

Mose smiled and quickly replied, "My mother's womb!" Then of course, in true Mose fashion, he laughed heartily at his own joke.

Carrie laughed, too. "Ach, I think he will be just fine. He seems to be getting back to his ornery ways *very quickly*." Carrie's eyes showed relief. She had never seen her husband this serious for so long, and

Mose and Carrie's children missed their dad's fun ways. She was glad the temporary stress was going to be lifted as soon as they could get Elizabeth, Karl and Willy moved.

As the books were getting closed down for the day, Lyle and Mose started laughing and talking. It did the whole group a lot of good to hear Mose joking around. It helped Mose to hear Lyle say that Dan would be happy with how much money was earned that day. Mose didn't realize how much he needed to hear that. He had always admired Dan's business skills and had felt the burden of representing Dan well as they liquidated his possessions. This responsibility was a heavy load to bear, and Mose wanted to do a good job for the brother whom he wished he could raise from the dead and bring back home.

Mose had a few minutes alone with Lyle to tell him how the horse and pony sales had gone. He had complete confidence that Lyle would keep it to himself. It wasn't that Mose was embarrassed about it but rather he just didn't need the information spread like wildfire all over the Amish community. Mose knew he could trust Lyle.

Mose recalled the sale of the horses: "I was most concerned about getting top dollar out of the horses. I was scared if I would have just sold them myself that people could take advantage of the fact that we needed to get rid of them. I got a letter from one of the horse investors from Kentucky, and he offered to buy them all for a ludicrous amount. I called him and told him I would sell them for that price. Within three days, I had received the check in the mail. A week after the check came, a caravan of horse trailers arrived to pick them all up. So easy. Just unbelievable."

"Dan would be so happy to hear that," Lyle said. "It sounds like God is working out all the details."

CORINA YODER

Chapter 4

Though the day of the sale was a sad one for Mose, it was the most fun day Karl and Willy had had in weeks. They both had friends who had come to the sale with their parents, and it felt good to laugh and goof off with their buddies again. They had both been working pretty hard to get ready for this day, and on sale day, they were able to watch other people do the work. It felt like they got to be teenagers again.

Karl stood a good head taller than Willy and they looked about as opposite as two boys could look. Karl was the spitting image of his dad with striking black hair and deep brown eyes. He carried himself with confidence and had a magnetic personality that could carry a conversation with anyone. Willy looked more like his mom's side of the family; he had light dusty brown hair with green eyes and a splattering of freckles across his nose. People smiled just by looking at him.

As Fred Christner was leaving the sale with his boys, Jerry and Joe, he asked Karl and Willy, "Would you two like to go fishing with me and the boys next week?"

"Are you kidding?" Karl said. "Of course, we would! Are you going to Fish Lake again?"

"No, not this time. I'm taking the boys to Lake Erie, and we are going to be gone for three days. A whole van load is going, and we would have room for the two of you. We will be staying in a cabin that we like to go to about every year."

Karl told Fred that they would check with Elizabeth first. When Elizabeth saw Karl and Willy approaching her, she also noticed Jerry, Joe, and Fred not far behind and figured they had something up their sleeves. When her two brothers told her about the fishing trip, she was excited for them. She told Fred she gave her permission for the two to go and that she would make sure they were ready bright and early Monday morning to catch the van.

Elizabeth was happy to see the boys so full of excitement. They talked about it until they went to bed that night. It was nice that they could all have a new focus and that it was such a positive and fun focus. She appreciated the fact that Fred had invited Karl and Willy along. Fred was always finding ways to encourage others; he had the gift of action behind his compassion – not just saying he cared about people and their needs but actually following it by doing something, too.

Fred's son Jerry was Karl's exact age, and his son Joe was Willy's exact age, so over the years, they had often spent Sunday afternoons together. In the evenings, the parents would go pick up the boys and stay to eat popcorn together, so they had enjoyed a lot of long talks at Dan and Sarah's.

Fred was certain that Dan would want his boys to have some fun, and he knew that if the roles were reversed, Dan would have gone the extra mile to look out for his boys, too.

The following Monday morning soon came, and the boys were awake before the sun came up, hardly able to contain their excitement. The night before, they got out a Road Atlas and saw the route they assumed they would take. They had guessed it would take about three hours to get there. They were close to being correct because as the driver, Glen Miller, was leaving the town of Middlebury, the boys heard him say, "The GPS says it is 175 miles and will take close to 3 hours."

Karl and Willy had the time of their lives at Lake Erie. They both loved to fish, and the cabin they were staying in was massive. The basement had a ping pong table, and the back yard had a basketball hoop. In between fishing and cleaning the fish, they played hoops and ping pong, but the best part of all was the loft all the boys slept in. It had a big screen TV, so they watched movies until they fell asleep which was an unusual treat since Amish people do not own TV's.

Lake Erie is best known for its walleye but also has yellow perch, small mouth bass, white bass, and channel catfish, a true fisherman's paradise if there ever was one. The weather and water temperature were perfect for catching fish. The fishermen running the Fishing Charter told them that the week before had been really rough, and a lot of men got sick from the waves tossing the boats around.

The fishermen told the Amish men, "You either got real lucky, or your God was looking out for you. We have been told that Jonah story before, and we wouldn't want to have to choose which one of you young boys we'd need to throw overboard!"

The Amish group and the rough fishermen all just laughed. On land, these two groups might not have had much in common, but on this boat, their mutual love for fishing and being on the open water brought an instant bond. They had a fun three days together.

The very first day, the fishermen and the Amish had agreed on one thing: the fishermen did not like the Amish speaking Dutch to each other. They couldn't understand what the Amish were saying, so they told the Amish guys. After hearing what made the fishermen uncomfortable, the Amish men then told the fishermen they would make them a deal: no more cussing from the fishermen, and the Amish would agree to speak English at all times. The fishermen laughed loudly at this request but quickly agreed to the deal. And each group kept its end of the bargain.

The boys could have lived here forever, but after the three short days were over, it was back to reality for all, especially Karl and Willy. As the driver, Glen, dropped them off at home, he told the boys "We'll be praying for you".

The harsh reality was, as the Miller boys got home, they wished they could tell Dad all about this trip. They did tell Elizabeth, and she happily listened. But they knew Dad would have really understood how awesome it had been.

Both boys had enjoyed having Fred take care of and look out for them, just like their dad used to, but the two brothers handled it in polar opposite ways. As they went to bed for the night, they both lay awake in their separate bedrooms thinking about their parents.

At age 15 Karl was just mad; angry that someone had taken away his parents. He lay in his bed mulling over the fact that someone could be so careless, and it ticked him off that he had to grow up so fast. This accident had ruined his summer plans. He had planned on enjoying this summer because he knew in July, he was turning 16. He had decided he was going to have a car and his fun and freedom as soon as possible. Now this jerk who hit his parents' buggy had ruined everything. Karl missed having his dad around and hated being in charge of *everything*. His heart felt anger and frustration.

On the flip side of things, Willy, at age 13, was much more soft-hearted. It made him sad to come home and to be reminded, once again, that his whole family was not there. He lay in bed and started crying. He thought about the times that he was nice to Barbara and Katie and how much fun they had together, but he also remembered there were days he was kind of mean and had teased them. Remembering those times made him cry all the more. He wished he would have been a better brother, and now it was too late. He wished he would have always listened to Mom and Dad, too. Instead of remembering what a kind son he had been, he started remembering times he could have obeyed more quickly. It made him feel very regretful, and he cried himself to sleep.

The next morning, in a bedroom close by, Elizabeth woke up around four thirty. Her heart started beating really fast. *Oh, good. It was just a dream*, she thought. She had been dreaming that she was at the Essenhaus waiting on her section of tables, and she had gotten behind in taking her food orders and could not catch up. She felt like her legs just wouldn't move, and her mind couldn't think. It was an awful dream. She lay there wide awake and then started laughing at some of the other nightmare waitress dreams she had heard. One of her waitress friends would have repeated dreams of having all the tables to take care of, *in the whole restaurant*. It was so absurd, but in the dreams, these situations seemed so real.

She decided she might as well get her day started early since she was wide awake anyway. Today was the big moving day to the new house. The trade made it so much easier for both families because they were leaving a lot of the furniture with each of the houses. It would still take a lot of work to move the boxes with all their things.

An Amish Mennonite friend of the family, Monroe Keim, had offered to bring his truck and trailer over to help the children move. It would take a lot less time that way, as opposed to using only a horse and wagon. The men loaded everything from the barn and the shed first. Then the women and girls also helped carry box after box out of the house. Once everything was loaded, the men hitched up the buggy that Elizabeth and Karl owned. They only had one single buggy since the double buggy had been destroyed in the accident. They still had two horses but were in the process of ordering a new single buggy for Karl to use.

Everyone got a bit quiet as loading came to an end. Elizabeth held her breath as Mose stepped forward to give the next directions for everyone.

Mose said, "I want everyone to ride over to the new house in your own buggies. I will take both horses in Elizabeth's buggy for her. We will all meet over at the new house to help unload the truck. I want only the truck driver to stay here and to wait on the children, out in the truck. I want us all to leave and give Elizabeth, Karl and Willy as much time as they need to look around a bit without all of us here." He then looked at the children, "Once you are ready, you can ride over in the truck. Take your time; we all know this isn't easy."

Oh, how thoughtful, Elizabeth thought. She was appreciative for the help but also needed a bit of space at this difficult point in time, leaving her childhood home.

The three children walked through the house first. Room by room, they just tried to drink it all in. They didn't cry but rather were deep in thought. It looked different seeing their dad's desk gone and Mom's sewing machine missing from its place in the house. They were taking both of those things along. The barn had been swept clean since the sale, so they were used to having that space emptier for a few weeks already. The place that made them all stop the longest was the backyard fire pit. They all remembered lots of hot dog roasts in the backyard full of laughter and friends. They all walked over to the girls' play house and the tree house above it. They had all played in the tree house that Dad had built with the boys' help when they were little. The boys climbed up to the top and both just sat there a bit. They both looked at each other. Karl said very gently to Willy, "It's gonna be OK. This is really hard. But we are going to be OK."

As they walked out to the truck, they all knew a chapter of their life was over. It would never be the same again.

Goodbye, Home Place. Thanks for all the good memories, Elizabeth thought as she wiped a tear from her eye.

The children had kept referring to the new house as "the new house" and the farm as the "old place," so they had decided to name the two. The farm they were leaving would be named "the Home Place," and the new one would be called something else. They still needed to name it, and they figured it would become apparent what that name should be over time.

Before they drove out of the lane, Monroe said a short prayer for the children. "Heavenly Father, we want to thank you for helping the children get through the past few months, and I ask you to please comfort all three of them at this time. Please heal their hearts and take away the pain and help them as they leave this home that they really loved a lot. Help them make new memories in the house they are moving to. In Jesus' name, we ask all these things. Amen."

"So where to? Where is the new house located?" Monroe asked.

Karl gave Monroe directions and remarked, "We used to live four miles from Ship, but now we are two miles closer."

When they arrived at the new house, the buggies were just driving in the lane, so it was perfect timing. The women and girls all commented on all the pretty flowers and the big ferns hanging on the porch. Elizabeth just smiled. She knew Joe and Amanda could have taken all of those along but instead left them for her to enjoy. She opened the front door and found a note on the kitchen table from Amanda. It read...

"Elizabeth, Karl, and Willy,

Welcome to your new home. We hope you love it here as much as we did. You will be in our thoughts and prayers.

Elizabeth, I want you to know that we moved over to my folks' house this last week so we could get this house cleaned real good for you so you don't have to do a thing. I had some church ladies come help me wash down all the walls and wipe out all the kitchen cabinets, bathroom cabinets. We even did some repainting to make sure it was all ready for you.

I know you aren't going to be expecting this in your bedroom, but Mildred Mast brought over a quilt your mom made for a benefit. Mildred just didn't feel right selling it and wanted you to have it. We all know your mom was such a giving person, and we want you to let us give you this quilt. I realize it's often easier to give than to receive, but we hope you like having something she made to welcome you here."

Elizabeth stopped reading the note and ran into the bedroom to look at the quilt. *Oh, this one!* Elizabeth thought to herself, reminiscing.

This was my favorite quilt that Mom ever made for the auctions. Elizabeth remembered asking her mom if she could make her a quilt exactly like that one, but then the accident happened, and Elizabeth forgot all about it.

"Wow! I feel like it's my birthday," she said aloud.

What a surprise that was! At about that time, all the people started carrying in boxes, and Elizabeth started directing everyone on where the boxes needed to go. She tucked the note into her dresser and was going to read the rest of it later.

The work was finished in no time. The entire kitchen had been unpacked and everything in the boxes put into cabinets. The clothes were hung into the closets and placed in the dressers. The men carried in the hutch that had been a wedding gift for Dan and Sarah from Sarah's parents, and a couple of women carefully displayed the dishes and bowls. There were boxes of books to place in the bookshelves, and very soon, it seemed like the house had their own family's stamp on it.

Willy and Karl had a few boxes with notes on them, instructing the ones who carried these boxes into the house *not* to unpack them. The women chuckled and thought the little notes were funny. But they respected that there were things they didn't want their aunts snooping through.

When the aunts saw the boys a bit later, one of them told the boys, "I hope it's OK that we opened the boxes you marked to not unpack. We read your diaries cover to cover!"

The boys laughed, and Karl replied, "We know you are joking because we don't have diaries!"

Another aunt said, "No, we didn't open your boxes. But, good grief, how much duct tape did you wrap those with to make sure we got the message?" And they all laughed.

The aunts were in the kitchen talking when the subject of duct-taped boxes came up again. One said, "I can see why the boys did that. Practically everything in their lives has been seen and inspected by others. And we had to invade their space again with the move. It's understandable that they just wanted at least *a few boxes* that no one else needs to see. They are going to be ready for some privacy around here."

As the men were finishing unloading the last of the barn equipment, Monroe's phone rang. It was his wife. She told him that their weather alarm had sounded and that bad thunderstorms with hail were being predicted. After hanging up with his wife, Monroe checked his Weather Bug app on his iPhone. He then told the others, "It looks like there's a storm about two hours away. If we all leave now, we can all make it home."

With that news, the day abruptly ended, and the buggies drove out of the lane, followed by Monroe's big truck.

Elizabeth, Karl and Willy sat on the porch for a little bit before Willy and Karl went to the barn to make sure the horses were OK in their new surroundings. As they were walking through the barn, they heard a cat meow. The sound surprised them both. They looked around for a few minutes. Then lo and behold, underneath the stairs was a cat with five baby kittens.

They headed back to the house to tell Elizabeth, who just remembered to finish reading the note left by Amanda.

The rest of the note said...

> "I wanted to tell you that we left one of our cats with a litter of five kittens. She's a really good mouse catcher, and it didn't make sense to take all of our cats along. We hope you enjoy her.
>
> In the refrigerator, you will find a lasagna casserole ready for you to bake. Bake it at 350 for 45 minutes."
>
> Love and prayers,
>
> Joe and Amanda

Willy entered the house and said, "Guess what we found? We found kitties in the barn."

Elizabeth smiled and replied, "I just read about it in this note from Amanda. She said they left the kittens for us to keep. The kittens will help us catch the barn mice. Amanda's note also said that she made some lasagna for us. So why don't you boys get your showers taken, and we can all enjoy our first meal in our new house."

The lasagna was the best meal they had in a long time, mostly because they were so relieved to finally be settled into their new house.

Chapter 5

The morning after the move, Karl and Willy woke up bright and early. It was such an odd feeling waking up in the new house. They were both surprised that they had not heard the storm during the night, but they could easily tell that there had been high winds. There were a few branches and leaves strewn about the yard. The first thing they checked on was the horses. It was apparent that the horses had not slept through the storm. The boys could tell the horses had more than likely witnessed the lightning storm and clearly heard the thunder, as the horses were restless and a bit antsy. It would also take them a bit to adjust to their new barn. The boys did the chores in less than half an hour, and that included talking to the horses to calm them down and checking on the kittens.

"These chores will be easy and fun compared to what we were used to having to do," Karl said.

"You betcha," Willy replied in agreement. "More time for fishing."

He paused. "I'm going to like living here."

"Me too," Karl said. "The best part about today is that no one is coming over. I was getting sick and tired of being around so many people. But I know we couldn't have done it without them. I am glad they were all willing to help us, but I was starting to feel like our privacy was invaded."

"I actually liked having so many people helping because no one noticed that me and some of the boys had gone back to the woods instead of working," Willy said with a smile.

"What?! You have got to be kidding. You didn't help carry boxes?" Karl asked in disbelief.

"Not one," laughed Willy. "We came back in time for some cookies. It was such a fun walk; we saw a pond just on the other side of that group of trees, in those woods. It has all kinds of big bullfrogs, and we are going to go frog gigging one of these nights. There are some big deer in those woods, too, and Johnny's dad has a hunting lease with the man who owns it. Johnny said he is sure his dad wouldn't care if we use these woods, too, as long as we always check with them during hunting season."

"I will let you off the hook this time for skipping out on the work," laughed Karl." I guess your connections with Johnny paid off, and this hunting property is going to work out better than I thought."

The boys picked up a few branches in the yard and hung the wind chimes on the front porch. They had decided to wait to hang the wind chimes until after the storm had passed, and they were glad they did. When the boys went inside the house, they were surprised that Elizabeth was still in bed sleeping. That was unusual, as she always woke up early. They figured she was just tired. They were right. She came into the kitchen just as the boys were finished making bacon and eggs for breakfast.

"What's going on?" Elizabeth asked her brothers. "I cannot believe it is 8:30. I must have been exhausted. I can't remember the last time I slept in like this. I must have needed the sleep."

As the three Miller children ate breakfast together, they felt as if they were on a vacation. No matter how much it hurt to leave the home place, they realized it was going to be so much easier to maintain their new five-acre property.

Elizabeth told her brothers, "This is the first time in months that I feel caught up. I don't even know what to do today. There's no work around here for today. What should we do?"

"Let's ride our bikes to the flea market," Willy said. "I wanted to get some firecrackers for July fourth."

"Sounds like a plan!" Elizabeth said, smiling, and they all went to change into their *going to town* clothes.

Much like any other Amish people, Elizabeth and the boys had *everyday clothes*, *church clothes*, and *town clothes*. When Amish people are working at home, they wear what they call their *everyday clothes*. On Sundays, they wear their *church clothes*. During the week, they also have another set of clothes that are nicer than the everyday clothes but not as good as what they wear for church, referred to as *shtat gleda* (*town clothes*), which would be worn to school or town.

They got their bikes and headed out toward Shipshewana with big smiles on their faces. They felt like birds set free from their cages. As they got closer to the intersection of Five and Twenty, they all got a bit quiet. They saw Joni Miller standing in front of his business, the Shipshe Service Center, and stopped to talk to him. Joni had been at the Service Center the day of the accident. Joni's fire and rescue squad experience had put boots on the ground instantly after the wreck, but there was simply nothing anyone could have done to save the family. It touched Joni deeply to see the children.

"Hey there!" Joni said with a friendly smile and wave. "It's good to see all of you. I often wondered how everything's been going."

"We're doing pretty well," Elizabeth said, "but it's hard coming here today. We haven't all three been here together since the accident."

"I heard you moved a little closer to town," Joni said. "That ought to be easier to get around, if you can bike into Shipshe."

"What would make it a lot easier would be a car," Karl said. "You know of any cheap cars I could buy?"

Joni laughed and said, "I'm selling one of my Harleys, but it isn't cheap. And I wouldn't want you to start out riding a Harley, either."

"By the way," Joni asked, "do you know who put the four white crosses in my flower garden? I think it was a really nice gesture in remembering your family."

The children said they didn't have any idea and that they really couldn't think of anyone they knew who made crosses. But they were intrigued. They walked over to the crosses and looked a bit closer at them. On each cross was written a different name in honor of the lives lost in the tragedy. The crosses read, *Dan, Sarah, Barbara*, and *Katie*, and each one had the words *gone but not forgotten* written on it.

Joni and the three children just stood there for a moment, wiping the tears from their eyes. They were all deeply touched at the kindness of someone in the community.

Karl wasn't comfortable with public crying stuff. He broke the seriousness of the moment and said, "Joni, I think it's pretty awesome that you have these flowers planted in a quilt shape. Your flowers all planted in the letters *HD* for Harley Davidson is the best one in the whole community. I never really liked flower quilts until I saw this one."

It lightened up the moment. The children said goodbye to Joni and thanked him once again for helping at the accident.

Crossing over the intersection caused Willy a bit of anxiety, but he did great.

The first stop was at Eash Sales to look at some puppies. Willy was trying to decide between a Golden Retriever puppy or a Goldendoodle, a mix between a Golden Retriever and Poodle. The owners, Marty and Joe said both kinds make great pets and are both very good natured dogs. Willy finally settled on a male Golden Retriever but added, "I'm also gonna get a female so they'll have each other when I'm not at home, but I'll need to get her from another litter."

"Are you sure you want to spend that much money?" Karl asked.

"Oh yeah, I have more money than I know what to do with. It's burning a hole in my pocket!" Willy said, laughing.

Karl and Elizabeth knew that Willy pinched his pennies and saved like crazy. Willy had a job detasseling corn and had worked pretty hard to establish his dog fund.

Elizabeth said, "OK, but you need to take good care of them. No complaining about the work it will take to train them."

They arranged with Marty Miller that the dog would be dropped off at their house later that week. As they were leaving Eash Sales, Elizabeth remembered that they had received a letter from Raber's Patio, asking the children to stop in at the store at their earliest convenience. She was not sure what they wanted but thought this would be a perfect time to find out, if they were in town anyway.

They found Ervin Raber and told him that they had received the letter and that they were just so busy with the sale and the move that they hadn't had time to come in yet.

Ervin was a friendly caring Amish man who knew the family situation well. He told the children that he had also been at the horse sale the day of the accident and had talked to their dad, "I still remember what we talked about. There were two young boys who had gotten in trouble with the law, and your dad was telling me, 'Ervin, we need to do something to help, what could we do to help?' That was the question that your dad was always asking, 'I wonder what we could do to help?' Whether it was for a widow or someone with health problems, he'd talk and start thinking of ideas, and the next thing you knew, it was happening. He could draft a crew to help in no time. That's why there were so many volunteers helping at your sale and the move. A lot of people think the saying, 'You reap what you sow' is negative, but it can be for really good things, too."

"Well, you children are probably wondering what I want. You will be surprised at what I'm going to tell you. You see all this Berlin Garden poly lumber furniture out here? Well, about a month before the accident, your dad had ordered and paid for a brand new poly lumber Octagon picnic table and seven Adirondack Chairs that he wanted for sitting around the fire pit. He said he was buying it as a surprise for the family."

"No way!" Elizabeth exclaimed. "Mom would have loved it. She was getting tired of staining the picnic table that we had. How often will we need to stain this new one?"

Ervin said, "You will never need to stain it because the color is in the poly lumber. You can even leave it outside in the wintertime. It's made in Berlin, Ohio, by a company called Berlin Gardens. The man who owns it is Sam Yoder, and his wife Ruby comes from the Fish Lake area. They have a lot of Amish workers, and it's really good quality outdoor furniture. You will like it a lot. It's easy to take care of, and it's pretty heavy, so it won't blow around in high winds like we had last night."

"Would you consider keeping two of the Adirondack chairs and letting us take a dog house instead?" Karl asked. "Willy just ordered some puppies, and we were going to have to build a dog house sometime this week."

"Sure, I can do that. Sounds like a deal to me. We will drop them off later in the week," Ervin told them.

The children thanked him and headed for the flea market. They were all quiet as they were all lost in deep thoughts about what just happened. They were surprised to hear about the lawn furniture but not surprised at the fact that one of their dad's last conversations was about trying to figure out how he could help someone. It sounded just like him.

Elizabeth smiled to herself as she realized that two gifts had come in the same week: first, the quilt and now the lawn furniture from her dad. It was almost as if their parents were stamping their approval on the children's new home.

The minute the children stepped into the flea market, they saw a sea of people as far as their eyes could see. It made the adrenaline rush through their bodies. Every year it seemed to grow bigger and more exciting than the previous year. It was, by far, one of the biggest tourist attractions in the state of Indiana, with over 900 vendors on 100 acres of land. It was open every Tuesday and Wednesday from May to October. People drove from miles around to bring their items to sell, and buyers flocked to it for the great bargains.

In the first two aisles, they stayed together, but Elizabeth kept stopping at booths with kitchen items and decorations for the house, things the boys were obviously not interested in. They had their sights set on finding ammo, tackle, and other important things, like hunting accessories. One of the vendors gave the boys a map of the vendor booths, and they started by highlighting all the booths they considered as priorities. They politely but emphatically informed Elizabeth that they had not come to the flea market to look at cookware. They decided to meet at 3 later that afternoon at the food pavilion, closest to the auction barn.

The boys were so happy to finally be moving faster and couldn't wait to get to the first booth. All of a sudden, Karl stopped and pulled Willy into a side aisle.

"Did you see Mildred Mast? We can't go down that aisle. She is going to make us talk for a half hour, and all she wants to know is how we are doing so she can to tell everyone else."

Willy said, "I hope she didn't see us. She means well, but I agree. We ain't got time for talking today."

As soon as Willy finished talking, three cute young Amish girls walked by and said hi. The boys didn't know them, so they just said hi and kept walking.

Without missing a beat, Karl tilted his head toward the girls and said, "Well, maybe we could reconsider what we have time for." The boys laughed but stayed on course.

They did a bit of bartering with a few vendors and got some new knives and a few new baseball cards. As they were walking down the aisles, they saw a few women posing to take pictures, so both boys jumped up in the air behind them. The woman taking the picture hadn't noticed, so the boys laughed at the thought that when the pictures were uploaded, the women would be surprised to see the Amish boys in the picture. They high fived each other and laughed again. It sure felt good to get to have a day that they could just be teenagers again.

Elizabeth was also enjoying her day and was thankful for the pleasant weather. It was fun to look at all the different collectibles and decorations. It wasn't like she needed to buy those things, but it just did her heart good to see the beauty and creativity. She spent time picking out a new candle. It was so difficult to choose because she enjoyed smelling all the unique scents. A woman asked her if Amish are allowed to have candles. Elizabeth politely smiled and said yes. Sometimes English people asked some pretty odd questions, but Elizabeth felt that sometimes the people just didn't know what to say to Amish people. Elizabeth did her best to always be friendly to people like that so they could see that the Amish are normal people who just dress differently.

Elizabeth decided to get an ice cream cone while she waited for the boys and was so happy to see her friend Suzanne, who was just finishing her shift. She came outside in the pavilion to talk and it was great to catch up.

All of a sudden the boys were back on the scene. They were grinning from ear to ear from the fun day they had. They said hello to Suzanne and also ordered two vanilla ice cream cones to enjoy before they left the flea market.

"Before I forget," Suzanne said, "a woman from South Bend came here last week looking to hire some Amish girls to help her clean her house. Her name is Cassandra, and I was wondering if you would be interested in helping me and a few others clean for her? I know you also work at the Essenhaus, but my job here stops in the fall, and I needed some winter work. She's willing to pay really well, and I got the impression that she could be quite interesting to work for."

"Interesting in a good way?" Elizabeth asked, laughing. "Let me think about it, and I will let you know."

CORINA YODER

Chapter 6

Elizabeth smiled as she watched Karl and Willy devour their ice cream cones. She could tell they had a fun day and was very happy to see them enjoy themselves. There was a pleasant breeze blowing through the flea market food pavilion. It felt good for the children to sit and rest for a bit. From this location, they could see a bunch of windsocks and flags dancing in the wind high above the booths. Those items were popular even on days with little breeze. But today was extra breezy, so vendors were going to make a fortune on those items since the very breath of God was giving them plenty of free advertisement.

The children got a kick out of watching the people walking by; there was so much to observe. It was ironic that a flea market could pull together so many people who were, by all outward appearances, extremely different. A lot of people came to Shipshewana to observe the Amish, but in all reality, it was also quite fascinating and educational for the Amish people as well. This town sure saw a lot of different nationalities. The population of Shipshewana is 677, but they yearly expect up to half a million visitors. The Lambright family, the owners of the Flea Market had helped put Shipshewana on the map.

A young Chinese couple, hands full of handbags, walked past Elizabeth and her brothers, talking rapidly. It was hard to tell if they were mad or just excited about something.

The elderly retired people were slowly milling around, just taking their good old time. They didn't seem to need anything but rather were just there for something to do. This age group enjoyed watching the antiques selling in the auction barn. At any given time, there could be as many as ten auctioneers going at the same time. Sometimes the auctioneer would pause long enough to ask a question about an old item. He would get his answer, and away he would go again, auctioneering off the next item. But those questions would typically open up a long conversation between total strangers. Normally it was the older people talking about "the good old days" and "remember when....."

The young moms with babies looked hot and frazzled while pushing the strollers. Some of the children were fussing and crying and didn't seem to be enjoying this outing at all.

There were also all kinds of Amish and Mennonite people out and about. It was easy to understand how the outside world could get confused by all the different groups within these religious communities. Some of the women wore white prayer coverings; some wore black doilies or veils. The caps or coverings were all worn as prayer coverings. They all had the same intent but were distinctly different in appearance.

The clothes that the Amish and Mennonites wore varied as well. Some of the Mennonite churches allow clothes bought in a store, and others require their church members to make and sew their own clothes.

Karl and Willy were wearing their homemade Amish clothes. Their mom had sewn the shirts and the pants. The boys called them "barn door pants" because they had buttons instead of zippers like a pair of store- bought jeans would have had.

Elizabeth was wearing a yellow dress that she had sewn herself. She had learned how to sew when she was only 12 years old and really enjoyed it. At first, she just helped her mom sew parts of the dress until she had learned how to assemble the whole thing from cutting it out to sewing it together and then hand stitching the hem. She had often helped her mom sew together parts of the boys' pants but had never completed any on her own. She knew she would more than likely need help to do that once the boys needed new pants. She hoped their pants would last for a while, but she knew they were constantly growing. "Growing like weeds," her mom used to say. It would be a lot easier if Elizabeth could go to an Amish store and buy them.

Elizabeth didn't want to ask for more help than she had to. She knew that there were some people in the Amish community who felt like the three Miller children should not be living on their own. In a big community like this one, there will always be so many kinds of opinions on any given subject. Some of the people, however, were very supportive of the children's desire to live on their own. They understood the privacy they wanted and needed. Others felt like Willy, age 13, needed more than an 18 year old to be his mom. What they all did understand was that Uncle Mose was only two miles away in case they needed anything. Living with Uncle Mose would be a backup plan in case plan A did not work out.

It might be that Elizabeth would live to regret taking on this role, but for right now, this was, by far, the best situation. Today was a great example, as they got to enjoy a full day of doing something that they all had wanted to do. Their parents had always told them to *work hard, play hard*. It simply meant that it is good to work hard but to also have an equal amount of fun. "Everyone needs a balance of those two," Dad had always said.

The loudest group in the pavilion was a group of women from Chicago who had come on a bus tour. There were approximately 25 of them, all wearing bright raspberry-colored tee shirts that said *We buy our Apples on Michigan Avenue and we dodge road apples in Shipshewana*. The women worked together in a high rise building in downtown Chicago. They felt like birds released from their cages and were enjoying a day in the country. They had agreed to all turn off their iPhones and iPads for the day. They were feeling disconnected from the world and enjoying every minute of it. They had freedom from their long to-do lists. For one day, there were no Twitter feeds, no Facebook posts, no Instagram pictures, no emails, no texts, no blogs. SILENCE, except for enjoying each other.

It was easy to tell which woman was the life of the party. A hilarious black woman by the name of Tanya was cracking jokes and making them all laugh hysterically. Tanya was in the middle of saying something when she saw Cletus Troyer walking toward the women. She started teasing Cletus as if they were the best of friends. Cletus Troyer was an Amish man who helped run a donut route in the Chicago area and had met Tanya at one of the donut shops. Through that connection, Cletus invited them to come to Shipshewana.

Cletus said, "Tanya, I could hear you carrying on a mile away."

Tanya's mouth dropped open, and she couldn't think of one thing to say to that. She had met her match, and she knew it. Normally she was always the one dishing it out on others, but a man – not just any man but an Amish man – had called her out. The whole group of ladies laughed and egged Cletus on.

Finally, Tanya said, "Cletus, you sure don't fit into the mold of all Amish being quiet and mild-mannered people."

Cletus laughed. "There's a false belief that Amish people are all the same. Just because we dress the same does not mean that God created our personalities and our preferences all alike. I know shy Amish people, and I know some who can't stop talking. We are often looked at as rigid people but are actually quite colorful."

"I am so glad to know that," one of the ladies said, "because I always had the idea the Amish were sort of boring. To me, it seemed as if they were all cut out of the same cookie cutter."

Cletus chuckled. "Well, we aren't boring. And speaking of cookies . . . are you ladies ready to head out to see the home of the world famous Rise and Roll donuts?"

The ladies gave Cletus a resounding *yes*, and with that, he walked with the 25 women out to the bus. He chuckled at the sayings on their tee shirts. In this neck of the woods, pieces of horse manure on the road were referred to as *road apples*. The locals and tourists did everything they could to not drive through them.

Almost all of the people who had been sitting in the pavilion were watching and eavesdropping on this interaction. Everyone was smiling, but they soon realized the entertainment had left the building. One by one, people got up and started back to their shopping.

Willy was not sure what answer he would get but decided he would ask.

"Can we stop at the sale barn to watch the livestock auction?"

There was a long silence, as both Elizabeth and Karl were trying to absorb what Willy wanted. Elizabeth looked at Karl and asked in Pennsylvania Dutch, "What do you think?"

Karl sighed. "Willy, are you sure you want to go there already? It will be pretty hard to go to Dad's favorite place. I will take you if you are sure, but I just need to warn you that it might stir up a lot of memories."

"Have you thought about that, Willy?" Elizabeth asked.

"Yeah, I've thought about it a lot lately. I didn't just think this up. No matter how long I stay away from there, it will still be hard to go for the first time," Willy said.

"That's true, Willy," Elizabeth replied. "When you two go to the Sale Barn, I will go pick up a few things that I need over at the Red Barn and Spector's. I will meet you at Jo Jo's Pretzel Shop right at 5. Don't be late."

As the boys walked toward the Sale Barn, Karl felt a strong, protective feeling come over him. Karl actually felt like he walked taller and felt almost father-like. He had never felt that before, and it surprised him that he liked how it felt. Sometimes Karl felt angry at the responsibilities and roles he was forced into, but this time, it fit like a hand in a glove. He realized how much Willy meant to him.

It didn't feel unusual or awkward to step inside the sale barn. It actually felt like they were coming home. They decided to walk through the back to see the animals. Today was the livestock auction, so there were cattle instead of horses. There were also rabbits, goats, pigs, and sheep. The boys talked about the rabbit factory they once owned. They had a good laugh. It had been a good idea at the time, but somehow, a cage had been left open one night, and a bunch of the rabbits ran away. They were sure they had fattened them up for the auction, but instead, their profits escaped.

Some of the sale barn workers recognized them and waved. The boys also saw a number of their dad's friends. The first glances revealed a vulnerable pain in the men's eyes. These men missed their friend who had died way too young. Seeing the boys was like pouring salt into an open wound, but very quickly, the men would mask their own hurts. Many would smile at the boys, say hello, and follow up with a remark about how good it was to see the boys. Amish people are typically gifted at hiding what they are thinking and feeling, but both the boys had noticed the lingering feelings of sadness on the faces of their dad's friends. Some of the men asked how things were going and were genuinely glad to hear that the move was a smooth transition.

The boys found a spot to sit and watch the auction. Karl glanced over at Willy and saw that he had a big smile on his face. *Like Father, like son*, Karl thought. He was very relieved that this visit to the sale barn went well. *Dad would approve,* he thought to himself. Karl only allowed a few seconds of thoughts to enter his mind. *I wish Dad was here. He always made me feel safe.* Abruptly, he switched the gears in his mind to focusing on the next cow they were getting ready to auction off.

When Elizabeth got to the Red Barn, she headed for the bookstore. She was ecstatic to find a new book written by Karen Kingsbury. Her mom used to love to read, too, and sometimes they were both reading the same book. Sunday afternoons were the best reading days. She also bought a book about dealing with death and grief. She wasn't as excited to find this one, but she hoped it would help her cope with the loss of her family.

She decided to skip going to Spector's. She just wasn't ready to go there yet. That was where her mom and sisters' had been right before the accident.

Elizabeth was very excited to go to the Davis Mercantile. It was one of her favorite places to go in Shipshewana. She loved meandering through the shops. Elizabeth walked up the Mercantile stairs to the top floor and, unexpectedly, straight into pain. She caught her breath as she felt like she had been hit with a ton of bricks. There was a birthday party with young girls going on. They looked like they were her sisters' ages. The girls were giggling and riding the grand carousel. When

Barbara and Katie were still alive, they always wanted to ride it. The horses were magnificent to see. It made Elizabeth feel like smiling and crying all at the same time. She soon realized after the deaths of her parents and sisters that grief could hit her when she least expected it. She felt like walking over and telling the moms to cherish every minute but was worried she may bring a depressing cloud over the party.

Elizabeth found herself on autopilot mode and headed out onto the back porch. She breathed in the smell of all the flowers and enjoyed rocking on the rocking chairs. Sometimes the porch was full of customers, but today was pretty quiet. Elizabeth didn't feel like being sociable. She knew she would need to get it together because the boys were meeting her very soon to eat pretzels. She decided she would be able to read the first chapter of her new Karen Kingsbury book. That was a big mistake. Five chapters later, she realized she might have missed her own strict meeting time.

Sure enough, Karl and Willy were just getting three Jo Jo's pretzels with cheese and three lemonades. The boys laughed when they saw Elizabeth and teasingly said, "Yeah, don't be late."

Before they ate, they all bowed their heads and said a silent prayer.

"I'm sorry," Elizabeth said. "I got a new book, and I was reading it back on the porch. I can't wait to read the rest of it. I was just going to read a little bit, but then time just got away from me. Whenever I read Karen Kingsbury's books, I feel like I am traveling somewhere." Elizabeth realized she was rambling off excuses.

"I really enjoy traveling," Willy said. He then asked, "Will we ever get to go on any trips again, like when we went to Niagara Falls?"

"I sure hope so," Karl said. "My goal is to see all fifty states. Some of my friends are talking about going hunting out West next fall. I'm hoping to save up enough money to go along. For me, that would be a dream come true."

"I would rather head out East," Elizabeth said longingly. "I want to see the New England states in the fall of the year. Glen Alma often takes vanloads out there to see all the colorful leaves."

"What did I hear you say Glen Alma does?" Alma Miller asked.

The children laughed. It was Glen Alma in person. They had not seen Alma come into Jo Jo's. Glen and Alma Miller were an Amish Mennonite couple that have maxi vans and a business hauling Amish. They go on a lot of local runs, but they also take a lot of Amish on long trips or vacations. Glen and Alma had taken the family to Niagara Falls, so they knew each other well.

"Oh, I was just telling the boys that I want to go to the New England states with you sometime. Fall is one of my favorite seasons," Elizabeth explained.

Alma agreed. "That's the prettiest time of the year to go out there. You let me know when you want to go. We just got back from Alaska. That was a trip of a lifetime."

"I would love to go to Alaska and deep sea fish sometime," Karl said.

"There are a lot of fishing charters in Alaska," Alma told Karl.

"How has everything been working out?" Alma asked. " I saw your Uncle Mose, and he said you moved to a new place."

"We really like it. It feels like ours now that we moved our things into it," Elizabeth replied.

It was time for Alma to pick up her load of women, so she said goodbye and told them she would be praying for them.

"She sure is a friendly lady," Willy remarked.

As they were finishing their first pretzels, Jo, the owner of Jo Jo's Pretzel Shop, came over to the children and asked the boys in Pennsylvania Dutch if they still had room for a couple of cinnamon pretzels.

"You bet! They're the best!" Karl said immediately.

They thanked Jo and headed outside to their bikes. What a great ending to a fun day in town.

Chapter 7

The Miller children found their bikes and were ready to leave town when Jo King stepped outside in hopes to catch a conversation with them. Her real name was Joanna, but everyone called her Jo. She was well known for her Jo- Jo pretzel shops.

Jo said, "I'm sorry that I didn't recognize you inside, but one of the Amish girls told me that you were Dan's children. I have been praying for all of you and wanted to tell you that I knew your parents. They were wonderful people and will really be missed by the whole community."

"Thank you. That means a lot," Elizabeth replied, "Some days are easier than others. For example, today, I went upstairs to the carousel and saw all those young girls, the age of our sisters, Barbara and Katie, and it just threw me for a loop. Grief hits us out of nowhere sometimes."

Jo gave Elizabeth a sympathetic smile. "Well, I want you to know that your dad's legacy of giving is going to continue over at Yoder meats."

"What do you mean by that?" Willy asked, looking rather puzzled. Karl and Elizabeth also looked like they had no clue as to what Jo was talking about.

Now it was Jo who looked surprised. "Let me guess. You honestly have no idea what I'm talking about."

"No, we really don't," Elizabeth replied.

"You weren't aware that your dad had a meat account open over at Yoder's meats for a lot of widows and struggling families?" Without waiting for an answer to her question, Jo began explaining how every single month, Dan would pay into an account and would tell any struggling family about the account. Apparently, over the years, he had spent thousands of dollars providing hamburger and other meats for people in need.

"No kidding," Karl said.

"Not only that," Jo added, "but he never wanted anyone to feel ashamed of needing help. He knew that Amish people sometimes struggle to accept handouts and he wanted to protect their dignity. In order to do that, he had created a secret code for this account so that people who used from it wouldn't be embarrassed in case there were other people in line. Your dad thought of everything."

"I have never heard of this," Elizabeth said. "Karl, have you?"

Karl took a deep breath. "Wow, now it all makes sense! I was often with him over the years when he stopped there to check on his 310 account. I just assumed it was meat for our family because when the account got low, he would send our cattle in to be butchered. I never asked him about it, and he never told me."

It was Willy's turn to add his two cents in the conversation. The words just gushed out of him, almost like an artesian well.

Willy said, "I was with dad one day, and he had stopped to pay on this 310 account. When he got into the buggy, he had a receipt and a piece of paper with a list of names on it. I was really tired because Dad and I were on the way home from fishing all morning, and we had left home really early. So I fell asleep. All at once, I heard Dad crying, but I didn't want him to know I was awake, so I just pretended to sleep. He was reading the names on the list and quietly praying in Dutch. I heard him say, 'God help them through these hard times. Help me know what else I can do for them. I feel so helpless, but I know you own the cattle on a thousand hills.' And then he cried some more."

Tears were welling up in Willy's eyes as he remembered this special time with his dad. He had never told anyone, but he had been deeply touched by his dad's prayers that day. Now it seemed to fill in the missing puzzle piece in his mind on why Dad had cried that day.

"Wow!" Jo exclaimed. "That was your dad's heart, and now he has a bunch of Amish men picking up where he left off. It will keep growing even bigger because more people were prompted to help out."

"Your dad started a ripple effect that outlived him," Jo continued. "The 310 account is from a verse in the Bible, Malachi 3:10, where it mentions that 'there may be food in my house.'"

"I have never read that verse," Elizabeth said," but I can just imagine we will find it underlined in his Bible."

"I bet you will, too," Jo agreed. "Have you ever heard him use the saying 'not on my watch'?"

All three children burst into a laugh. Karl said, "Only about a million times!"

He continued. "This saying was no secret in our house. He would find out something was wrong somewhere with someone, and he would pray for them. In his prayer, he would use the saying 'not on my watch will we neglect to care, not on my watch will we neglect to help, help us to do all we can to show love and that we care.'"

"It sounds like he had a watchman intercessor's gift," Jo concluded.

"What in the world is that?" Willy asked.

"In the days of the Bible, the watchmen would sit and guard the walls to protect the city. Today, though, an intercessor is simply someone who prays for others."

"Oh yes, he did do that a lot," Elizabeth replied, as her brothers nodded in agreement. "Thanks for telling us that story."

Jo smiled. "Well, I better get back inside. We still have a long line of customers wanting pretzels. I'm really glad to meet the three of you."

"It was good to meet you, too," Karl replied. "Better get back to work so you don't get fired."

Jo laughed as she waved goodbye to the Miller children.

When the children reached the Blue Gate Restaurant, the traffic was still pretty heavy on the St Road 5, so they decided to take the Ship-Middlebury Road about a mile east to avoid crossing the 5 and 20 intersection again. The very thing that was a blessing to the community with all the consumers also made it a challenge to get around on the roads at times.

They waved at the Amish man giving carriage rides, and Karl read the sign on the Blue Gate advertising the newest show: *Josiah for President.* He laughed. "I think it ought to say *Karl for President, from Shipshe to the White House.*"

A man sitting on a bench beside the road overheard Karl's comment, and he laughed out loud. He hadn't expected to hear an Amish person say that, and it struck his funny bone. He said to Karl, "I'd vote for you." They both laughed and smiled as the children rode away.

The traffic was lighter on the Ship-Middlebury Road, but they still needed to be cautious. A lot of tourists were not accustomed to driving around horses, buggies, and bikes. Sometimes they were so focused on taking pictures of the Amish that traveling on the roads with them became dangerous. As soon as they reached the first country road turning south, they took it. They were making great time until Elizabeth noticed her tire going flat. It was too far to just walk the bike home, so at the next Amish house, they turned into the lane. They didn't know who lived here, but they were soon going to find out.

Elizabeth caught her breath as she saw the young man strolling out of his shop. *Of all people*, she thought, *it was John Hostetler. Oh great . . . why couldn't this be some old grandpa's house?*

He looked surprised to see them but greeted all three with a big smile.

"Well, what happened to your tire?" John asked, turning his attention toward Elizabeth.

"I'm not sure . . . it was perfectly fine until we got on this road," Elizabeth replied.

"We can take it into my shop, and I will take a look at it," John said. "I'm afraid it won't be an easy fix today, but I was just hitching up the buggy to go over to my folks' house. I can just take you home right now, and I can bring the bike some other time, after I get it fixed for you."

"Oh, I hate to be a bother," Elizabeth hesitated.

"You are absolutely not a bother at all. I would be glad to help out," John replied.

"OK, I will go tell the boys, and then I will go with you in the buggy."

What irked Elizabeth is that John seemed genuinely happy to be at her service. She could tell that he thought she was worth his attention and time and also that he enjoyed helping her. It all made her feel good, but at same time, she didn't like owing him anything. Most girls would have loved the attention, but Elizabeth wasn't most girls.

Elizabeth stepped out of the shed, walked over to Karl and Willy, and explained to them what John had said about the bike and also about taking her home. Karl started laughing.

Elizabeth said, "Stop it right now. This is not funny. I hope no one sees us two. We don't need tongues wagging about nothing."

Karl and Willy continued to laugh all the more to see Elizabeth's calm blue eyes a bit ticked off. She was stunningly beautiful and normally real calm and level headed. This situation rattled her because it was completely out of her control.

The boys left John's to ride their bikes home, and Elizabeth prayed a quick prayer for their safety on the road, a habit she had started since the accident. As Elizabeth waited for John to bring the buggy around to the front of the shed, she started remembering things she had heard about him.

Elizabeth had seen John in crowds before but had never met him before today. John was known as the most eligible bachelor in the whole area as he was twenty-four and had already made a considerable amount of money. Some of her girlfriends had told Elizabeth in the recent past that John thought he "was really something"; but she noted that he was very down to earth and easy to talk to.

Elizabeth's dad had taught her to watch out for charmers, and she was trying to discern his motives and intentions while remaining friendly but not flirty. *Flirty* and *forward* were not words ever used to describe Elizabeth Miller. They wouldn't be words to describe her today, either.

Before they got into the buggy, John untied the horse and patted the horse on the head. He was gentle and kind to his horse, and his care for the horse reminded Elizabeth of something her dad would have done.

At the end of the lane, John stopped the buggy and said to Elizabeth, "I know that Dan is your dad, but I wasn't sure about your name. I'm John."

"I'm Elizabeth, and my brothers who went on ahead with their bikes are Karl and Willy." She proceeded to give him directions to their house.

As they left his place, Elizabeth asked, "Did you just recently move into this house?"

John said, "I moved here about a year ago. It used to be my Daudy Fry's house. No one ever thought I'd join church or move back to my Amish hometown. I never imagined I'd ever put down roots back here in Indiana."

"Where did you live before this?" Elizabeth asked.

"The easier question might be where I didn't live," laughed John.

"Well, what happened was, I went out West with my family one summer. I had just turned eighteen, and when we stopped in Montana on our last leg of the trip, I knew I wanted to stay. So I went to a local drilling rig and got a job. My parents tried talking me out of it. I told my dad I would shrivel up and die inside if I had to leave the West. I had gotten a taste of it, and I had to have it, a bit like a shark getting a taste of blood." He laughed and then continued. "I told him that I would still send him money until I turned twenty-one. It was quite the experience; the supervisors loved me because I knew how to work hard. The owner ended up moving me from place to place. I got so many promotions and raises. It was surreal. My favorite areas were in the heart of Texas. My bosses owned cattle ranches, and I had all-access passes to their places. They trusted me like family. They took good care of me and even taught me how to invest in oil and gas."

"My dad missed me a lot, but he came to visit me in Texas. He always told me he could understand why I loved it. My mom would bring me cookies and homemade food. The ranch hands thought she was an angel straight from heaven. Every single time she left, though, she would cry and ask me when I was moving home."

He paused for a short time. "I honestly never thought I would, but one October, I realized I had not seen the fall leaves changing colors and had not smelled the autumn weather in years. I knew it was high time I head home. That very day, I turned in my two weeks' notice.

Fourteen days later, I loaded up my pickup and headed north. At the Texas state line, I pulled off the side of the road, had a good cry, and had yet another one as I crossed the Indiana state line. I knew this was not a visit. I knew I was moving home. I don't know how I knew, but I just knew."

"Wow!" Elizabeth exclaimed. "What an interesting story. So full of adventure."

"I don't know why I told you some of that," John replied. "I've never shared that about the crying at the state lines with anyone. You must have a good listening ear to get that story out of me."

He looked a bit vulnerable, like he had just surprised himself by opening up that easily to this girl he had never met before today. He had basically let down the guards around his heart and welcomed her right in.

Elizabeth replied, "My dad constantly had people tell him stories, and they would often say, 'I have never told anyone this,' so I must get it from my dad. Don't worry. I won't send the story to *The Budget.*"

They both laughed.

"How did it make you feel to see the leaves that year?" Elizabeth asked.

"It's funny that you should ask that. I got home on a Friday afternoon, and all the oldest grandchildren had come over to help Mom and Dad with all the leaf raking. They had about forty big old oak trees, and it was an endless job to keep the leaves raked. I drove in the lane, and there was a big welcome home committee all in place. The nephews took me and threw me into a pile of leaves the size of a mountain. They were ecstatic to see me. Mom came out of the house, and of course, she started crying because she was so happy to see me. Dad almost fell over backwards! He knew I never took vacations in the fall of the year, and somehow he also just knew that I was home to stay.

"It was good to be back, and I can still remember what we ate for supper that night: meatloaf, mashed potatoes, and custard pie. I realized, no matter what, family is really important."

"I agree," Elizabeth replied. "Our family was very close, and I just wish we'd have had more time together."

"I can't even begin to fathom what you and the boys have gone through in the past few months," John said sympathetically.

"It's been difficult, but a lot of friends and family have really gone the extra mile to show their support," Elizabeth explained. "My Uncle Mose has been a real blessing to be willing to carry the heavy burden of this for us. I couldn't have done this without him."

"People in this area sure speak highly of both your dad and Mose," John said. "I hear nothing but a lot of respect for both men."

"Well, they had a mom who was always telling them the two most important things in life were to love God and love others. She didn't take excuses or whining or diverting from that goal in her own life and in her eight children's lives."

"According to a lot of stories I've been told, she did a good job of passing that on," John replied.

John's horse was fast, and Elizabeth was home before she knew it. It was a bit awkward for Elizabeth when they passed other buggies on their trek to her home. She hoped no one recognized her with John. She just didn't want any rumors started about the two of them.

As they drove in the lane, John commented on the nice place they had. "It looks quite welcoming."

"Yes, I see it as our safe haven, after everything that happened this year," explained Elizabeth. "I miss the home place at times, but this has been exactly what we needed."

"Safe Haven," John repeated. "Sounds like a good place to heal."

As Elizabeth climbed out of his buggy, he said, "I will get your bike fixed as soon as possible and get it returned to you."

"Thank you for helping us out today," Elizabeth said. "We really appreciate it."

As John drove away, Elizabeth walked out to get the mail and noticed a buggy coming up the road.

Chapter 8

As the buggy got closer, Elizabeth saw the horse slowing down to turn into their lane. That's when she realized it was Uncle Mose. It did her heart good to see him. She was glad he was here because this sure had been an eventful day. She had some questions she was dying to ask him.

Mose jumped out of the buggy. Before he even said hello, he asked, "What in the world was John Hostetler's buggy doing coming from here?"

"Hello to you, too," Elizabeth said as she started laughing. "It's not how it looks!"

"What is that supposed to mean?" Mose asked.

"I can understand why my dad used to call you Mose with the nose," she retorted with a laugh.

She explained the whole ordeal about her bike, and Mose chuckled. But a look of seriousness also crossed his face.

"John's a great guy, but just be careful because there's a row of girls who wish he'd look their way. The fact that he hasn't has actually broken a few hearts," Mose told his niece.

Elizabeth replied, "Uncle Mose, you know that I appreciate the concern, but seriously! John only gave me a buggy ride home because my tire went flat. You act like we are getting announced to be getting married in church this Sunday."

"Lisbet, Lisbet, I guess you are right," Mose said. "I realize that I came off pretty strong. Just be careful. I think your heart has had enough heartache for one year."

"You actually sound like Dad," Elizabeth said with a smile," well, except Dad never called me *Lisbet*! You can be assured that no one else on this planet ever gets to call me that."

It was true. She hated that nickname, but for some reason, she had allowed Mose to call her that since she was just a little girl. She knew an older woman by that name, so she thought it sounded like a grandma's name.

"I need to talk to you and Karl if you both have a minute," Mose said.

"Definitely, come on in," Elizabeth said.

When the three of them were all sitting around the table with some fresh garden tea, Mose said, "I just wanted to touch base with you two now that we have both farms settled up financially. I want you both to know that there was plenty of money from the sale of *the home place* and the equipment sale to cover this new place. There is also quite a bit of money left to support the three of you for a long time. I will continue paying the gas bills, property taxes, and things that are substantial, but I will also set up a checking account that you can both write checks out of as you need things."

Mose continued. "It was a lot of work, but it was very important to your dad to look out for his family. Every year for the past five years, he made me sit down with him, and he would go over a list of things he wanted me to do for him if he, as he said it, 'should ever beat the race to Heaven first.' It used to really get on my nerves because I hated to talk about stuff like that. In hindsight, I'm so grateful that God prompted him to do that because I would not have known where to begin if he wouldn't have written out a detailed will and also a list of places where he had left different important papers. Instead of a nightmare, it actually went like clockwork."

Karl added, "Dad always said, 'Fail to plan, plan to fail.' It's good he listened to his own sermons."

Elizabeth chimed in. "I am very thankful that Dad planned ahead for this, but I also want you to know, Mose, that we couldn't have gotten through this without you. It was a big relief to us to have your help."

Karl nodded his head in agreement and said, "That's for sure. I would have had no idea how to do all of this stuff, so thanks, Mose."

"We need to be grateful that your dad was a good money manager and had money saved for this type of emergency," Mose replied. "I still have people wanting to help out, and it is a lot of the same people your dad had helped out throughout the years. They needed help during tough times, and now they are back on their feet and want to pass it on to others."

"Mose, did you know that Dad had a meat account at Yoder's?" Karl asked. "We just found out about it today."

"Yes, I did, and he would have told you about it once you were older," Mose replied. "One thing I want both of you two to do is to keep this information that your farm is paid off and that there's money left to live on to yourselves. I don't want someone taking advantage of you children, and I will do all I can to protect your private affairs. The Amish community is great at rallying together, but it can also be a gossip mill if the wrong people find out things that truly are none of their business."

"Do you both understand that this information is not to talk about to friends, neighbors, other aunts and uncles and not even people you date? Your dad would want you to guard this very close to your hearts. If people ask you any questions, just send them to me. You can just tell them that Uncle Mose is the one handling all that information. If they actually come to me, I will know they want to help out. But if they just want to be rude and nosy, they probably won't bother asking me.

"Do you both understand this reasoning? Mose asked.

"Yes," Elizabeth said. "Thanks for shielding us and having a plan in place to take the pressure off of us children."

When Karl opened his mouth to answer the question, his words were full of wisdom and understanding, as he had done quite a bit of growing up in recent months. "Yes, Mose, I heard you loud and clear. It makes a lot of sense to keep this information private. I wasn't sure why you had asked Willy to go outside and watch your horse for you while we talk, but I can see why it's best if Willy doesn't even have a clue about this stuff. I think we need to keep his childhood intact as much as we can."

Mose nodded in agreement. "That's exactly right, Karl!"

Karl added, "If Dad were here right now, he would tell you that you did a really great job in the past few months wrapping up his affairs."

Mose took a deep breath and let that sink in because he knew some nights were quite sleepless and that he had done a lot of praying to God for wisdom. They all three sat quietly for a time. The grandfather clock was the only noise in the room.

Finally, Mose replied, "Why, thank you, Karl. That means a lot to me. I often prayed for God to guide me. My favorite Bible verse is James

1:5. It says, 'If any of you lacks wisdom, you should ask God, who gives generously to all without finding fault, and it will be given to you.' The verse helped me to know that it's OK if I don't always know what to do. I can always ask The One who does know."

"I like that promise," said Elizabeth. "Mom had taught me about a prayer. The prayer she told me she said the most was, 'God, I need your help.' I've prayed that a lot since she died."

"That's a great prayer to pray," Mose said as he stood to his feet. "Thanks for the tea. I better get going; I told the kids that I would take them fishing after supper tonight."

Mose thanked Willy for watching his horse. As Willy was heading into the house, Willy informed Mose, "He's a really calm horse. You don't need to worry about him causing you any trouble."

"Good to know," Mose said, smiling.

Karl had followed Mose out to the hitching rack where Mose had tied up his horse and buggy.

"Mose, I have a question for you. I've been thinking how nice it would be if I could buy a car once I turn sixteen. I've been looking forward to my own set of wheels for years."

Mose looked like he wanted to run for the hills. The role he played (and had always played) was one of the fun uncle, and now he was being asked to destroy his nephew's dreams. He had no idea how to navigate through this question, but he knew the answer he had to give.

"Karl, I have dreaded you asking me this question!" Mose said honestly. "Trust me, I knew you would ask. I have lain awake on many nights thinking about the answer I need to be ready to give you. You know that your dad and I had cars when we ran around as teenagers. You having a car is not something I personally am against. I think your dad was the same type of Dad, too. You know this, right?"

"Yeah," Karl replied. "I knew Dad had a car, and I figured you wouldn't care, either."

"Well, here's my predicament," Mose explained. "There have been many Amish people who gave me money for your living expenses, and that money does need to last for a lot of years. I know that some of the Amish people who gave would not have a problem with you owning a car, but there are also some who would be upset if they gave money to help and then would see you spending money on a car. There are still a lot of them who think cars are very sinful and wrong."

"I'm not going to beat around the bush or give you false hope. I have to tell you no, Karl, we can't buy you a car."

The mature man Karl had portrayed earlier in the house disappeared. He looked like an angry six year old as he spewed out, "I don't know why Dad couldn't have just stayed home from the sale barn that Friday. It wrecked my whole life!"

Both Karl and Mose were shocked at the words that Karl had just spoken. Karl hadn't even realized he felt that way.

Very kindly, Mose said, "Karl, I can understand why you could feel like that right now, and I want you to know that I care about how you feel."

Mose meant every word. He had thought the same thing a number of times but never expressed it out loud to anyone. Anytime he thought it, he quickly repeated the verse in Romans 8:28: *We know that all things work together for good to those who love God and to those who are called according to his purpose.* Mose knew Karl needed an ear to listen to him, not a sermon, so he kept this verse to himself.

"I know you do, Mose. This whole mess is just so unfair!" Karl stated. He then sighed heavily. "Let me know if you change your mind."

As an afterthought, Karl added, "Thanks for the good news earlier."

As Mose rode home in his buggy, he remembered how free he had felt when he had first gotten a car. Even though it was hard to tell Karl no, he knew he had made the right decision. He refocused his brain on thinking about his own young children. He was glad they weren't teenagers yet, and he wasn't willing to miss out on a fun night fishing. He was going to treasure every minute he could because he knew this life was just a one-shot deal.

Karl was preparing for an evening of being mad when he heard a knock on the door. It was Roger Smith, an English neighbor from *the home place.* Roger wanted Karl to come with his son and him to the batting cages for a few hours. Roger had no idea what had happened earlier in the evening with the devastating news Karl had received about not getting to buy a car. But Karl couldn't forget it.

The batting cage was great therapy and an amazing way to vent his anger in a constructive way. While they were at the batting cages, Roger commented a few times, "Wow, Karl! That hit would have been a home run. It's too bad you weren't playing in a real game tonight." The two hours felt like ten minutes, but Karl had burned off some steam in the process.

As Karl fell into bed, he realized he was completely drained by the day's highs and lows. One comment that he had made entered his mind. He remembered saying, "This mess is just so unfair." His mind instantly went to the most influential woman he had ever had in his life, his mom. It was a saying she never allowed her children to say unless they wanted her to teach for about five minutes. He could hear the whole spiel in his mind. If they ever said the words "life's not fair," their mom would say, "You're right. Life is not fair. You have food to eat, and a lot of others don't. You have a house to live in, and a lot of others don't. You have your eyesight, and a lot of other people are blind."

The Miller children had just learned that unless they had time for a long talking to, they shouldn't use that language. She also expected good attitudes. The refrigerator was often covered with little papers with handwritten sayings, all written by Mom. The one he remembered best was *gratitude improves the attitude.*

Sorry, Mom. I blew it today, Karl thought.

Karl was almost drifting off to sleep when he heard these thoughts through his mind: *Karl, you are doing really well. This has been tough to handle, and you are strong. I am pleased with you. Stay in the game.*

Karl couldn't believe what he had just heard. He knew it must have been God speaking to him because those were not his own thoughts. It was the first time he remembered hearing something so clearly. He felt validated in how hard things had been and encouraged by the blessings. He felt strengthened as he felt the discouragement leaving him.

Karl slept better than he had in months and woke up feeling well-rested. He saw that he woke up a half hour before his alarm was even going to go off, so he gave himself some time to just lie in bed and think. He hadn't realized how much he had been anxiously waiting on the news about their finances. That was a weight that he would not need to bear anymore. It was a relief to know that it would not be up to Karl to pay the bills. Dad's saving and planning had provided for them. The thing that had helped him sleep most of all, though, was the message he had heard from God last night.

Karl felt like those special words were going to keep him alive through this blizzard-like life circumstance he was facing. Three of Karl's cousins had told him many stories about hunting out West. On one occasion, these three brothers had been caught by a blizzard before they could get back to base camp. They had no choice but to wrap themselves up with the elk hide they were transporting out. They were nearly frozen and knew hypothermia was a serious threat to their lives. They hunkered down for the night and prayed for a miracle. The next day, the wind died down, and they safely got back. All of them knew that God used that tough elk hide to save them from freezing to death.

Somehow Karl felt like God had wrapped him up in elk hide with the words he spoke into his weary bones. He thought of the cousins lost in the blizzard conditions. They had walked in circles for hours, and Karl realized that he had felt a bit like that, too. He had also felt lost and alone and unsure how to navigate life at times. When the brothers awoke the next day, they were glad to be alive and were shocked at how close they were to the cabins. The wind had died down, and they could easily see the path out before them. That's like Karl felt today. It was a new day, and he could see the path in front of him.

The path wasn't a literal path but rather a mindset. Karl's new mindset was *I am doing well. This has been tough, but I am strong! God is pleased with me. I need to stay in the game.*

Karl knew everything was different because he was experiencing a feeling of internal calmness. He was shocked at how much better he felt today. He was experiencing peace, but he wouldn't have even been able to name it as such. The truth is that any teenage boy has enough life changes to process through, even if everything in his life is normal. No boy of Karl's age would know how to face a tragedy of death of this magnitude.

As Karl walked toward the barn, he looked up at the early morning sky before dawn and realized how bright the stars were. He saw the moon was turned in the shape of a smile. Karl smiled back at God and whispered into the darkness, "That's cool."

Chapter 9

Elizabeth sat up in bed and looked around in shock. It was still pitch black all around her. She realized she had just woke up from a dream. The dream had seemed so real that she lay in bed thinking about it. In her dream, she had seen her dad in Heaven. She was sure of two things: It was definitely her dad, and it was definitely heaven. But what was confusing about her dream was seeing her Amish dad sporting a tattoo on his right arm that said *faithful to a thousand generations.* He was laughing with two other men, and it all seemed so natural. It did her heart good to see him laughing and joyful, though only in a dream. But what was that tattoo all about?

The Amish normally speak of the hope they have of going to heaven, but some Amish people believe you can know for sure. It would have been hard for Elizabeth to explain to others about her dream, about the peace she felt seeing her dad in heaven. Others might doubt the dream was from God because of the tattoo. She would ponder this over and keep it close to her heart. She decided to only ask her brothers about it and then keep it to herself. She didn't want to appear crazy.

Elizabeth made the boys biscuits and gravy before she got ready to go to work at the Essenhaus. She told the boys about her dream and asked if they ever dreamt about their parents. The boys said they couldn't remember having dreams about their parents. Elizabeth had been a vivid dreamer since she was a little girl, and this dream was the most colorful dream she had ever had, not to mention the only one she had ever had about Heaven.

Elizabeth had enough time to read a few sympathy cards while she waited for the workers' van. She was so thankful for all the cards they received in the mail after the accident. Someone had written about the accident in *The Budget*, a newspaper printed in Ohio, and the children were still getting cards and prayers from people they didn't even know.

Sometimes they had money in them, sometimes a handkerchief, and sometimes a prayer. It was a custom she found to be very kind. In *The Budget*, Amish and Mennonite people from several different states write on a weekly basis about what is going on in their communities. The Amish and Mennonites used this method of communication long before Facebook became popular.

The ride to work was pleasant for Elizabeth, as the women asked her about life at the new house. They admired the pretty flower gardens and hanging plants on the porch.

Elizabeth was honest and said," I can't take any credit for those. Joe and Carrie left them for us to enjoy. I love sitting on the front porch swing. It's like a restful sanctuary with all the flowers and butterflies. If there's a nice breeze blowing, my mom's wind chimes almost put me to sleep. It's so relaxing."

It felt good to talk to women who were her mom's age. As the van approached the Essenhaus, she once again breathed a prayer of thanks to God for this job. The owners, Bob and Sue Miller, were a wonderful Christian family to work for. All of the managers and shift supervisors had been so supportive and understanding of the time she needed to have off for the funeral, sale, and the move.

Back in the 1970s, Bob and Sue had moved from Sugarcreek, Ohio, to Middlebury, Indiana. They had purchased a small 24-hour truck stop known as Everett's Highway Inn and had turned it into an Amish-style restaurant. Those were the humble beginnings of The Das Dutchman Essenhaus. It grew so much that now it is one of the largest restaurants in the state of Indiana. The restaurant can seat over 1,000 customers at a time and on busy days will serve over 7,000 guests. In a one-week period, the restaurant may use up to 2,100 dozen eggs, 2,700 pounds of white sugar, 60 gallons of apple butter, 3.5 tons of potatoes, 3,600 chickens, 3,090 pounds of roast beef, and 2,990 heads of lettuce, to name a few items.

People sometimes questioned why Bob and Sue would be closed on Sundays, but they held true to their convictions that Sunday should be a day of rest and time for worship and family fellowship for their employees. God had blessed them richly for that decision. They gave the credit to God for the success of their restaurant. They taught their own children the value of hard work and now had them involved with running the business.

Over the years, the Essenhaus grew into a destination point. They then added the Essenhaus Inn and Conference Center that could hold weddings, reunions, and large events. They advertised it as *a pleasant surprise in Northern Indiana Amish Country.* After a delicious meal in the restaurant, a patron could also shop in the bakery attached to the restaurant. The smell of freshly baked bread and pies permeated the air, and the hardest thing to do was to choose which one of the thirty kinds of pies to take home.

The men loved events like the classic car and tractor shows. The women love to spend hours shopping at the gift shops. The children enjoy the miniature golf and also going up into the silo. The shows and dramas at Heritage Hall are fun for the whole family. But most tourists ultimately love to take a horse-drawn carriage ride. The winding lane that leads down past the pond and Inn crosses an old covered bridge.

The Essenhaus workers are a mixture of Amish and English workers. It is very common for the workers to feel a bit nervous around each other at first if they have not ever been in contact with the opposite before. However, it normally doesn't take long for them to get to know each other. There was always something interesting to learn about each other's cultures. It is nothing unusual to hear an Amish worker teaching the English workers how to say words in Pennsylvania Dutch. The favorite two sayings are *ve bisht do*, which means *how are you?* Another common one is *vas is da numa*, which means *what is your name?*

One of the funniest days in the kitchen happened when one of the Amish cooks was cleaning close to a vent, and her cap got sucked out through the vent. It was only funny because she laughed the hardest and was quick to say it was an older cap. She did ask to be taken home, though, because she just didn't feel comfortable going without a covering in public, and that request was highly respected. For her, being out in public without her prayer covering was like being only half-dressed.

When Elizabeth arrived at work that day, she helped set up tables for four different banquets. This included cutting pies and loading trays full of various cream pies and baked pies. When that task was finished, the waitresses sat down to eat together before the lunch rush. Some of them were discussing the new Obamacare health plan and how it would affect their lives. Of course, different waitresses had differing views of the subject, but the Amish ones were a bit unfazed by it all. Instead of having health insurance, the Amish typically just help each other pay hospital bills and have fundraisers and sales to help cover costs. Elizabeth really enjoyed the banter among the waitresses because they were all so different, and she loved to see how riled up some of them got about things they really felt strongly about.

One of the English waitresses named Toni was married to a cop. She said her husband had just spent most of Saturday night at a big Amish party. It was a mess because most of the girls didn't have driver's licenses, so they had no identification. When the cops showed up, a lot of the kids went running through cornfields and woods. One of the Amish waitresses started laughing and looked down at scratches all across her arms. Toni said, "Oh, Sarah, were you there? You kids made my husband's job a living nightmare last Saturday night. You know I love you Sarah, but I just don't understand all this rumspringa stuff.

The conversation was about to get really interesting when the first banquet group arrived. The men and women hurried around the table, found their favorite pieces of pie, and quickly ate the salad. It was hilarious to see their eyes when they saw the big dishes of fried chicken and big heaping bowls of mashed potatoes. They were a loud, expressive bunch of customers and repeated over and over that this was the best food they had ever eaten. This was the fun part of the day, watching the customers smile and enjoy themselves. The waitresses kept busy refilling the bowls and platters because this particular banquet was all-you-can-eat style.

It had been a fun day at work, serving mostly banquets for Elizabeth. She thought she was finished waitressing for the day when she saw the hostess seat someone at one of her tables. It was a young guy in his twenties all by himself. As Elizabeth glanced out into the dining room, she thought, *why did he have to be seated in my section?* She was turned off by his tattoos and instantly assumed he was a rough character. She was pleasantly surprised and actually shocked at how gentle and polite he was. She began to feel bad for prejudging by outward appearances. He ordered a beef Manhattan and devoured it in no time. He then also ordered a piece of pecan pie with ice cream.

When she handed him his bill, he said, "My name is Ridge. I'm a Christian, and I sensed that God wanted me to tell you that the dreams you have been having have meaning."

Elizabeth about fell over. Still in shock, she said, "How did you know? I've only told my two brothers."

Ridge replied, "I didn't know. The Holy Spirit just told me. I've taken some classes on dream interpretation. Maybe I can help you figure out your dreams."

This is really weird, Elizabeth thought, as she looked around her section. She made sure all her tables were completely finished and did not need her. She then turned to Ridge and said, "I keep having different dreams. The most recent one was a dream of my dad in heaven. He was with two other men laughing and talking. He was Amish before he died, and now in the dream, he was in heaven and had a tattoo on his arm. The tattoo said the words *faithful to a thousand generations.* What do you think it means?"

"Oh, that's cool. You got to see him in heaven and having fun in the dream. A tattoo on your dad's arm in the dream doesn't mean that he got a tattoo in heaven. It is just symbolic, or indicating that it is a permanent promise. The saying on the tattoo is part of a verse - let me look it up on my phone." After just a few seconds of searching, Ridge said, "It's in Deuteronomy 7:9. 'Know therefore that the Lord your God is God: he is the faithful God, keeping the covenant of love to a thousand generations of those who love him and keep his commandments.'"

"Could I just text this verse to you?"

Elizabeth just laughed and said, "No, I don't have a phone because I'm Amish, but you can write it on this placemat."
"So all Amish don't have cell phones?" Ridge asked. "I use my iPhone for almost everything."

"Some Amish people do, but I don't," Elizabeth replied.

"Back to the subject of your dreams," Ridge said. "Obviously, God wants you to know that your dad is in heaven. That has got to be reassuring because my dad is not saved, and if he would die, he would not be going to heaven. God also wants you to know that He will stay faithful to your dad's covenant of love. God also wants your family to keep loving Him and keep His commandments. I have a strong sense that you will need this promise in the coming weeks, so I encourage you to memorize this verse and get it into your bones. I know that sounds kind of weird, but sometimes we need promises that actually strengthen us in the marrow of our bones. I sense this is one of those. In the dream, your dad had it tattooed on his arm, but I believe you will need this tattooed on your heart."

Elizabeth glanced at Ridge's armful of tattoos and said, "I think that will be easy to remember." They both laughed.

"Do you mind me asking what happened to your dad?" Ridge asked a bit hesitantly. "Unless you would rather not talk about it. . ."

"I'm OK with telling you about it," Elizabeth said. "My parents and two sisters were killed in a buggy accident in February of this year. I have two younger brothers who are still living. It's still pretty raw yet, but God has been helping us heal."

"That is a lot to deal with!" Ridge said and then quietly added, "Now I understand why I got rerouted."

"Rerouted?" Elizabeth asked.

"I am riding my motorcycle across the country, from California to the East Coast," Ridge explained. "I take whatever route the Holy Spirit directs me to take. I have a Facebook page, *Riding with Ridge*. It tells my story, if you ever want to read it. The reason I said I got rerouted, I slept in Indy last night and had assumed I'd be in Pittsburgh tonight, but I woke up this morning and knew I was supposed to head north. I ended up here in Amish Country. I was hungry, so I Googled *Amish restaurant*, and here I am. I've learned to trust the Holy Spirit's voice and guidance. I believe this was a divine encounter, and I will be praying for you and your brothers."

"I am thankful to have met you. Thanks for looking up that verse for me and helping me understand my dreams," Elizabeth said. "Be careful out on the roads, and I will pray for your safety."

"Most important thing, get that verse into your bones, and keep trusting God," Ridge repeated. Then he added, "If I never see you again in this life, I'll see you in the next."

As Elizabeth gathered the tips off all of her tables, she saw a postcard with Ridge's tip. It had a picture of Ridge on his motorcycle with the Golden Gate Bridge behind him. At the top, it said *Riding with Ridge* and had his cell number. At the bottom, he wrote a short note: "Have a great day. Remember Deut 7:9. I will be praying for your family. Call me if you need anything."

Elizabeth was walking toward the waitress station and reading the postcard when a customer at a table across the room from her own section stopped her. The woman said, in a condescending voice, "I couldn't help noticing that young man you were talking to. You are such an innocent young Amish girl and need to be cautious about whom you trust."

Elizabeth was surprised by the woman's rudeness. She politely listened but didn't really reply to her. Inside, Elizabeth fumed as she walked back to the kitchen. She thought, *I'm not telling her what we were talking about. I don't need to defend myself!* Of course, Elizabeth knew she needed to be wise.

The obvious call on this woman was that she herself was obnoxious and misjudged Elizabeth's friendliness for ignorance. One thing that Elizabeth was not, was dumb. After all, she thought, *woman, do you know that I know how to speak three languages and that your body odor is awful? Have you ever heard of deodorant?* She then started giggling to herself. Elizabeth obviously couldn't say out loud what she was thinking because in restaurant work, Elizabeth just had to follow the rule of the customer always being right. Plus, her mom had always taught her that if she couldn't say something nice, it would be better not to say anything at all.

Elizabeth tucked the postcard into her purse. She knew she would be cautious and careful but felt irritated that she had been questioned by someone who had no idea what she and Ridge had talked about.

She soon forgot the comment as the Essenhaus host, which today was the owner Bob Miller, repeated over the loud speaker throughout the entire restaurant, parking lots, and all of the gift shops, "Feta Coo, party of one."

"Feta Coo, party of one."

And finally, "Last call for Feta Coo."

All of a sudden, Elizabeth and the other Amish waitresses realized what Bob was saying. They glanced out to see the two maintenance men bent over laughing. *Feta Coo* means *fat cow* in Pennsylvania Dutch, and the maintenance guys had written it on the wait list when the host wasn't looking.

The work at the Essenhaus was hard work, but the employees also made sure they had fun. They loved playing practical jokes on each other.

The Amish waitresses went over to Bob and told him he'd been had. He could also speak Dutch so he fully realized what he had been saying. It took a bit to compose himself after he realized the joke. He almost couldn't stop laughing to announce the next customers. He knew for months he would probably hear a "moo" from these two men any time he saw them.

How would he ever live this down?

CORINA YODER

Chapter 10

The next few days, Elizabeth worked on memorizing the verse she dreamt about. She wrote the words out on an index card and carried it around with her as she did the house work.

Know therefore that the Lord your God is God; he is the faithful God, keeping his covenant of love to a thousand generations of those who love him and keep his commandments. – Deut. 7:9 (NIV)

Her parents had loved God and taught the children that it was important to obey Him. Her favorite part of this verse was the *He is a faithful God* part. She still couldn't believe that God had sent a total stranger to give her a message. She hoped Ridge was safe out on the interstate. She remembered what he said right before he left: "If I never see you again in this life, I will see you in the next."

She had never had anyone say that to her before, but then again, she had never met someone who was crossing the U.S. on motorcycle, either. She prayed that he would be careful and that all of the vehicles around him would see him. She had learned from this past year the devastation a split-second mistake can make.

Elizabeth felt awful for prejudging Ridge. She realized he was quite a gentleman who loved God and wasn't scared to talk about Him. Meeting Ridge reminded Elizabeth of the story in the Bible about John the Baptist, which was one of her dad's favorite stories to read to the children. He explained that John was looked at as an odd character. He stood out by wearing unusual clothes, eating different foods, and not being scared to speak up and tell people things God wanted him to say. On this Earth, he was not always accepted, but Jesus said, "Among those born of women there has not risen anyone greater than John the Baptist." (Matt 11:11 NIV)

Dad had often told the children to "never judge a book by its cover" when seeing people because God often uses the least likely of characters for great works. Sometimes the ones the world views as weird are the very ones God chooses to use.

God will choose whom He will use.

Another one of Dad's favorite Biblical characters was David. The story Dan had repeatedly told the children was the time David wasn't invited to his own anointing. Every time Dad would tell the story, he would remind the children that even David's own dad, Jesse, had not thought to consider God might choose his youngest son to be the chosen king. When the prophet Samuel showed up to anoint one of Jesse's sons, he immediately thought it would be the oldest son. But God looks at the heart, not outward appearance. Jesse presented son after son, seven of them, and God told Samuel no to all of them. Finally, Samuel the prophet asked Jesse, "Do you have any more sons?"

So Jesse told him, "The youngest, he's out taking care of the sheep."

Samuel said, "Go get him," and all of the older brothers had to stand and watch David be anointed.

Dad often noticed the people others overlooked, and he was not easily impressed with people who always wanted to be so important that they ran over others.

Elizabeth was glad the incident had happened with Ridge because she needed to learn from it. She realized how it felt rotten to be misjudged by the rude customer, too.

The week was full of excitement. Karl and Willy had worked hard to clear an area for a fire pit. An Amish concrete crew came to pour the cement. When they were finished pouring it, the boys made Elizabeth come out, and they all three placed their hands into the cement. They all etched their names underneath their hand prints. It was the first thing at this farm that was stamped by the children, and it made for a fun memory.

The next day, the poly lumber chairs were delivered. Ervin and his son came along to help the boys assemble them. The boys could have probably figured out the assembly on their own; but Ervin and his son were known in the community as people who go the extra mile. Ervin's sweet wife had even sent along an ice cream bucket full of cookies.

The finished outdoor area looked sharp. The boys could hardly wait to light a fire. That evening, the children roasted hot dogs and marshmallows and made s'mores. They stayed up late sitting around the fire. Something about sitting around a fire was just mesmerizing, and they could have stayed up all night talking. The weather was just perfect for this kind of evening, too. The flames on the six tiki torches danced in the slight breeze blowing across the yard.

This particular evening began a nightly ritual of fires in the fire pit. It was the perfect place to talk, laugh, and bond. They needed each other. Without realizing it, they had created a perfect place to heal and make new memories.

The boys had found a dead tree that they could cut up for firewood, and it kept them supplied for a long time. Mose also told them that he would take them into his woods to get more wood. He had a lot of old trees that needed to be cleared. More than likely, it would be snowing when they did that.

Soon after their first night around the fire at their new home, Willy's long-awaited day finally arrived. The two puppies were coming. The male came from dogs owned by a Mennonite couple from Millersburg, Dewayne and Lori Yoder. It was easy to tell Dewayne's five children had played with the male a lot. He was full of energy and so much fun. Willy decided to call him Rex. The next day, the female came from E & S Sales, and she was much calmer. Her personality was the complete opposite of Rex's. Willy came up with the name Bella, and he was entertained by the two dogs for hours.

Elizabeth and Karl couldn't believe how much Willy laughed. They had the windows open and could hear Willy talking to the puppies and laughing at them. It was like medicine for all three of their wounded hearts. He figured out that Bella loved retrieving balls and trained her well. Rex couldn't have cared less about retrieving, but he loved water. The children bought a little blue plastic swimming pool, and Rex would get into that pool every chance he had.

At first, the cats hissed at the puppies, but it didn't take the kittens long to befriend them. Before long, it was not all that unusual to see them all lying around in the summer sun napping together. But at night, the boys always put the puppies into the barn to keep them safe. They didn't want them to run away or take any chances with coyotes getting to them.

One night when they were eating supper, Elizabeth told the boys, "I thought up a name for this house. What do you two think of Safe Haven?"

"Oh yeah, I like it," Willy said. "It feels true. I feel safe here."

"What do you think, Karl?" asked Elizabeth.

"Oh, I don't know," Karl replied. "It fits, I guess, but it could also be called the Hunters' Hangout, if you ask me."

Willy came up with the solution. "Why don't we call the farm the Safe Haven, and then we can use that little barn at the back of the property for the Hunters' Hangout. We could keep all our hunting gear out there so we don't get the dog smell on them."

"Sounds like a good compromise," Karl said, laughing. "You are not just getting your way because you are the oldest, Elizabeth! We all have equal voting rights on stuff like this."

"Actually, shouldn't the youngest get the say?" Willy said.

"In English, it isn't called *the say*. You would say, 'Shouldn't the youngest get to choose?'" Elizabeth explained. "Mom had to teach me correct English words a lot."

Elizabeth was laughing as she started telling the boys a story about herself as a little four-year-old girl. "My favorite story about my early years of speaking English was hilarious. I was with Mom and an English driver, and when we came past a new neighbor's house, I told the driver, 'Our new neighbors just pulled in there.'

"Apparently, the driver looked and looked for something that looked 'pulled in,' like a wagon or something. She couldn't see anything like that, and she couldn't figure out what I meant. The driver asked me again about the new neighbors, and I very assertively explained to the driver that the new neighbors were high. Mom had been busy helping you younger boys with something and hadn't been listening to what I was saying to the driver. When the driver asked Mom if the new neighbors did drugs, that's the first time Mom realized my English might need a little help. The driver and Mom had a good laugh when Mom explained that 'moved in' means 'pulled in' in Dutch and that

Amish people call English or non-Amish people 'high' in Dutch. It doesn't mean high on drugs. Mom assured the driver the new neighbors who just moved in were not criminals."

"That's funny," Karl said.

"I know," said Elizabeth. "I bet some of the teachers around here could write books on funny sayings that we Amish children say at school."

"Speaking of school," Willy said, "this is my last year. I thought the eighth grade would never get here. We should probably go to the school to change our address and make sure the bus driver knows where we moved to. I'm pretty sure it would still be the same bus driver because the route I went on used to go close to this house."

"We can stop at the school on the way over to Merle's to help get ready for church," Elizabeth said. "I will be going the next few days, and you can both go with me to help get their shop ready for church."

The next few days were spent helping get Merle's house, yard, and shed ready to host the Sunday church service. The friends and neighbors of the family hosting church in the Amish community come to help clean the homes from top to bottom. Windows get washed, and everything gets organized and ready. The women prepare the food, and the men prepare a place to tie up the horses and buggies. Sometimes hay wagons are used, and other times, people unhitch their horses and put them into the barns. It all depends on how large of a barn or shed someone has. It is a lot of work to be the host for church, but if people help each other, the work goes easier.

Elizabeth woke up early on Sunday morning to get ready to go to church. The Amish church they would be attending today was at their Uncle Merle's house. Merle lived in a different church district, so it would take a little longer to get there. As Elizabeth caught a glance of her brothers coming down the stairs all dressed up to go to church, she was shocked to see how much Karl looked like their dad. She hadn't noticed when he was wearing his everyday clothes.

Immediately, Elizabeth remembered an interaction between her parents she had observed. She was on the porch looking into the kitchen area. Elizabeth had seen her mom's face and eyes light up when she saw her dad enter the kitchen all dressed up for church one Sunday morning, in his Amish Sunday best clothes. He saw it, too. Without missing a beat, her dad had played an air guitar and sang the words "every girl's crazy about a sharp dressed man." She had seen both of them burst out laughing, and he gave her mom a big hug. Elizabeth had never heard that song played before until one night she was with some kids at an ex-Amish guy's house. They were watching *Duck Dynasty*, and the theme song came on. It was the same song Dad had sung to Mom. Elizabeth realized it must have been '80s music her dad used to play on the guitar when he was a teenager. She liked the fact that her parents had stayed close and still had fun together. She wanted a relationship like that someday.

It was a very pleasant day for a buggy ride. On a lot of the country roads, the clip clop of the horseshoes and the wheels on the buggies turning were the only sounds not a part of nature. The wonderful thing about a buggy ride is that it is slow enough to enjoy the beauty outside. The butterflies were fluttering everywhere. They seemed born to spread joy. The flowers were blowing in the breeze, and the water in the creeks was gently running over the rocks and stones. It was a perfect summer day. The children even sang a couple of songs on the way, but mostly they just sat quietly, enjoying the ride.

As they approached Merle's, they saw they were some of the earliest ones to arrive. The boys dropped Elizabeth off at the house so she could go help her aunt. Then they unhitched their horse and put the horse in the barn. They gave him water and some horse feed as well. Merle's boys were glad to see Willy, and he told them all about his new puppies. They took Willy back to the hen house and showed him a new rooster they had gotten. The rooster was a handful, they said, and had a mean streak in him. Merle saw the boys and reminded them they better keep their clothes clean for church. He knew how ornery three young boys could be and shut down any plans they might have had to train a wild rooster. Boys will be boys, he chuckled to himself.

The church service was held inside Merle's shed. The Amish preachers stood in the front of the shed to preach the sermon. There was no pulpit or microphone. Henry Mast had the aufung (the beginning), and when he was finished preaching, Jonas Keim had the main part of the service. Then a few preachers gave testimony to what he had spoken on. Everyone sat on backless benches. The women sat in one area, and the men sat in another area. The songs were sung in High German, and a song leader would lead the songs, not up front but just from his seat. They sang songs from out of a songbook, but they were all sung *acapella*.

Today, the sermon covered John 10, primarily in High German. The different preachers also mixed in some Pennsylvania Dutch and English. The preacher had a Bible, but the Amish people do not normally carry their Bibles to church with them.

Elizabeth was so happy to hear the sermon because Jonas Keim was preaching, and he explained that John 10:10 says that the thief comes to steal, kill, and destroy. She agreed wholeheartedly that sometimes it is the enemy who kills. She thought of her parents and sisters and remembered many well-meaning people telling her it must have been their time to go. Some people had even indicated that this accident must have been God's will. It made her fill up with aggravation every time she heard anyone say that. Today, she realized that the Bible even backs up her belief that sometimes it is not God's will or God's timing but rather the enemy's. She felt relief flood her soul because she just couldn't understand how God would plan such an awful tragedy for their family. She hoped she could learn more about this verse later on.

During the service, Elizabeth helped the Amish women pass around snacks for the little children to eat. The church services are kind of long, so the crackers and pretzels help to keep the little ones from getting hungry or fussy. It was wonderful when you were little, but once you were too big to be considered a child, it was hard to pass on without wanting to eat some.

Elizabeth also helped get the food ready for immediately after church. It wasn't a large traditional Amish meal but rather sort of like a snack to tide everyone over for the buggy ride home: homemade bread, Amish peanut butter spread, apple butter, cold cuts of meat and cheese, and Amish church cookies.

Willy, his friend Johnny, and his two cousins, Roger and Ryan, quickly ate and then ran off together. Their first stop was to check on the rooster. They teased him a bit and then headed for the woods. The boys showed Willy and Johnny the big black walnut trees they harvested walnuts from. Roger explained that they gather them in the fall and then sell them to an Amish man from Rentown. He pays the boys by the pound, and both boys were able to purchase new guns from last year's walnut money. Willy's business-savvy mind started thinking of the woods behind their new house. He was picturing some cash in his hand. When the boys got back to the house, they realized Johnny's parents had been looking for him, and they were ready to leave. Willy asked Johnny's dad if he could look for walnuts in the woods that Johnny's dad was leasing.

Johnny's dad said, "Why sure, Willy! Help yourself. You can get all you want."

"Much obliged," Willy said as he waved goodbye.

Karl was eating at a table full of young sixteen- to eighteen-year-old guys. The conversation quickly turned to the fact that a bunch of their families were going to be camping at Twin Mills over the fourth of July. They were telling Karl that he needed to come watch fireworks with them.

Chapter 11

For the Millers, camping at Twin Mills for the week of the fourth of July was a long-standing family tradition. Mose and Carrie always made it a priority as well. While Dan had worked in the trailer factory for several years, this time was his only designated week of summer vacation. He also got two weeks off over Christmas. When he started working at home with the horses full time, they continued keeping this particular week of camping intact.

This year, the children decided to go camping for just a long weekend. They thought the puppies were a bit young to be away from Willy for a whole week. The truth was that Willy would have missed the puppies too much. It took Karl and Willy most of the morning to gather up all the tents and camping supplies. Elizabeth worked on preparing the food and filling all the coolers. They could hardly contain their excitement. They had always looked forward to camping. Karl had asked Pete Miller, an Amish friend who was seventeen, to give them a ride to the campground. Pete was also going to camp, so he said he'd be glad to swing by and pick them up.

When Pete drove in the lane, he had Keith Urban blaring on his radio and was grinning from ear to ear. Karl was pretty impressed with Pete's new Chevy pickup, and Pete was excited to show Karl all of its bells and whistles. Karl was genuinely happy for Pete and was thankful he had a friend who had a vehicle and could drive. The boys loaded up the camping gear and then headed for the house to help Elizabeth carry out the food coolers.

Karl thought Pete was a blast to be around when he was cracking jokes like a comedian, but it was like a switch flipped when he was around Elizabeth. Pete got all polite and thoughtful. When Pete started his truck, he turned down the music to a reasonable volume. Karl would have preferred to drive with the music blaring and the windows down. To top it all off, Pete asked Karl, Willy, and Elizabeth if they would want to go see the fireworks with him on the fourth.

That was the straw that broke the camel's back. Why would Pete want to include Willy and Elizabeth, Karl thought to himself, rather annoyed. So Karl abruptly answered, "I want to go with you, but these two already had plans with my Uncle Mose!"

Karl decided if he wanted to have any fun with Pete this weekend, he would need to do all he could to keep Pete far away from Elizabeth. Sure, Karl was glad Elizabeth wasn't ugly, but sometimes she distracted his friends. That was a bit annoying at times. He didn't feel bad for uninviting his brother and sister because Elizabeth actually thought some of Karl's friends were rather immature. Karl knew she would never see those younger guys as dating material. Only in Pete's dreams would Elizabeth ever be interested in him, Karl thought to himself.

When they all arrived at Twin Mills, they soon found Mose and Carrie's camping spot and unloaded all their gear at the site next to it. Mose was happy to see them and got right to work setting up the tents. He was cracking jokes left and right, and he had all three children laughing in no time. It seemed completely normal to be hanging out with their family. It wasn't that everyone didn't miss the rest of the family, but this was starting to be the new normal. It wasn't that they were all blocking out the truth that the loss had happened or that they weren't missed. They were just making new memories, and Mose was bound and determined to make this trip a fun weekend for everyone.

Early on, after the death of the four, Mose made a choice that he was not going to allow grief to consume his life. He had lots of life to live and was not about to be dragged into a pit of despair.

He knew people who dealt with grief, death and loss in a crippling way. They seemed to allow their own lives to be cloaked in death. Mose knew others who dealt with the grief and asked God to heal their broken hearts. The ones who let themselves feel the good, the bad, and ugly seemed so much more able to handle life. He made a choice to repeatedly choose the healthy path of grieving the traumatic deaths.

Mose hadn't talked to Karl since the night Karl got mad at him about not getting a truck. He noticed Karl had a good attitude, and he was thankful. He knew that sixteen year olds could sometimes be temperamental and that the age between being a boy and a man could be awkward.

The minute all the tents were set up, the boys changed into their swimming trunks. They rode their bikes to the swimming pool and spent the rest of the day having fun with their friends. Elizabeth had looked forward to reading her new book, so she spent the afternoon lounging in a hammock. She just loved the trees, and the weather was perfect. For supper that evening, they roasted hot dogs and grilled some corn on the cob. Carrie had brought radishes and carrots from her garden. It was the perfect summer meal. After they were all finished eating, they lounged and talked for a long time. When the younger children were ready to go to bed, Willy and Karl were ready to get their evening started. They had brought a bag full of quarters to use for games up at the arcade center. When the children were sleeping in the tent, Mose and Carrie came back out to the fire.

Elizabeth said, "Why don't you two bike up and play ping pong for a while? I can stay here with the children."

"You don't need to ask me twice," Mose replied. "I haven't beat Carrie in ping pong in almost a year."

Carrie laughed. "It's not that we haven't played. I'm just better than he is." Mose laughed at his wife's response.

Mose and Carrie biked away, looking like two sixteen year olds who were excited to go on a date. Elizabeth smiled and let her mind think about a few young men she had thought of some over the years. She didn't waste her time on these thoughts a lot, but just seeing Mose and Carrie reminded her of the kind of relationship she wanted someday. The man would definitely need to be a strong leader like her dad had been. She didn't like wishy-washy guys without any backbone. She also wanted a man who loved God. Life was hard, and she knew it would be even worse without God.

On the evening of July fourth, Elizabeth, Willy, and Mose's family watched the campground Patriot Parade. It was fun gathering up candy and seeing the different themes of each decorated golf cart. The first golf cart was playing the song "Born in the USA" loud enough to wake the dead. After the parade ended, a lot of the campers sat on the beach and watched the fireworks from a nearby town. Some of the people who lived beside the lake also shot off some fireworks across the lake. The campers ooh'ed and aah'ed throughout the entire show. A group of junior high cheerleaders passed out sparklers to the children and did a dance performance with sparklers to entertain the crowd before the fireworks began.

The Amish and English were intermingled, and everybody was laughing and having fun, until a man walked up in front of the crowd and quieted everyone down. The man introduced himself as Pastor Smith and said, "I would like to pray a blessing on America together tonight." He then proceeded to pray a beautiful prayer. Elizabeth had peeked during the prayer, and she saw Amish men and women praying beside English people dressed in patriotic clothes. It was a touching experience for the whole group, and it reminded all of them how blessed they were to live in the U.S.A.

Karl had gone with Pete and some other guys to watch some bigger fireworks at the Goshen fairgrounds. They didn't expect to get back until pretty late. Elizabeth didn't fall asleep until she heard Pete's truck drop Karl off, and she thanked God he made it back safe and sound.

She thought about Karl's birthday coming up in a few weeks and realized she needed to get used to Karl being gone a lot more. Even at eighteen, she felt more like his mom than his sister. She had a few thoughts about what she wanted to get him for his birthday, but she would need Mose to help her in order to pull off the element of surprise.

The next morning after breakfast, she told Mose her ideas, and Mose said he would help make it happen. The rest of the weekend flew past, and by the time they got home on Sunday afternoon, all three were exhausted. They had a bit too much sun, and all of the clothes smelled like campfire. They dumped a big bag of dirty clothes and towels in the wash house. Elizabeth had her work cut out for herself on Monday. She did have a brand new wringer washer, which helped a lot. She was also thankful for the two extra-long wash lines because tomorrow, those would be full to the gill. The puppies were so excited to see Willy, and he played with them until dark.

The next few weeks also flew past. The weather was hotter every day, but they did get a lot of work done in the pasture area and on the hunting shed.

Bright and early on July 18, Karl got his first birthday gift. He was finally sixteen. Elizabeth and Willy surprised Karl and did all the chores for him. They told him to get dressed and ready to go eat breakfast at the Five and Twenty with Uncle Mose. Mose had lined out a driver to pick both of them up. During breakfast, Mose told Karl that he was taking him to get a phone for his birthday. Karl was so excited. He had not expected this gift, so it made him really happy. They had a fun morning together, and as they left the Verizon store, Karl was beaming. He had an iPhone 5 and the world at his fingertips.

Mose left Karl at the Verizon store and had the driver take him to a few other stores. By the time Mose got back, Thunder, the Verizon employee, taught Karl how to program phone numbers and how to text. Karl was stoked because for years, he had to carry a list of phone numbers in his wallet and use the phone shanty. Thunder was used to the Amish who were phone first timers, though, and showed Karl what they carried in order to charge his phone without electricity. It was a battery-operated charger powered by solar energy. Thunder also helped Karl set up a Facebook page and helped him search for his friends.

While they were working together to set up Karl's Facebook account, Thunder started laughing.

"What's so funny?" Karl asked with a smile.

Thunder replied," You have only had this phone for an hour, and you have 25 people already asking to be your Facebook friend. Do you know this Pete Miller?"

"Oh, yeah, he's one of my best friends," Karl said. "Why did you ask?'

"Well, he asked you if you want to go to the Elkhart County Fair tonight in Goshen," replied Thunder. "Do you know how to reply?"

"I have no idea how to reply, but I want to go with him," Karl stated.

Thunder found this so interesting. He had customers who had children the age of four and five who knew how to operate their parents' smart phones. He also had a lot of Amish friends who were in their rumspring years. Thunder's boss learned to always let Thunder deal with the young Amish kids because he had Amish neighbors all of his life and was good at interacting with them.

Thunder explained to Karl that his new Facebook friends were now posting happy birthday on his Facebook wall. He also told Karl that he had 20 more friend requests. One by one, he read the names, and sure enough, Karl knew them all, so Thunder taught him how to accept their requests, too. The last friend request was by a Bill Yoder. After Karl accepted his friend request, Bill wrote, "Happy Birthday, Karl! Dad wants to know if you want to work for his construction crew (starting Monday)?"

"What the heck?" Thunder said. "You were just offered a job on Facebook? I have never heard of that before. You Amish kids sure know how to network."

Soon after Karl's job offer came through Facebook, Mose came back and overheard what Thunder said. "What happened?" Mose asked.

Karl said, "Thunder got me set up with my phone, and we added Facebook. Just now, Bill Yoder asked if I want to work for Yoder's Construction, starting Monday already."

"What did you tell him?" Mose asked.

"I didn't answer yet," Karl replied. "What do you think?"

Mose was very supportive and shared what things he had been told about the business. "That's a good Amish crew to work for; Bill's dad is known to be a good contractor. He does very neat work and pays his guys well."

Thunder asked, "Why would he hire Karl without doing an interview?"

Mose said, "Here's the deal: Bill's dad knew Karl's dad before he died, and he knows that any son of Dan's would be a trained worker."

Karl and Mose shook hands with Thunder and thanked him. Thunder said, "I hope you like your phone and the Demolition Derby. You had better enjoy your last day off before you start the job you never applied for."

"That's true," Karl said, laughing. "I will!"

When Karl got home, he showed Elizabeth and Willy his new phone. They were glad to finally have a phone at the house. The closest phone booth was about a mile away, and in the winter time, that distance may have been too far to travel. It was nice to have a phone readily accessible, in case of emergency.

He also showed them his Facebook account and told them about his job that started on Monday.

Elizabeth made Karl's favorite pulled pork sandwich for lunch and had wrapped a few gifts for him to open. The first box was really heavy and had a bunch of clay pigeons for target practice, along with a few boxes of ammo.

"Oh, sweet! Thanks a lot!" Karl said. "Willy, do you want to go out and practice shooting targets this afternoon? Hunting season will be here before we know it."

The boys had fun shooting targets but didn't want to do it too long, or it would make the horses too restless. Willy stayed in the yard and played with the puppies, Bella and Rex, until they were all three exhausted. Elizabeth made some lemonade and brought it out to the front porch. She and Willy sat and talked, and it seemed to her that Willy was getting used to the fact that his sisters were in Heaven. He talked about how much both girls would have liked the puppies. Willy decided that Barbara would have preferred Bella, and Katie would have liked Rex better. It was pretty insightful, and Elizabeth agreed with him.

When Karl came out of his room, Elizabeth and Karl almost didn't recognize him. He was dressed in denim jeans and an American Eagle tee shirt.

"Don't I look handsome?" Karl asked, while strutting around to show them all angles of his outfit. "Can't you see the line of girls wanting to date me? I will just need to tell them, 'Back of the line, Baby.'"

All three children burst out laughing. Karl was becoming more like Uncle Mose every day.

"You look pretty sharp," Elizabeth said. "But when did you get those clothes?"

"Pete took me shopping on the weekend of July fourth," Karl replied. "He's coming pretty soon, and we are going to go get my hair cut before the fair tonight. My haircut doesn't really match the outfit."

The children could hear Pete coming up the road before they could see him. He sure liked his music loud. Karl and Pete headed for Middlebury to style Karl's hair. Pete always brought his buddies to this particular salon for their first haircuts after they turned sixteen. He had become friends with the women who worked there. The salon owner finally started giving Pete free haircuts for every new customer and just for his free entertainment. He was full of a lot of hot air but was really likeable.

This was Karl's first experience at the Elkhart County fair. It was always held at the Goshen fairgrounds. They walked around the fair, took a few rides, and ate some fair food. Then they headed for the grandstands to watch the Demolition Derby. They found a bunch of friends to sit with and enjoyed the pre-derby entertainment. A couple of the Amish girls had Karl pose for some pictures beside some of the cars. They showed him how to upload the picture onto his Facebook profile. While watching the derby, he couldn't believe how people drove recklessly into each other. It was a great evening for Karl and his friends.

At home, Elizabeth and Willy played a game before he went to bed. This was the first night that she felt like she was missing out on her teenage years. She missed having Karl around, but she wanted him to get to have fun, too.

Chapter 12

Karl told Willy all about the Demolition Derby the following morning. They decided to go fishing back in the woods and also scout out black walnut trees. They got busy gathering up their fishing gear, and Elizabeth was watering plants on front porch. As the boys were walking toward the barn, they noticed an unfamiliar car drive in the lane. It was a rusted out old junker of a car. The children were instantly uncomfortable, but because they were already outside, there wasn't much to do except find out who this was and what this person or people wanted.

A scruffy-looking man who looked like he had just rolled out of bed got out of the car and walked toward the boys. He must have been around the age of 50.

"Are you the Miller children whose parents were killed in the buggy accident?" he gruffly asked.

By this time, Elizabeth had walked over to her brothers and had heard the blunt and almost rude question. They hesitated but were almost ready to answer when all four of them saw a buggy driving in the lane. It stopped the conversation. The man asked, "Are you expecting someone?"

The Miller children saw Elizabeth's bike on the back and knew right away who it was. They all just stood still and watched John Hostetler get out of his buggy and walk toward them.

Willy blurted out in Dutch, "We are glad you are here! We don't know who this is!"

Instantly, John took charge of the conversation and asked the man, "May I ask what your name is and what can we do for you?"

The man replied, "My named is Greg White. I'm Blake's dad. Blake was in that accident that killed the Miller family. Am I at the right farm?"

The children nodded yes.

Greg cleared his throat and said, "Well, I just wanted to come tell you that we ain't got much, so please don't think about suing us."

Karl and Elizabeth looked pretty puzzled by this odd request. They couldn't figure out what in the world he was talking about.

John spoke up again, "Sir, I'm not sure why you are here because it was an accident. We Amish people are praying that Blake gets out of the hospital soon and are glad that his life was spared."

Greg got agitated, and an angry scowl soon covered his face. "You must not know where that worthless piece of trash is headed to. He's not getting out of a hospital to walk free. He went straight from the hospital to the state pen. I knew he would end up in prison one day. I've told him that he's been nothing but trouble since he's been five years old. I was right. That was not an accident that he drove his truck into your family's buggy. He was drunk that day. I hate him for what he's put me through all my life. I wish he'd have never been born!"

The children had never heard such anger toward anyone before. Greg White was just getting good and started. It was like he was spewing out venom. His face got all red, and it was scary to watch.

He began cussing but slowed down a bit when a police car drove in the lane.

John glanced at Elizabeth, and they both looked relieved to see the police officers arrive. The two cops got out of the car and joined the conversation. They looked at the children and asked if everyone was all right.

Greg said, "Oh yeah, we are all fine. I just wanted to apologize for my son."

Karl spoke up and said, "I don't know what is going on here, but this man claims he's Blake White's dad. He also claimed that Blake was drunk the day of the accident, and now he's here begging us to not sue them."

One of the cops took Greg White off to the side and spoke to him. He asked him to leave and never return to the Miller house. The other cop asked the rest of them to sit down on the chairs by the fire pit. The cop said, "I'm pretty upset that Greg White came to your house like this. We got a call this morning from someone in the community telling us that he was asking people where you children lived. I was the officer who found out that Blake had been drunk the day of the accident. As you children know, he was in really serious condition in the Fort Wayne hospital, and none of us thought he would make it. He was never tested for his alcohol level the day of the accident because he was literally hanging on by a thread. He was in a coma until last week. Two days ago, I went down to the hospital to visit him with a friend of mine from my church. We got to visit with him, and he started talking about the week of the accident. We couldn't believe how good his memory was. He explained exactly what happened."

The cop continued. "My friend who came with me runs a recovery program at church, and he had been helping Blake. Blake had become a Christian nine months earlier and was successfully kicking an alcohol and drug addiction. He was clean for six months and doing great. The week before the accident, Blake lost his job at one of the trailer factories that he had worked at for ten years. It was a big layoff by new ownership, and they cleaned house on the best paid workers. It devastated Blake, and he had got scared and depressed. The day of the accident, he started drinking in the forenoon. He had then decided to drive to an area out in the woods, one he hunted in, to end it all. He was on his way to take his own life when he ran into your parents' buggy. The accident and being taken to hospital saved his life."

The cop, John, and the children all just sat quietly for a bit.

The cop had tears forming in his eyes but pulled it together for the sake of his professionalism to explain more. "He has had a really tough life. You met his dad. It took a long time for him to forgive his dad for a lot of things that happened in his childhood. Blake wanted me to come to talk to you children. He asked me to tell you that he is so sorry for the trauma he has put your family through. He is devastated and extremely full of regret. He knows it might take a long time to forgive him, but he would ask for your forgiveness. I was not expecting to hear this confession when I went to see him in the hospital. Quite frankly, I wasn't sure if he would ever tell anyone what happened. He would have been released from the hospital to go home. He was honest and realizes he will be in prison for a long time. It was by far the hardest arrest I've ever made."

The officer then paused, allowing everyone to process all of this information. Then he asked, "Do any of you have any questions?"

"Oh my," Elizabeth said. "This is awful. It was terrible enough when we thought it was just an accident. Now there is so much more to process. Dad would definitely want us to forgive him. Right now I just feel so bad for his life. I even feel bad for his dad. He must be miserable being so angry. I can see why Blake started drinking in the first place. I want to write him a letter sometime. I just want some time to think about it before I do."

"What about the rest of you?" the cop asked. "Do you have any questions?"

Karl cleared his throat and said, "I start a new job on Monday, and I won't be here during the day. I don't want that Greg White coming here again, 'cause if he does, I'm going to get mad about it. I'm the only one with a phone, and Elizabeth wouldn't be able to call you cops if he comes again. Thank goodness you all showed up today!"

"We actually do have a pager system for a few of our Amish people in the area," the cop explained. "We have had some Amish people turn in drug dealers. They wear pagers in case of any situation of retaliation on their Amish families. I will have both Elizabeth and Willy wear them. Greg White should be leaving town immediately, and his home is four hours south of here, so I doubt you will have any more problems. We had told him not to come out here, and we apologize that he didn't respect our request. I think he just feared being sued by you kids, but we know you aren't those types of people."

"That man needs help," John said. "It sounds like Blake is better off than his dad is. I would have been scared to grow up under his roof."

"I agree," the cop said. "Unfortunately, that is how a lot of people live."

As they were finishing up the conversation, the second police officer walked up. They all heard the car Greg White was driving leaving the farm.

The second officer said, "Greg White better not show his face here again, but just to be safe, we will bring you pagers to wear." He looked at John and said, "Could you hang around here for a couple hours until we get back and get everything in place?"

Elizabeth wasn't sure what John was going to say to that, and her mind instantly thought about lunch.

Her mind started running. *What will I fix for us to eat if he's here? I would have planned a meal if I'd have known!* Her mind started fretting. Immediately, she made her mind calm down. Then she asked herself, *what would Mom do? Think!* She remembered they still had pulled pork left from Karl's birthday, along with pie and cake. She felt immediate relief.

She heard John say, "Not a problem. Yes, I can stay until you all get back." Then the cops left.

John and the children could not believe what had just happened. Willy was sure to tell John again that he was glad that John was there at the time. Elizabeth and Karl both nodded their heads in agreement.

Karl said, "I just got my phone, but it was in the house, and I didn't want to leave Elizabeth and Willy outside while I ran in and called the cops. Plus, I don't even know the number for the police station."

"I am glad I could help out, and I'm glad I was here, too," John said. "I have a phone for my business, too, and I carry it with me except when I go to church. I can help you program the police and other emergency numbers on speed dial. It's pretty easy."

As they all walked toward the house, Elizabeth was thankful she kept the house neat and tidy because she had not expected to have company today. For sure, she wasn't expecting John Hostetler. But she couldn't deny that it just seemed comfortable for all four of them. As they stepped into the house, John looked around and smiled. Then he said, "This is a really nice place you have here." He even commented on the front porch and all the flowers.

"Yeah, we love it here," Karl said. "I will go get my phone."

Willy went out the front door to check on the puppies, and all of a sudden, it was just Elizabeth and John.

She said, "It seems like you always get us out of predicaments. Thanks for fixing my bike and helping us today. I don't know what we would have done without you. Karl does a good job taking care of everything around here, but today would have been pretty scary if we would have been here by ourselves."

"I agree. I was even freaked out by that guy," John said.

"You were?" Elizabeth asked, surprised. "I couldn't tell. You hid it well."

"I've seen a lot of rough characters, but he's got a lot of nerve trash talking his own son like that," John said. "I wish he'd go serve Blake's sentence. It's pretty obvious Blake never got an ounce of affirmation or love from his own dad."

"You're right. I can't imagine all he has lived through," Elizabeth replied.

John reached over to place his hand on Elizabeth's shoulder. "You have lived through a lot, too, in the past few months. Today was a lot to go through. Are you doing OK?"

About then, they heard Karl coming down the stairs, and John pulled his hand back.

Elizabeth had been a bit surprised by the gesture, but it felt comfortable. "Yeah, I think I will be all right. I often wish I could tell Dad stuff that happens because he always seemed to know how to handle things."

"You had a great dad, that's for sure," John reassured her as he turned his attention to Karl's phone. "Wow! You have an iPhone five! That's an awesome phone."

John helped Karl program the fire department, ambulance, and police station. He then also programmed his own cell number into Karl's favorites and told Karl he could call him day or night if he needed anything.

Elizabeth had gone to the kitchen to set out lunch, but every now and then, she glanced into the dining room area at the two young men. She couldn't believe how normal it felt to have John here. It didn't seem awkward at all. She had to get some pickles in the basement, and as she was walking down the stairs to get them, she reached her hand up to her shoulder where John had touched her. She thought to herself, *he really genuinely cared about how I am doing.* But of course, the practical, responsible side of her brain said, *focus on making lunch. For Pete's sake, anyone would have cared after this forenoon's event.*

They ate pulled pork sandwiches, some leftover birthday cake, and a freshly baked custard pie. John commented a few times how good everything was and even told Elizabeth that custard was his favorite pie, and this particular one was the best he had ever had. He then laughed and said, "Just don't tell my mom I said that."

After lunch, the guys all helped bring the dirty plates to the sink. Elizabeth washed the dishes and cleaned up the kitchen while the guys sat and talked at the kitchen table. It didn't seem unusual, although it was.

All Karl had to do was ask John one question about Montana. Like a primed water pump, John started telling story after story of his days out west. It was fascinating to all of them, and Willy even ran and got an atlas so he could see where the states were that John was telling them about. He told about hunting trips up in mountains, camping in the rough, carrying bear mace in case of bears. The insanity of the adventures made for really exciting stories. The retelling of John's adventures kept Karl and Willy at the edge of their seats, and John seemed to enjoy reliving each story he told.

Karl told John that he would like to go hunting elk with some friends this next winter. John said, "I got connections to help make that happen if you are serious. I'd even want to go along if you have room for one more guy."

Elizabeth felt her heart beating really fast, and the feeling of intense panic came over her. John noticed the change in her demeanor instantly and knew immediately what had happened. Elizabeth had just heard the dangerous stories he had told, and now Karl wanted to go live that out. He could understand why Elizabeth would be fearful of losing Karl, too. She had too much loss for one year to want to risk more loss. Graciously, John then leaned in and told Karl, "Save your money for a few years, and you can afford a better hunt."

Somehow, John just understood Elizabeth. He felt protective of her. He barely knew her, but he felt like he had always known her. That made absolutely no sense at all, but it was the truth.

One officer finally returned with the pagers. To her, these pagers actually looked just like pocket watches. The department had them specially made for the Amish because they looked like something the Amish would actually own. They would need to keep them charged up and only use them in case of an emergency. It sounded easy enough. The police explained that most people who wear them never even need to use them, but it was better to be safe than sorry.

One of the questions Elizabeth asked the cops was if they would need to go to court over the accident Blake had. She hoped they wouldn't because the court process makes most Amish people very uncomfortable. The officer reassured her that she would not. He explained that if a drunk driver hits and kills someone, then the state would press charges against the drunk driver. It would be considered involuntary manslaughter. Elizabeth was very relieved that it would not drag her brothers and her into the legal side of things. The Miller children and John thanked the officer and walked with him to his car. The boys decided to skip the fishing that day and went to put away their fishing poles.

Elizabeth walked with John to his buggy to unload her bike. She thanked him for everything. He wouldn't let her pay for the bike repair bill and told her to call if they ever needed anything.

Chapter 13

Elizabeth watched John's buggy drive away. The police car carefully maneuvered around the buggy and drove out of sight. She instantly felt alone and told Karl and Willy that she was going to take a nap. The day's events had her feeling emotionally drained. She wrapped herself up in her mom's quilt and had a good long cry. It felt like there was a big boulder on her back. This new information was too much to carry without her parents. Today, she missed her mom the most. She wished that she could ask her some questions. Her mom always knew exactly what to say to encourage her children. She prayed a lot for them, and it showed. If Mom had something she was worried about, she would turn it into prayer. She claimed it was hard to do both at the same time. She had often told the children that worrying will actually add more problems, while praying will bring answers.

At this moment, Elizabeth didn't feel like praying about anything! Instead, she just wanted Mom to come home. She knew that she would have been able to instantly tell if her parents liked John Hostetler. Elizabeth was almost certain her parents would have really enjoyed his company, but she had no way of knowing for sure. She was trying to sort through how she felt about him, too. It seemed every time he was in their lives, they needed his help with something. He made her feel taken care of, and today, she had felt protected by him. That is exactly how her dad had always made her feel, too. She shuddered at the thought of how different her dad was from Blake's dad. It made her grateful to have grown up in a good home.

She thought of how Mom would have calmed them all down with her words. It made Elizabeth question if she could do a good job being a mom to Willy. She punched her pillow in frustration because she wished it wasn't a responsibility she needed to carry. The truth was, all who were around her could see she was doing an amazing job. Elizabeth had made the choice to essentially become a parent to the boys, but it sure was not the easy route. She thought about her eighteen-year-old friends, and most of them were still enjoying their freedom.

As she lay in bed thinking about everything, she got the impression of a row of dominos falling over. She thought about how the tragedy had started with a negative domino effect. She wished she could push them backward and change the domino effect to a positive one instead, starting with Blake staying sober, not losing his job, the new owners of the trailer factory not unjustly laying off the guys, Blake having a great childhood. Like an unstoppable freight train, her mind just ran on and on. Finally, she pulled the brakes and stopped her thoughts. She told herself, *you can't change the past! No amount of wishing will change it.*

Finally, she whispered a prayer. "God, I need to stop trying to figure this all out because it is going to drive me crazy if I don't turn it over to you. Please help me get some rest and trust you with all of this, in Jesus' name." Within minutes, she fell into a peaceful sleep.

Karl and Willy had also crashed onto the two couches in the living room. They were exhausted, too. The breeze was blowing the curtains, and the wind chimes were gently playing in the breeze. Before the boys fell asleep, they both heard Elizabeth crying. They exchanged glances but didn't say anything. They could both see the pain in each other's eyes. They understood because both of the boys were overwhelmed with the day's events, too. It hurt both of them to hear Elizabeth so sad. Normally, she was upbeat and worked so hard to bring a cheerful atmosphere into their home.

That evening when Karl's friends stopped in to pick him up, he told them he wouldn't be going along. Elizabeth was surprised at that kind gesture because she knew he had been looking forward to going to the fair again. Instead, the three children built a fire in the fire pit and enjoyed a quiet evening on the deck. The fireflies were out in full force. The moon was bright, and so were the stars. The stars were twinkling, and Elizabeth, Karl, and Willy could easily see the Big and Little Dipper.

It was one of the most serene nights they had all summer. It felt like God was up close and personal, and the children sat and talked about their four family members in Heaven.

But talking about their treasured family made all of them cry at different times. They also had an interesting conversation on what Heaven would be like. They talked about Blake White and how awful his home life must have been. They even felt sad for the miserable life that Greg White was choosing to live. Being that mean must have come from his own pain. It was hard telling what kind of childhood he had and now was passing on to his kids.

It was tough to handle so many feelings at the same time. The Miller children talked about what Dad would have advised them to do with this new information. They knew without a shadow of a doubt, he would have encouraged them to forgive. He used to always say, *not forgiving someone is like dragging a dead corpse around with you. It just weighs you down, and there's no life in that.* He would also say, *bitterness is like drinking a poison in hopes it will hurt the person who wounded you.* These were just a few of the things their dad had repeatedly taught them over the years. His wise words, they knew, would stick with them forever.

On Sunday morning, the three children did their chores and then rested because it was what they called their "in between Sunday," which meant they did not have church that week. Amish people only have church every other Sunday. On the Sunday that they don't have church, they rest and still practice the Sabbath Day. They don't do farm work or mow the lawn, but they do feed their animals and milk cows if they have some.

The Miller children were invited to Mose and Carrie's house for lunch. They couldn't wait to tell them all about Greg White and the news about Blake as well. The children rode their bikes, and Karl pulled a cart behind his bike. Elizabeth started getting mildly annoyed with the boys because they kept goofing off with their bikes. She had spent a good amount of time baking a pecan pie and two chocolate cream pies, and they were in the cart. She was imagining that Karl was going to flip the cart on the side, and her pies would be destroyed. She finally told the boys that if they dumped the pies, they would need to go home and make some before they could come eat. They laughed, but they listened.

When they arrived, Mose welcomed them into the back porch. They instantly smelled the delicious meal Carrie was preparing. It smelled just like Mom's kitchen, and all of their mouths started watering. Elizabeth helped cut the pies and then filled all the bowls with steaming hot food. Carrie had made poor man's steak, mashed potatoes, green beans, fresh lettuce salad, (straight from the garden), homemade bread, apple butter, and red beets. Each dish looked amazing.

It was good to be with Mose and Carrie and their children. They enjoyed hearing what their young, rambunctious cousins had been up to recently. The little two year old climbed up onto everything, and they had to constantly protect him from getting hurt. Mose reminded Karl about some of the things Karl used to do when he was just a little whippersnapper.

Karl just laughed and said, "No, I was the perfect little boy always sitting around reading books or twiddling my thumbs."

"Oh my, we wish! Mose said. "You gave us all quite a few scares."

"Speaking of giving us a scare," Karl continued, "you should have been at our house yesterday. We had quite an experience." Karl told Mose and Carrie all about Greg and Blake White.

Mose was surprised to hear the fresh news of Blake's confession. It rattled him to think that none of this would have happened if Blake had not been drinking.

Elizabeth also shared with Mose and Carrie what she had heard Jonas Keim preach about, the sermon on John 10:10.

Elizabeth said, "I have never believed that this accident was God's will. It rubbed me the wrong way if people told me that it must have been their time to go. When I heard about Blake being drunk, it confirmed my gut instinct. I remembered those verses that Jonas Keim had read out of the Bible. I knew this accident and these deaths fall under the first part of that verse in John 10:10 where it says, 'The thief comes to steal, kill and destroy, but that God comes to bring life and to the full.'

"I see this accident as something God did allow, but God was not the author of it. I know that what we do with what happened is up to us, though. We need to choose a good response to it. I just really wish that people would stop saying 'this must have been God's will' to evil tragedies because the Bible clearly states that sometimes it is not His will. It must hurt God when people blame Him for the thief's destruction. I want to learn to not quickly say something is God's will."

Mose agreed with Elizabeth and told her that people sometimes say ignorant things when they don't know what else to say. "Hearing that Blake was drunk and driving would definitely fall into an illegal category, even by the law, so of course it was wrong. So sin was the author of that and not God's will at all. You are onto something, Lisbet. I do agree with you that there is nothing bad that has happened in this life that God can't turn around and use for good."

They sat and talked for another hour about anything and everything. Mose knew how to make them laugh but also kept it serious at times and encouraged the children to forgive Blake. Karl was pretty excited about his new job with Yoder Construction that started first thing on Monday morning. Mose asked him if he had a good tool belt and all the things he needed. Karl told him that he was planning on taking his dad's belt and tools because they were still fairly new.

"Switching the subject a bit," Mose said, "Elizabeth are you going to the singing tonight?"

Elizabeth was surprised he asked because she hadn't been able to go much of anywhere alone since the funeral. She normally stayed home with the boys. The singings were for the Amish youth to gather together and sing songs. They were held on Sunday evenings at different homes.

"I wasn't planning on it," Elizabeth answered.

"You need to go spend some time with your friends tonight," Mose insisted. "Willy can stay here overnight, and I could use his help tomorrow with some of my calves."

"I can take you to the singing," Karl offered. "I have some friends who said they were going, too."

The bike ride home was less stressful for Elizabeth. The boys were still a bit obnoxious, but at least there was no fear of pie being dumped. On this trip, she was able to laugh at their silliness. Willy packed a bag of work clothes and his overnight things and rode his bike back to Mose's house. He wasn't scared of biking alone, but he did take along the pocket watch pager the police had given him.

After Willy left, Elizabeth and Karl got dressed in church clothes to go to the singing. It felt a bit strange to be going, but she was excited to go see her friends. She also loved to sing and couldn't wait to do that again with a group of young people. They took the buggy and had a good talk on the way.

When they were walking toward the shed where the singing was going to be held, Elizabeth saw Suzanne. They greeted each other with a quick squeeze of hands. Suzanne said, "It's high time you got to come! I have missed you at the singings."

Elizabeth enjoyed the evening and sang her heart out. A few songs about heaven brought some tears to the corner of her eyes, but she knew she was going to see her family again one day. And it was true. Heaven will surely be worth it all.

After the singing was over, Elizabeth and Suzanne were talking with a group of girls. Suzanne mentioned that they could use Elizabeth's help cleaning at Cassandra's on Monday.

Elizabeth replied, "I have off at the Essenhaus on Mondays, and I could go along tomorrow. What time would the driver pick me up?"

"Be ready at seven. It takes about an hour to get to her house," Suzanne replied.

Bright and early, on Monday morning, Karl left for his new construction job, and Elizabeth was on her way to a brand new experience. She had never helped clean for English people before, so she hoped she'd learn how to use their appliances rather quickly. It didn't take long for Cassandra to make them all feel welcome. Her house was very big, so she took different girls to different parts of the house. Elizabeth was relieved that she was asked to dust the dining room and living room. She knew how to do that chore with confidence but was a bit nervous to dust some of the expensive items Cassandra had sitting around.

Cassandra was a very sophisticated 50 year old woman with black hair and piercing blue eyes. She loved stylish clothes with flamboyant colors, with purple being her favorite. She truly carried herself as royalty.

It was obvious that Cassandra was very wealthy and enjoyed living her life of luxury. Her dogs were more pampered than most children. In fact, the dog's trainer was stopping by right at the time the girls started cleaning to take the dogs for their morning run. It was just unheard of in the Amish community. *Oh for Pete's sake,* Elizabeth thought. *The Amish dogs get exercise chasing cows.* She soon started giggling to herself. It felt so good to laugh.

Cassandra asked the girls to stop working around 11:30 and to come into the kitchen area to eat. She introduced the Amish girls to the cook named Senora Sanchez, who was the sweetest Mexican woman. It was an interesting lunch because Cassandra was full of questions for the Amish girls. She wanted to know everything about the Amish that she could learn. She explained that she had moved to South Bend from New York City and had not known much about the Amish until she visited Shipshewana.

The last question Cassandra asked was how many people were in a typical Amish family. The other girls all spoke first, and then Elizabeth's turn came. Her throat was so dry, and she couldn't speak the words out loud. She looked around the table in a moment of panic. The question had just thrown her for a loop because minutes before, they were all laughing and talking. Now the table was quiet until Sarah finally spoke up.

"It's really hard for Elizabeth to talk about this, but she just lost her parents and two younger sisters in a buggy wreck."

Cassandra's face drained of color as she reached for her heart. "I am so sorry to hear this. I understand exactly how you feel."

Elizabeth thought, *you have got to be kidding. . . one of these people who thinks she knows how I feel. . .*

Cassandra continued on in her sentence and quietly said, "I also lost both of my parents in a plane accident. I would give up all this money if I could just bring them back." Elizabeth soon realized that Cassandra *did* understand.

And just like that, the fun lunch ended. Cassandra pulled Elizabeth off to the side and asked her if she had already received the money from her parent's life insurance policies to cover her living expenses. Elizabeth told Cassandra, "No, my parents did not believe in life insurance policies. The church had gathered a collection to help pay for some expenses, and the farm was sold to cover the rest."

"I've heard of people who can't afford life insurance, but I've never heard of people not believing in a life insurance policy," Cassandra admitted.

"Among our people, we help each other a lot," Elizabeth explained. Then she asked, "How old were you when your parents died?"

Cassandra sighed out loud and said, "I was twenty-one. I remember it like it was yesterday. I was in my final year of college, and it happened immediately after my Christmas break began. My parents were flying from Paris to New York City, and they never made it across the Atlantic. Two hours from LaGuardia Airport, their private plane crashed into the ocean. I am an only child, so I was devastated. I wasn't able to finish college that year because I was an emotional train wreck. They had been my whole world. Fortunately, my parents had surrounded themselves with three very loyal trustworthy employees who had worked for our family for years in our home. They were almost like family to me. They helped me settle in a new apartment close to Central Park, and I sold the house. My parents left money for the employees to retire on quite nicely. The employees, to this day, still check in on me."

Elizabeth felt deep compassion for Cassandra and said, "I am sad to hear your story. That must have been very difficult to face by yourself, so I'm glad to hear you still stay in touch with them."

At this point in their conversation, one of the girls had a question for Cassandra, so their talk would have to be put on hold.

Chapter 14

Cassandra hugged the girls as they were leaving and repeatedly thanked them for their hard work. She handed each of them envelopes with their checks inside. Some of the girls opened theirs on the way home, but for some reason, Elizabeth thought she should wait until she got home. The van ride was about an hour long, and the first half was spent talking about what an experience it was working for Cassandra. They all thought she was a very interesting woman and couldn't fathom one person living in such a big house all by herself. Elizabeth told the girls what had happened to Cassandra's parents, and they all agreed that must have been really tough losing both parents.

"It was hard losing my mom and dad on the same day, but at least I have Karl and Willy," Elizabeth told the others. "I can't begin to imagine facing life all alone at 21."

During the last part of the ride home, the conversation switched to one of the girls and her wedding plans. They talked about different dress fabrics and menu items, all things girls enjoy talking about. A couple of girls gave the bride-to-be a bunch of unwanted silly advice, which got the whole van load laughing. For Elizabeth, it was a refreshing change to get to hang out with girls. The conversations at home were often about the things the boys were interested in, like guns and animals. She knew that she needed to make more of an effort to spend time with her friends. She hadn't laughed that hard in months.

Back at the farm, Mose and Willy spent most of the day moving the calves into a new area of the barn. Willy enjoyed helping Mose because he was a lot of fun, and it was also good to be around a dad figure. Willy had been taught a lot about horses from his dad, but learning more about calves was fun. He thought the calves seemed like cheerful, happy animals, and he loved how each one had unique spots.

Mose claimed that some people enjoy eating cow tongue. Mose noticed that it about made Willy gag at the thought, so when they went in for lunch, Mose made it a point to ask Carrie if the cow tongue was ready.

Willy tried to hide the horror he felt, but Mose saw it and burst out laughing.

Carrie said, "Willy, I wouldn't make that for you! We are having meatloaf."

Willy thought it was funny, but he said, "I hope there's no cow tongue ground into the meatloaf. I was about ready to say I need to get home and check on my puppies."

For Willy, it was good to be with two adults. They asked him a lot of questions about how he was doing, and he really enjoyed the conversation. They saw life through the same lenses as his parents had, so it felt very comfortable at their table. He didn't feel like a visitor at all. That was a great feeling for Willy, so it seemed odd when Mose paid him for the work.

Willy told him, "You don't need to pay me. I was just glad to help." Mose insisted he take the money and told Willy that all the work the two did together would have taken him three days to do alone.

Willy smiled most of the way home, and every time he thought of the cow tongue, he started laughing. He was thankful that he had such a hilarious uncle. He decided this world needed more people with a good sense of humor like Uncle Mose. Laughter was good medicine. Willy was a lot more like his dad. They were both very deep thinkers and always trying to figure things out. His dad had told Willy, *Deep thinkers are sometimes their own worst enemy. Sometimes you just gotta get out of your own head and simply trust God will work things out.*

He was glad his dad had pointed that out and had explained the differences in the personalities of Mose and Karl. He said they were more wired for fun and didn't see the need to analyze things so much. Neither was right or wrong, just different personality types.

Mose had also really enjoyed being with Willy. He whispered a prayer to God to thank him for such a great nephew and asked God to keep him safe as he biked home. Mose would definitely ask Willy to help again because he had done a great job.

Mose often bought 20 calves at a time to raise for beef cattle. He had built up a regular customer base, and most of his customers wanted him to butcher a whole beef cow for them every year. At present, he had more people interested in organic meat than ever before. One of his customers was Professor Samantha Linch from Goshen College. Samantha had a son with a lot of food allergies. She brought Mose all kinds of research information on searches she did on wheat allergies, free range, paleo friendly, gluten free, and hormone free. Mose would feel like he was sitting in her class every time she stopped by, but it had educated him a lot on how to raise his animals and on how to advertise how he raised them as well. Her husband, Tom, owned a web design business, so in exchange for meat, Tom built a website for Mose that advertised his business.

Tom would create the price lists according to the prices he found on other organic websites and would raise the prices repeatedly. Mose was often shocked at the high prices people were willing to pay for organic, free-range eggs and whole chickens.

He would joke around to Carrie about going out to lay his hands on his flock and pray over them. When Carrie would want to butcher 20 chickens at a time for themselves, he would give her a hard time about eating the profits. He was just teasing her, but they laughed at the good prices they got for the animals they raised. If he came into the house smelling like animals, Mose always told Carrie, "I smell like money, Honey."

When Mose initially started talking about raising animals without all of the steroid shots and chemicals, some people thought he was a bit much. He could tell how they would kind of smirk at his ideas, but now that his "crazy" business venture was becoming very successful, he often said, "Now I'm laughing too. . . all the way to the bank."

Karl loved his job from the very first day that he started working for Yoder's Construction. Mose was right; they were a great company to work for. Chris Yoder, the owner, did a lot of the office work and did the bidding of the jobs. He had two crews, and each had six guys. Karl's friend Bill ran one of the crews.

Bill was only eighteen, but he made running a construction crew look effortless. A lot of the men were older than Bill, but they all highly respected him as their leader. It was easy to tell that he had a special way about him. He treated the men with utmost respect and highly valued their opinions.

A Methodist church had hired the men to finish out the inside of a steel pole building for their new church house. Karl helped one of the Amish men assemble the walls on the ground. Some of the walls reached the 29-foot ceiling, and Karl was glad he didn't need to help with installing those. It didn't seem to faze the other workers, but for today, Karl felt safer on the ground. He hoped that over time, he would get used to working up that high. He remembered a joke his dad had told him one day when they had to work on the barn roof. His dad had told Karl, *Falling off the barn roof won't hurt you. It's the landing at the bottom that will hurt you.* Karl smiled to himself as he thought of his dad. He knew his dad would be proud that he even landed this job and would have encouraged Karl to do it well.

The day went by quickly because the pace of the crew was consistent. They were smiling and moving. No one was standing around complaining or wondering what to do next. It was like a well-oiled machine. Everyone knew his part of the task at hand and did it.

When break time rolled around, they all went out to the custom-built break trailer. Each guy had a place to keep his lunch bucket in the trailer. The trailer also housed a small fridge to keep their drinks cold. Best of all, Bill's mom had made a big pan of cinnamon rolls. The pan was set out for everyone to share on a table in the trailer. Karl asked if the cinnamon rolls were a daily occurrence, and all of the men laughed.

One of the guys replied, "Not every day, but about once a week, one of our wives will make cinnamon rolls and send them for everyone. Each of us men brags about the fact that his wife's cinnamon rolls are the best." The men all laughed because it was true. It was a standing joke with the crew.

The English driver was the only one who said, "My wife refuses to bake me any cinnamon rolls. She's a fitness instructor and tries to make me eat healthy all the time. A lot of her food and cooking is really good, but every now and then, I go over to Pete's house after dinner in hopes that they will offer me some of their supper."

Pete laughed and said, "It's true. We know what he wants if he comes at that time of the evening. The funniest night was one evening that we were eating banana soup. He took one look at it and said he didn't want any."

The Amish men and boys all laughed. They all knew what banana soup was. It was simply pieces of bread in milk with bananas or strawberries poured over it. It was a refreshing, cool meal on hot summer days.

It was also a cheap way of feeding a family. Normally in the summer time, the dish is eaten cold, but on cold winter days, it can be eaten with heated milk and bread pieces. Some people call that *bupply soup* (baby soup).

A few men lay down under a shade tree and took short naps, while the rest just sat and talked a bit longer. Before long, they were all back at work again.

At 2:30 sharp, the crew stopped working. They all gathered to talk about the plans for the next day, and for the last half hour of the day, they all cleaned up their work zones. Brooms came out, and everything looked neat and orderly.

Bill took Karl off to the side and asked him, "How did you enjoy your first day? And did you have any questions?

Karl replied, "I really enjoyed it a lot. I can't believe we are already done for the day. It went really quickly."

Bill explained that the last half hour of every day is used to clean up in order that the next day is always a clean slate.

"My dad started that habit years ago. His construction crews used to work until 6-6:30 at night, and it ended up making the workers much too drained. It cut into family time and was creating resentful feelings in marriages. He prayed about it and felt prompted to change things up. He decided to shorten the work day and increase the hourly wages so the crew members all could continue making what they were taking home before but always stopping at three o'clock. This generosity changed the morale of the workers, and they all gave it 100% while they were on the job site. My dad believes in blessing others and being generous."

Bill continued, "His accountant told my dad that it would never work, but he chose to follow God's prompting and try it anyway. God has richly blessed him ever since with good workers as well as a lot of consistent jobs. God's wisdom trumps an accountant's mindset."

It was kind of unusual for two teenagers to get into a conversation about God, but it made sense to Karl. Bill's dad reminded Karl of his own dad. They were both Amish businessmen who prayed about their business dealings, and it showed.

When the boys got home, they helped each other do the chores. Then Willy played with the puppies for a little while. Bella was the better ball fetcher, and anyone who watched her could tell that she thought she was really something in her retrieving abilities. Rex loved being put up on the trampoline and jumping with Willy on it. They played well together if Willy wasn't around, but if he was, they got possessive and competitive for Willy's attention. They both seemed to want to be his favorite.

Karl showered and then sat and scrolled through Facebook on his iPhone. Elizabeth heard him laughing and went to see what he thought was so funny. A waitress from the Essenhaus had posted a video of Bob Miller saying, "Party of one, Feta Coo," and someone had taken a cow that was mooing and clipped it into the video. It was hilarious. Elizabeth assumed it was Clete who had videoed it and posted it on the Facebook group called, "I'm not Amish, but I speak Dutch." Clete had better watch out. He was baiting for retaliation.

"Would you be able to find a 'Riding with Ridge' site?" Elizabeth asked Karl.

"Sure, I just punch it in the search bar," Karl said. "It's right here. Wow, he has a sweet bike. Who is he?"

"He's a guy who ate at the Essenhaus, "Elizabeth explained. "He's riding from California to the East Coast. Does it say where he is today?"

"Yeah, he took a picture with the Liberty Bell in Maine," Karl said. "And it shows him on a beach on Cape Cod, so he made it from coast to coast."

"Can you look to see if he wrote about Middlebury?" Elizabeth asked Karl.

Karl had to go through a lot of photos and posts before he found a picture of the Essenhaus.

Elizabeth had gone into the kitchen to make some food when Karl found the blog attached to the Essenhaus post.

He read the title of the blog post: **"Never doubt a reroute."**

Last night, I had got a great night's sleep in Indy, and I had anticipated being in Pittsburgh by tonight. However, when I woke up, I knew that I was supposed to head north instead of east. So I headed north and ended up in Amish Country. I was hungry and Googled restaurants. The Das Dutchman's Essenhaus came up, so I got a table, and it didn't take long for the Holy Spirit to start telling me things to tell my waitress. You have got to understand this was the first Amish person I have ever met, so that was a new experience. I wish I would have a picture to post of her, but I do not. Some people describe the Amish as being plain. There was nothing plain about her . . . she was stunningly beautiful.

So just remember, we make our plans, but God orders our steps.

With God, it wasn't a reroute. It was on his route for me the whole time.

Pray for my new Amish friend and her family. She's definitely a prophetic dreamer. Pray that God helps her understand her dreams.

> As I am out riding with the horses and buggies, the thought that keeps coming to me is that waves of mercy are coming to this region.

Riding with Ridge —June 2014

"Elizabeth, come here. Ridge wrote about you in his blog," Karl told her.

"Are you serious?" Elizabeth asked, not even trying to hide her surprise.

"I think you made a good impression on him," Karl said laughingly.

Elizabeth also laughed when she read these words from Ridge: "There was nothing plain about her. She was stunningly beautiful."

"I would love to read some books on dream interpretation," Elizabeth said, "In the Bible, Joseph was a dreamer, and a lot of his were dreams with meanings."

"He sounds really interesting," Karl said, as he continued reading blog post after blog post of interesting places Ridge stopped and people he met. Every day Ridge wrote about God directing his road trip.

The evening flew by with supper and the three of them playing a game of rook before they all went to bed. It felt good to just do something light-hearted together. It had been a great day until they realized they were out of lady finger popcorn. This was what was considered a major crisis in the Miller family. In this house, running out of popcorn was just as serious as running out of something as important as toilet paper.

As she was getting ready to crawl into bed, she saw her purse with the envelope sticking out of it. She tore it open and saw a letter with her check. The letter read, *Elizabeth, I feel a deep connection to you because of our lives being forever connected through similar tragedies and want you to please consider working for me part-time. Love, Cassandra.*

Elizabeth was extremely grateful for the check and was surprised at the amount because it was more than the other girls had been paid. She was glad she had not opened her check on the way home. She would definitely enjoy both jobs because they'd give her variety. Her dad had always said, *God is Jehovah Jireh.* That means *God is a provider.* Dad was right. She knew this was God's way of providing for her and the boys.

Chapter 15

Elizabeth was scheduled to work at the Essenhaus from three to close for the next two days. That meant she got to be with Willy during the morning hours. Elizabeth had called a driver to pick them up at nine in the morning to take them to get Willy registered for school, as the first day of school (August 12) was quickly approaching.

Elizabeth could hear the excitement in Willy's feet as he trampled down the stairs. It was funny how she could tell which of the boys was coming down the stairs by the way his feet would hit the wooden stairs. Willy normally came down calmly, and Karl went a lot faster. But today, Willy was rearing to get going.

Wearing a huge smile on his face, Willy said, "I'm going to put Bella and Rex in the dog kennel to keep them from getting into trouble while we're gone, and then I'm ready!"

Elizabeth laughed and said, "OK, just do it quickly because the driver will be here in five minutes."

Almost immediately, Willy was back in the house. Elizabeth questioned him, "Are you sure you put them in already? You were barely out there."

"Yes, yes, yes, good grief! Go see for yourself," Willy said, a bit agitated. "Every day you tell me I take too long with the puppies, and then when I am quick with them, you question if I did it right. What's up with that? I would think you should be complimenting me."

Elizabeth's mouth dropped open. She asked, "Are you telling me that I tell you that you take too long every day?"

"Yes, every single day, since I got them," Willy declared emphatically. "I get kind of tired of that because I think I do a great job of being responsible for them. If I was neglecting them, I could see why you'd complain about that, but I don't think Mom would have gotten on me like you do."

"I'm sorry, Willy," Elizabeth apologized, her heart sinking. "I didn't realize that I was doing that, and I didn't know you felt like this."

Elizabeth paused. "Why didn't you say something? I can't read your mind."

"Well, now you know, and I feel better because I got it off my chest," Willy then smiled at her. "I know you don't mean to be bossy, but it sort of comes out that way. I know I'm the youngest in this house right now, but I'm not incapable of carrying the load on some things. I feel like you don't trust me when you question the things I do or don't do."

"Hmmm, that's interesting," Elizabeth said. "That book on personality types I just read says that people who have your personality are very loyal, trustworthy people. Let me guess . . . nothing hurts you more than when you are questioned or doubted?"

"That is exactly right! It makes me feel like you don't trust me," Willy said. "It hurts when you do that."

"Wow, Willy! I'm really sorry," Elizabeth said, with kindness dripping off her words. "I will stop doing that to you. Immediately. I want you to forgive me for that. I want you to know that I wasn't seeing you as incompetent at all, but I obviously caused you to feel that way."

"It's OK," Willy said. "I forgive you."

"No, Willy, it's not OK, but thanks for forgiving me," Elizabeth said smiling. "I will watch my words from now on."

They heard the van driving in the lane and quickly gathered up the paperwork and information they needed for the registration. Elizabeth tucked all of it into her purse, and out the door they went. They were always promptly ready when van drivers arrived. They had been taught that it was rude to make van drivers wait unnecessarily. Her parents had always set this good example. Her dad had taught them that if they expected the van driver to be promptly on time, then they should be on time, too. Their time is also valuable. Another one of Dan's favorite sayings was, *don't be burning daylight*. It was his way of teaching them not to waste time. He believed that life was meant to be lived with a purpose.

"Good morning, Edna," Elizabeth greeted their driver. "I guess the first stop will be Westview Junior High School. We need to register Willy for school."

"Sounds good," Edna replied. "You looking forward to school starting, Willy?"

"Yes, I can hardly wait," Willy said. "I'm in eighth grade, so this is my last year already."

"Have you ever considered going on through high school?" Edna asked.

"I have thought about it," Willy replied. "I told my dad that I really liked learning things in school, and he said that school was easy for him, too. A lot of my friends despise studying, but I think it's fun."

"Well, that's good to hear," Edna said. "What is your favorite subject?"

"It's a toss-up between math and history. I love learning things from the 1800s, but the math is just second nature for me. I don't have to study much for those classes. My dad often told me that I should become an accountant. Every year when he got his taxes done, his CPA would tell him that he should consider teaching other business owners how to keep records. They thought he was the most organized record keeper in the area."

"That would be a good career for you if you are gifted with numbers," Edna mused, as they pulled in to the school driveway.

As Willy and Elizabeth walked toward the school, they saw the football team running nearby. When Willy was spotted, a few of his friends yelled, "Hey there, wild Will!" Willy laughed and waved at them. It was good to be back.

The first person they saw inside the school was the principal of Westview Junior High School, Randy Miller. He came right over, grabbed Willy by the shoulder, and said, "How's Mr. Miller doing today?"

"Pretty good, and how's the other Mr. Miller doing today?" Willy laughed.

"That depends on if you can stay out of trouble this year," Mr. Miller chuckled. "Are you Willy's sister?" He looked at Elizabeth.

"Yes, my name is Elizabeth," she said. "It's nice to meet you."

Mr. Miller's demeanor changed as he said, "My condolences on the loss of your family. I was just joking about Willy causing trouble. He's a great kid, and we really enjoy having him here."

Mr. Miller was called away, and as Willy rounded the gym corner, he spotted his friend Joe Christener with his dad, Fred. The two boys were so excited to see each other. Almost immediately, Willy asked if Joe could go home with him for an overnight stay.

"I keep on hearing the frogs out in that pond at night," Willy said. "We need to go frog gigging and silence a few of those."

Fred laughed and said, "I think tonight would work out if you boys save me some to fry, too."

"We have a 25-per-person limit a day, so we'll try to get the biggest ones," Joe said.

Frog gigging consisted of the boys going out after dark and using flashlights to spot frogs in the edges of ponds and then spearing them with long frog gigging spears. The ends of the spear looked almost like a big fork. According to the boys, the bigger the frog the better.

"Now I am not frying those things for you," Elizabeth informed the boys. "I won't clean them either. I have to work tonight and Wednesday night at the Essenhaus."

Fred understood because his wife didn't like to help with the cleaning, either, so the plans were made for a "guys-only frog fry" for the following evening.

After the boys were registered for school, Elizabeth and Willy asked Edna to stop at E & S, and their crisis was soon averted: the Millers were once again restocked on lady finger popcorn.

Joe's house was the last stop, as he needed to get his everyday clothes to go frog gigging. Edna also helped the boys with some odd looking items and asked, "What in the world is this contraption?"

"That's our frog gigging equipment," Joe replied. "We use these spears to stab through the frogs and then we fry them up and eat them."

"That sounds disgusting to me, but I hope you have fun," Edna stated.

When they got home, the boys quickly changed. After they ate a quick lunch, the boys headed outside. Elizabeth could hear the boys shooting hoops, talking, laughing, and playing with the puppies.

They came inside to get some empty ice cream buckets and said they were going to go back to the woods to look for black walnut trees.

Elizabeth told them to be careful but have fun. "I don't want you two to go to the pond without Karl being here. I'm leaving for work at 2:30, and Karl will get home around 4 today. I trust you two to hold down the fort while I'm gone."

"Yep, we'll take good care of the fort," Willy said, smiling. He had heard the word *trust*, and that spoke volumes to him. Elizabeth had heard him, listened, and switched her words to be affirming instead of demeaning.

The next few days flew by at the Essenhaus for Elizabeth. It was the busiest season of the year, and the waitresses were kept running from the minute they walked in the restaurant at 3 until the last table of the evening. After they were finished working, they would normally grab a bite to eat before cleaning up.

One of the English waitresses, Nolita, wanted to know, "Why do you Amish and Mennonite people call people by two names? I hear you ladies say, 'Almie Crist's or 'Merv Irene's.' Why do you do that?"

The Amish girls started laughing. Elizabeth explained, "That's funny! We just do it naturally without thinking about it."

Nolita continued, "Another thing I just heard you say: 'We are going to Wayne's for an ice cream supper.' We English people would say, 'We are invited to the Smiths' house.'"

"It's true, we do," Elizabeth said. "Well, part of the reason we do that is because if I would say, 'We are going to the Yoder's for something, there are thousands of Yoder's, Millers and other very common names and it could get confusing. Also, among the Amish and Mennonite, there are lots of similar first names, so to clarify which one we mean, we say the husband and wife's name together. Then sometimes if we don't know who someone is, we use the grandparents' names, too. You might hear someone say, 'He is Roger R's, John's, Jonas's .' We all know what it means, but it probably sounds odd to outsiders."

That explanation helped the English women to better understand the Amish.

"The one thing I noticed," Roxanne said, "is that if I have English people who want chili, they order a bowl of chili, but if Amish people order chili, they order a bowl of chili soup. You Amish waitresses call it chili soup, too."

They all had a good laugh as they headed back to work. Nolita attempted to speak Pennsylvania Dutch as she told everyone, "Vella, Schtada Uhbutsa," which meant *let's start cleaning up.*

When Elizabeth got home, the boys were still out frog gigging. The boys had waited to go until it was dark, and then one of the boys shone a spotlight on the bullfrogs while the other two used the gigging tools to secure "the meat." In about an hour's time, they had caught close to 50 frogs and decided to call it a night because Karl needed to be up bright and early for work.

Elizabeth was in the kitchen getting a drink when all of a sudden, she heard a song blasting somewhere in the house. She about jumped out of her skin. She realized it was Karl's phone and ran to answer the phone. It was her friend Suzanna wanting to know if Elizabeth could help at Cassandra's on Thursday.

"Let me calm down a little," Elizabeth said. "I was here by myself because the boys went gigging for frogs, and I didn't know Karl's phone was here. All of the sudden, his music started playing. I must have jumped a foot off the ground. But yes, I can help on Thursday."

When the boys got back to the house, they were pretty happy with their successful evening. They laughed when Elizabeth told them about jumping when Karl's phone rang.

"The house was all quiet, and all of the sudden, I heard Jason Aldean singing, 'How do you like me now?' I think your volume is turned on too high, too," Elizabeth laughed.

Karl thought it was hilarious and replied, "Well, it takes that volume to wake me up for work. I actually set two alarm clocks and put one across the room so I have to get out of bed to turn it off. One of my friends had to put an alarm clock in a big stainless steel bowl so it caused more racket. I bet that noise could almost raise the dead."

Wednesday evening, the night of the guys-only frog fry, soon came. Fred held true to his word and helped the boys clean and fry the frogs.

He also brought some fish from the Lake Erie trip. He had the boys form an assembly line. Some cleaned and others battered, but he did the frying. He told the boys that there's sort of a trick to learning how long they needed to be fried, and it's easy to over-fry them. As the first batch was just getting out of fryer, Mose showed up. The boys teased him about coming after the work is done.

"No problem," Mose said. "I can take this corn flake potato casserole that I was waiting on right back home."

"Oh no, you can stay," Karl decided. "That's my favorite."

They ate frog legs to their hearts' content and finished their meal with watermelon for dessert. It was the perfect summer meal. They all pitched in and helped clean the place up. They didn't want to upset the queen of the castle by leaving any frog residue lying around.

After dinner came game time. They had two sets of bag games and played until dark. Then they lit a fire and sat and talked around the fire pit for a few hours. Since they all had such a great time, they decided the guys-only frog fry needed to become a yearly event.

When Mose and Fred were leaving, they both noticed that Karl and Willy had both thanked them numbers of times. They realized how much it meant to the boys and decided to make an effort to do more things with them.

Elizabeth was impressed with the men's clean-up efforts because she could hardly tell they had been there. It sounded like they had a lot of fun. They had saved some watermelon for her, and she ate her portion before heading off to bed.

On Thursday, when the girls arrived at Cassandra's, they noticed that Cassandra looked a bit disheveled. She told them she hadn't slept very well. It looked like she was exhausted. She asked the girls to clean out closets and reorganize them. The girls would bring out box after box, and Cassandra would go through them. She chose to give away a lot of things she no longer wanted to keep. She had found a Restore that used the sale of the store's profits to fund Habitat for Humanity houses. It made her happy to pass on things she no longer needed to others who might not be able to afford them, but it seemed to take an emotional toll on Cassandra as well.

Finally, she said, "This 'purging' of sorts is harder than I thought it would be. A lot of these items were in storage after I sold my parents' house, and I haven't gone through these things in a number of years. There are a lot of memories that get stirred up as I go through them."

The last thing they sorted through was a lot of games. She had mostly board games. Cassandra asked Elizabeth if she and the boys ever played games. Elizabeth told Cassandra that they did play games all the time, so Cassandra filled a big box with about 10 different games and told Elizabeth that she could have all 10.

The girls spent the rest of the day going through Cassandra's master closet. It was a bit odd how uncomfortable they all felt in the master bedroom and bathroom areas. It seemed depressing and sad every time they were in those areas. Though the décor was cheerful, that area of the house felt so gloomy. It made no sense why it felt that way.

Elizabeth and Suzanne had never seen so many clothes in their lives. Cassandra could tell they were looking at them, so she started telling them what events she had attended and where she wore the different gowns. Then she opened a locked safe area and showed the girls her exquisite jewelry.

She asked the Amish girls, "Do any of you girls have any jewelry?"

A couple of the girls told her that they had jewelry from the mall but nothing of this quality.

Cassandra told Elizabeth to come to the mirror. Cassandra put a diamond necklace on Elizabeth's neck. It was flashy and extravagant.

It looked hilarious because Elizabeth had on an Amish dress, Amish cap and a necklace that Cassandra said was worth thousands of dollars. Cassandra got her phone out and wanted to get some pictures.

It was a fun day because they got to go with Cassandra to deliver the items to Restore. Then she needed to go to Shipshewana, so she took the girls home. Elizabeth was the last one to be dropped off, and Cassandra helped her carry in the box of games.

Cassandra looked around the yard and the porch and commented, "It feels so peaceful out here in the country."

"We named this house the *Safe Haven*," Elizabeth said. "We feel like God brought us here to heal."

"I can see why you love it," Cassandra said with a smile. "I will see you next week."

With a hug and a wave, Cassandra was off.

CORINA YODER

Chapter 16

The August heat in northern Indiana is known to drain a lot of energy out of a person. August 1st was one of those days, a scorcher. By 6 o'clock that evening, the muggy humidity ushered in a fierce thunderstorm. It was the most violent storm the Miller children had ever seen. All three of the children were in the living room until Karl noticed the eerie-looking colors outside, prime time for when the Midwest experiences tornados. He checked the weather on his phone and saw the thunderstorm watches change to tornado warnings.

"We need to go to the basement," Karl said with urgency after he read the warnings.

"I'm going to run out and get Bella and Rex and bring them into the basement with us," Willy said. "I don't want them to be scared."

"There's no time, Willy!" Karl said emphatically as they all headed for the basement. "You can't go out in this storm. We need to get to the basement right NOW!"

As they were hurrying to get downstairs, Elizabeth asked Karl, "What is the difference between a watch and a warning?"

Karl read from the Weather Service site: "A watch occurs when conditions are favorable for a thunderstorm or tornado. But a warning means severe weather is imminent where there could be high impact damage."

Willy asked, "What does *imminent* mean?"

Karl explained, "In everyday language, *imminent* means something is likely to happen at any moment. They are telling people to take shelter."

Elizabeth remembered going with her parents into the basement at the Home Place and that Dad and Mom used to pray for protection, so that's what she did at that moment. It was terrifying because of the dark swirling clouds. The sky darkened with clouds that looked dangerous and vicious. The wind came in strong gusts, and it felt like the roof would be taken off at any time. The storms lasted for a few hours, but it really felt like an eternity. They stayed in the basement until the storm gradually calmed down. As soon as they felt safe to do it, Karl went out to check on the horses, and Willy ran for the dogs. Thank God they were all safe, and it looked like the trees were all OK in the yard. There were a few things blown around but nothing major.

Karl's phone soon rang. It was Uncle Mose checking to see if they had survived the storm and if they were all at home.

"Yeah, we are OK," Karl said, "but it sure was nerve-wracking. I was freaked out because it felt like a tornado was about to take our house down."

"That's awful. I'm thankful you are all OK. I was really worried because I haven't seen a storm like this in years. The cold front pushed in, and the temperature dropped down 20 degrees in an hour's time, so that's why the crazy unrest in the weather came about. Oh, by the way, can you tell Elizabeth we still need her to babysit tomorrow?"

"I will remind her, and thanks for calling," Karl said. "I'm glad you are all OK, too."

Mose felt his body relax as he left the phone shack. He had been holding his breath until he knew that Dan's three children were all unharmed. He had never been anxious like this before the buggy accident. He didn't want to start now, either, and he breathed a prayer: *God, help me trust You instead of worry.*

The next day, Elizabeth babysat for Mose and Carrie so they could go to South Bend. Elizabeth was very thankful that the weather was calm when she had the little ones. Willy went along to help her. It was almost unbelievable what a difference a day could make. It was a very sunny day but with cooler temperatures. It was so pleasant that they took the children out to play on the swing set and in the sand box. It was hard to fathom that only hours earlier they had felt unsafe and in danger.

It was a miracle that nobody in the region was hurt or even killed, but they found out that a tornado had completely leveled a big barn near Emma Town. The Amish owners lost some livestock, which would be difficult for the owners. Their buggy horses were very dependable and would be hard to replace. The good news was that the family was in the house only a short distance away, and nothing was touched on the house. More than likely, within weeks, the barn would be rebuilt. That's the way the Amish do things.

When Mose and Carrie got home, they were happy to hear that it had gone well.

"I rarely leave the little ones, so they don't always do all that well for others," Carrie said. "By the way, Willy, I made you a couple of school shirts and two new pairs of pants, too."

"Are you kidding? That's awesome! I didn't know you were going to do that," Willy said. "Thanks a lot. I needed a few new ones for school, but I hated to ask Elizabeth because I knew she was busy."

"Oh, Willy, I wasn't that busy," Elizabeth told him. "You could have told me. But this will help a lot, Carrie."

On the bike ride home, Elizabeth and Willy talked about how kind Carrie was to sew for Willy and to surprise him, too.

Elizabeth added, "I think it was even more thoughtful that she made you a blue shirt and grey pants, your two favorite colors."

Willy added, "It sounds like something Mom would do."

"Yeah, you're right," Elizabeth agreed. "And Willy, never be scared to tell me if you need me to sew something."

The children ate supper together before Karl left for a softball game. Karl joined a local softball league, which caused his social life to grow into a busy schedule and a very full calendar. His team had a mixture of Amish guys and town guys, so they would hang out with a mixture of Amish girls and town girls. They even got to travel to Ohio and Illinois for tournaments. Those traveling weekends proved to be Karl's favorites.

Sometimes Elizabeth and Willy would go watch a game, but Karl would often get a ride from a teammate to each game. Some drinking typically went on after games, which greatly concerned Elizabeth.

If Dad would have still been alive, Elizabeth knew exactly what he would have told Karl. When she had turned 16, her dad had warned her that drinking was illegal for her. He told her that it put her at the risk of being arrested, not to mention the fact that getting drunk could put her into some pretty vulnerable situations. Elizabeth was a rule keeper by nature and didn't care for beer, so this was not something she was overly tempted to do. Her parents weren't demanding and forceful about it, and that motivated her to keep their trust. She wanted to be wise about her surroundings and what she consumed. Some teenagers weren't very close to their parents, but Elizabeth was thankful her mom and dad had worked hard to keep their communication lines open.

Now Karl, on the other hand, was a fun-loving person. If there was a rule, he normally wanted to push into the boundary. Elizabeth reminded Karl that a lot of his softball friends were underage.

"Don't be a worry wart, Elizabeth," Karl would tell her. "We have a lot of fun playing at the softball games, and we don't let things get out of hand afterward."

She didn't want him to get carried away. As a teenager, their dad drank a lot, and it was not something he wanted for his own children. The accident now served as a big reminder how brutal the effect of alcohol can be. It made her angry that it stole her family, and she wanted Karl to take what she said seriously.

Karl's current life focus was socializing, so he saw no need to waste time talking about the alcohol. The team all really liked him. He was a great player, so he instantly made a lot of friends. Everyone on the team kept asking Karl when he was going to have a cookout for them. He finally told them if they beat their biggest rival that he'd have them over. When the girls heard Karl say that, it was pretty well planned out and set in stone. They pulled off that win a week later.

Karl asked Elizabeth if he could host the team cookout. Elizabeth told him he could if they all helped to bring the food and clean up. She also added the "no beer" reminder.

Karl worked hard to get ready for it. He set up the volleyball net, and they had hot dogs, hamburgers, and a bunch of corn on the cob. Everyone seemed to enjoy being together, and they ranted and raved about his food. He was glad that his dad had taught him how to grill at a young age. The girls had asked everyone to bring a side dish or dessert, so with 20 people in attendance, there was plenty of food.

As the guys got done eating, the competiveness came out in them, and before long, there was a volleyball game going.

One of the town guys had the idea to play Amish versus English guys. The minute the game started, the Amish guys started calling the next play in Dutch. The English guys soon realized that plan wasn't good after all, complaining their "secret language" made the competition unfair. They all laughed. It was a friendly game, but both teams wanted to prove their playing was superior.

It was a great evening until the sky started to get an eerie look to it yet again. Soon it began to storm. Everyone grabbed a few things and headed for the house. If the Millers would have had electricity, it would have just gone out anyway.

They headed for the basement with their lawn chairs. This particular storm wasn't as bad as the storm on August 1st, but they still decided to go to the basement. The basement was a big open room that was concreted and had concrete walls. They had an area with a table set up, so the girls sat at that. The girls noticed the box of games Cassandra had given Elizabeth, so some of the girls pulled a few of them out. The third game down was an Ouija board game, and two of the girls knew how to play it.

Before long, the girls had a group of kids standing around them as they showed the others how the game can tell answers to any questions. Some of the guys thought it was a bunch of baloney, so one of the girls said, "OK, you ask it something."

One of the Amish boys, John Henry, asked, "Who is my bishop?" The Ouija board answered correctly.

"You've got to be kidding! Where'd you get this game, Karl?" John Henry wanted to know.

"Elizabeth got it from a woman she cleans for in South Bend," Karl told them.

Willy had been in his bedroom until it got stormy, and then Karl told him to come to the basement, too. Willy watched quietly as the girls asked the board game questions, and they laughed hysterically about whom the game said they were going to get married to. He was fascinated but knew he had better just stay out of the way or Karl might chew him out for talking with his friends too much. He was curious how this game worked.

By the time Elizabeth got home from work, the storm had calmed down, and all the guys were in the living room. The girls were washing up the last of the dirty dishes. She was glad that Karl had respected her wishes and that they were helping to clean up. Kara, an English girl, was helping dry the grilling platters.

"This weather sure is unsettled the last while," Kara said to Elizabeth. "It seems more like spring weather. I have read the book about the Palm Sunday tornados that went through this area back in 1965. My mom was in those, and she always tells us that when we are trying to decide when we should go into the basement, that it's better to be safe than sorry."

"I agree," Elizabeth said. "When I was at work tonight, the lights at the Essenhaus blinked, but we never lost power. It got pretty windy, and the Middlebury sirens went off, but we were all safe." "Is it pretty busy this time of the year at the Essenhaus?" Kara wondered.

"Oh yes, this is our busy season," Elizabeth replied. "We normally have waiting lines on the flea market days and on the weekends. The flea market customers are normally hot and tired this time of the year. We can serve a lot of them in a short time frame because they are hungry and drink a lot, too. Every now and then, we get customers who are upset at how long they had to wait. But once they get their food, they realize that it is worth the wait. Around Christmas time, we serve a lot of banquets, and it's all decorated with Christmas decorations."

"I've thought about applying for a job there," Kara said.

"If you do, you can use my name as a reference," Elizabeth offered. "It helps to know people who already work there."

In the living room, Willy sort of felt in the way, so he went back up to his room and finished a book he had been reading. He kept hearing Karl's friends talking and laughing loudly. He realized that he missed having Karl at home since Karl turned 16. It seemed like all Willy had was a lot of losses and changes this past year. It made him feel sad and all alone. He thought of Rex and Bella and was glad he had both of them this summer. It was the only significant, new thing he had since the accident. Well, of course the new house, too. He missed the big barn but didn't miss the work load. As he lay in bed, he thought about the Ouija game and wondered how it worked. He finally fell asleep as he heard cars and trucks leaving.

Karl kept his word on not having any alcohol at his own party, but the ball games brought out the alcohol in full force. It was very upsetting to Elizabeth whenever Karl would come home drunk. He wasn't mean, but he was loud and obnoxious. She was worried that the guys who drove Karl home might have been drinking as well. It made Elizabeth so angry at him and his choice to do the exact same thing that caused their family's accident.

Karl's drinking caused a lot of arguments between the two of them. She could not understand why he thought he had to drink to have fun.

It made her feel unprotected by Karl. She resented his ability to be so carefree.

Karl wasn't intentionally trying to hurt Elizabeth, but instead, he drank for fun and to numb his own pain. It angered him that it angered her. He started viewing Elizabeth as a "Miss Goody Two Shoes" who always did the right thing.

He was a second born who didn't like to be forced into roles that didn't fit him yet, like being the man of the house. When he drank, he felt young and invincible. It helped him forget his responsibilities and the fact that there was an ocean of pain that the accident had caused him. He didn't like to think about it when sober because it was too painful.

The conflicts between Elizabeth and Karl escalated. They argued about everything, and it left Willy with mixed emotions. He could understand both sides. He believed them both. Sometimes it was more peaceful when they were both at work and Willy got to be home alone with the puppies. The puppies were growing and would fight for his attention, but they were also close friends with each other as well.

Elizabeth often complimented Willy about the good job he was doing with the puppies and how responsible he was. That was a 360-degree turnaround for her! That was the nice thing about Elizabeth. She was open to hear correction. Karl, on the other hand, just got more bullheaded.

One afternoon, when Karl and Elizabeth were at work and the animals were lying around sleeping, Willy remembered the Ouija board game and decided to try it out. This game fit his grid because he was such a deep thinker and always wanted answers to things. At first, it felt weird asking a game questions, but it soon became a magnetic pull that Willy was hooked into. He would still play with his puppies and scout for walnut trees with the neighbor boys, but nothing else seemed to be as fun anymore. The game intrigued him, and he lost interest in other things.

Elizabeth could not figure out what had happened with her kind, caring brother Willy. He would talk back and was often very rude. Almost overnight, his demeanor drastically changed. He became moody and depressed. Karl, on the other hand, was living the life of a carefree teenager who didn't seem to notice that Elizabeth was stressed out from carrying a heavy load.

Both boys were a handful, and soon Elizabeth felt in over her head. A switch had flipped in this house, and it was not for the better.

Chapter 17

The one positive thing about all of the area's recent storms was that the cooler fronts that pushed through made the weather more pleasant for sleeping. The biggest downside of not having electricity is (for most Amish people) a lack of air conditioning in the summer. It seemed to Elizabeth that air conditioning could be OK'd by the church just like heat is in the winter. But, to the church leaders, it wasn't viewed the same. Air conditioning was thought of as a luxury, something that one could live without. The other reason is that the furnaces could be run on gas, and the air conditioning needed electricity. Most Amish lived off the electric grid. As is in every culture, there were some exceptions to those rules, like for health reasons, if a family was renting, or if the family simply finagled a way to bend the church rules.

Elizabeth lay in bed and tried to fall asleep. She was restless, shifting from side to side. The tragic accident had its sixth month mark coming up. It caused Elizabeth to feel like she was trapped and strapped onto an emotional roller coaster ride that she wanted to get off but could not. What made it even worse was that she was such a level-headed, calm soul by nature. She normally took things in stride and had never been depressed in her entire life. She remembered as a little girl losing a kitty and being sad, but the other ten kittens soon helped her move on. Her life had been sheltered and safe. She had no previous training for climbing the mountain of grief that she faced on the path in front of her. It was a night of very little sleep. She woke up almost every hour. Anxiety was like a blanket cloaking her.

The next morning, Elizabeth woke up feeling like she was at the end of her rope. She started second guessing if she should be raising the boys, wondering why she thought she would have the ability to be a parent. She knew she was in over her head and felt like a complete failure today. She was ready to admit defeat and throw in the towel. She had seen this house as the Safe Haven, but right now, it felt like a place of gloom and doom. It didn't feel so safe anymore, and the tension was more than she could bear.

Mose had asked for Willy's help for the day, so as soon as both boys left for the day, she allowed herself to fall apart.

She felt out of control and let the tidal waves of grief wash over her: gripping, tangible fear mixed with anger. Her thoughts were totally irrational and would come into her brain but then spin on to another thought and then on to the next.

Anger came up toward Blake, followed by compassion and pity for his life with his dad. The insanity of her mental thought process was like an Oreo cookie. Black, white, black, white, good, evil, good, evil.

She realized she forgave Blake but wished she could find all the bottles of alcohol in the entire world and break them into a million pieces. If she could personally open all of the cans of beer and dump them herself, she would have. She was convinced that alcohol was the worst form of poison that existed on Earth.

Actually, though he was still living, alcohol killed the life Blake White had. He wasn't actually dead, but the alcohol locked him into a prison cage that would keep stealing his life away. Day after day, year after year, like a sand-filled hourglass that was repeatedly turned over and over. She understood Blake was human, and he could be given grace to not make good choices every time. But God was God.

The insanity of it all caused her to question God.

She screamed out loud at God, *Why didn't You stop the accident?*

She continued on out loud. Her hands were moving with every question as if He was standing in front of her. She chopped the air with both hands at each statement and question.

"I can't do this! I can't raise the boys alone! It's way too hard. You gave me more than I can handle, and I'm so mad at You. I wonder if You even care about me! If you did, wouldn't you be doing something to stop things that are happening to us? How much is one family supposed to bear? How much until it's ENOUGH???! How am I supposed to know what to do? How am I supposed to know how to be a mom and a dad? People who thought this was not a good idea must have been right. How could I be so stupid? I thought You were going to help me, God!"

She felt deep shame and embarrassment that she would look like an absolute fool in their eyes. She calmed down just a tad and, in a bit of a sadder, softer voice, continued.

"The thing that makes no sense at all is the way I am willingly pouring out my life for Karl and Willy, but yet it feels like they both just seem to add stress on my life and don't seem to care. It feels like You set me up to fail at this, God. You could do something to change all of it. I give and give and serve and sacrifice, but yet they seem to just take it for granted and scoff at carrying their load. It all rests on my shoulders, and it's all up to me."

Her anger at God just kept pouring out of her: "It seems like You have left this house, and You don't even care about us! It's like everything that happened with the accident could have at least earned me *some* things that could go easily. So instead of all the things I had to lose as far as my family, my house, my home of all those years, my safety in my dad protecting us, his help, Mom's cooking, the girls' laughter and fun, and now all I'm left with is two boys who just don't seem to understand me! *I wish I'd have died too!"*

"It's worse that some of us made it and the rest left because it's almost like we are just surviving, like we just move around but aren't even fully here. If I admit this to people, they will laugh because they will think I was too weak to do it. But it's not because I'm weak. I'm just tired! The battle is just too fierce, and I can't get out of this depression. The cloud moved into this home and is suffocating us with grief. *I just want to drop off the Earth to never return."*

She was back to ranting at the top of her lungs in anger. At a God she could not even see.

The house was empty, so she felt fine spewing. And she did.

As soon as she verbalized the thoughts in her head, she felt such relief, but feelings of guilt came soon after because she knew God had provided so much good and help and worked out many things along the way. But right now she felt good to just tell Him exactly how she felt.

It was not normal among the Amish to yell at God, and Elizabeth was shocked that she had. She thought if he is a good Dad, like her dad was, then God would hear, listen and do something! She informed God that if her dad were there on Earth, he'd do something!

She then uttered her final words: "If you are real, God, I need you to prove it to me. I don't hate You. I just don't understand You. I need your help."

Her brain was full of thoughts. Her mind was spinning, and she knew she needed to calm herself down. She knew exactly what she wanted to do. Her favorite thing to do was to go horseback riding, something she hadn't done in a long time, not since Dad died. She knew where she'd feel the most like her dad was with her and talking to her, and she needed to know what he would tell her to do.

She headed out to the barn. She had not taken Stella, her horse, out to ride since they moved here, but she knew it would all come back to her. As Elizabeth allowed Stella to gallop down the lane toward the woods, her heart felt alive for the first time in weeks.

Stella felt free, and so did Elizabeth.

Out in the woods, her cyclone of thoughts stopped. She could just ride and clear her head. She let the tears run down her cheeks.

Elizabeth hung on tightly as Stella's hooves pounded as she galloped down the trail leading through the trees. Elizabeth instantly felt calmed by the woods. It felt different out there, as it had a certain serenity that calmed her to the bones. She slowed Stella down and had her walk slowly on the path that overlooked the creek. The creek had a little bit of water in it, though not much, being that it was August. She found the tree with the swing tied to it. She stopped Stella and hopped off. Elizabeth helped Stella go over to the creek to take a drink. Then she tied her to a nearby tree.

As Elizabeth sat on the swing and looked at the trees blowing in the breeze, she was almost mesmerized by the leaves.

It was as if God himself was blowing gently on the tops of the trees. The birds were chirping away and singing their songs. She thought to herself, *I need to do this more often.*

In the distance, she could hear the train rumbling along the tracks and honking in the distance. She knew that within ten minutes, the train would rumble through these woods and cross over her favorite spot along the creek.

Elizabeth could feel God's presence with her. She wished she could talk to her dad. He would have such good advice. He always did. She sat and thought about her situations with both boys and thought to herself, *what would Dad tell me to do?* She had been around him for 18 years, and so she knew his mindset. His mentality and thoughts started coming into her head.

The first thought that came into her head was how he had once told her that people who tell you that God won't give you more than you can handle were lying. He had told her never to believe that. He had witnessed a lot of devastation in the lives of people he had reached out to and helped over the years. He told her no one is prepared to handle some of the things he saw some families go through.

Instead, he taught his children that God will help us through anything, but if we could handle everything, we wouldn't need God.

She ran that thought from her dad across her situation. Dad was right. She couldn't handle all of this. It was too much to handle, but she was glad to be reminded that God could help anyone through anything. She was glad that her dad had been a great teacher and that he took time to speak wisdom into her life. This advice could easily be applied to her circumstances.

She could almost hear him saying a list of quotes: *Now is not the time to give up. Better days are around the corner. Keep looking up. It gets the darkest before dawn; the battles are won in the mind first.*

Dad could have been a motivational speaker, she thought and laughed.

She heard the train getting closer, so she went over to calm Stella and make sure she didn't try to break free. She didn't want her to be spooked because it would be a long walk home for Elizabeth if she lost her ride.

She knew she needed to clear the air with her Creator.

"God, I'm sorry I got so mad at you." She then prayed aloud. "Thank you for calming me down, God. I have so many insecurities and fears. Thanks for the thoughts on walking through these things. I'm sorry that I said I don't want to live. Please forgive me for saying that. Please show me a sign if you think I can do this with the boys, and please send me help to figure this stuff out."

As she headed home, she felt refreshed and was again confident that their situation would all work out.

She thought to herself, *Wow, I feel closer to God after yelling at Him.* She had thought it would cause Him to pull back from her, but it was neat how He felt the closest He had ever felt. Her hope and faith was going to be restored. She felt more peace than she had in a long time.

When Elizabeth got back to the barn, she put Stella away. Stella seemed to have a smile on her face, and Elizabeth wondered if she missed Dad, too. She decided to make an effort to go horseback riding again soon. It was very therapeutic.

Elizabeth caught herself singing as she walked out to the mailbox. The song "What a Beautiful Day for the Lord to Come Again" flowed out of her heart. As she sorted through the mail, she saw a card with a letter inside. It was from a woman she had never met before, Susan Yoder.

The letter was addressed to Elizabeth. Susan wrote, *God prompted me to write and encourage you and to tell you that you are doing a good job.* She added that she would like to come over and visit Elizabeth and offered to help her with anything she might need help with. The letter went on to say that she understood loss and grief because she had lived through it, too. She told Elizabeth that it takes a healing journey of going through the anger and pain and asking God to come heal it.

"Wow! A sign! I had asked for a sign, and this is my confirmation sign." She spoke these words aloud. Elizabeth then put her hand over her mouth in disbelief and laughed. She couldn't believe it. The timing was impeccable. Elizabeth could not wait to meet this woman. Susan had left her phone number for a phone shed recording machine and asked Elizabeth to leave her a message on which day would work to come over.

Elizabeth had a good feeling about all of this. In the letter, Susan mentioned being a friend of Mose and Carrie, so Elizabeth was sure this was a good thing.

The first day of school was August 12th and was quickly approaching. A lot of eighth graders dreaded the end of summer, but Willy looked forward to going back to school. He was very excited to get to see all of his friends every day.

Mose and Carrie invited Karl, Willy, and Elizabeth to go out to eat at the Blue Gate Restaurant and also bought tickets for the five of them to go see the show *Josiah for President* at the Blue Gate Theater. They hired babysitters for their own children because they wanted to be able to fully enjoy the evening with their niece and nephews. They told the children it was to celebrate Willy starting the last school year. The Amish graduate after eighth grade, so this year was a monumental one for Willy.

The show was a hit with all five of them. It was nice to have a couple of adults to be with again, and obviously all three were on their best behavior, so it almost seemed like the good old days.

August 12th soon came, and school started with a fun bus ride for Willy. It was going to be a great school year; he could tell. At school, he was everyone's friend. The Amish kids liked him, and the English kids did, too. He was the consistent friend to all.

One day when Willy was at school, Elizabeth spent the day catching up on the laundry. She used the wringer washer in the wash house and then hung the laundry out to air dry on the wash line. When it was dry, she brought it into the house and folded it all on the kitchen table. As she was taking Willy's clothes into his room, she felt an odd feeling in the room. It caused her to feel uneasy. She couldn't put her finger on why and had never felt like this before. As she went to put his socks into the dresser drawer, she noticed a game sticking out from underneath his bed. She pulled the quilt up and saw it was the Ouija board game. Beside it, she saw a long list of questions and answers.

That's weird, she thought. *He must have brought this game up from the basement and, for some reason, didn't want me to know.* She had thought he was in his room reading a lot lately. It made chills go up her spine, but she wasn't exactly sure why. She thought to herself, *Maybe this is why he's so different lately.* But she wasn't sure what made her feel so uncomfortable about the game.

This is why I need a mom around here, for times like this when I'm not sure what to do, Elizabeth thought to herself. She wasn't mad anymore but rather just stating the facts. She couldn't wait to set up the day for Susan to come over. She looked at the calendar and chose a few days that could work. She decided that when Karl got home, she was going to use his cell to call Susan's number and get this hopefully fruitful relationship started.

Chapter 18

The hopeless despair slowly lifted off Elizabeth. Not much had changed, but there seemed to be a rainbow of promise over her life again. The hope that things would turn out for the best was returning. It's hard to have faith without hope and hope without faith. They go together like salt and pepper. Sometimes, in order to rebuild our faith, God has us look back at His faithfulness in the past. That is precisely what Elizabeth decided to do that day.

Elizabeth took the calendar off the wall in the kitchen and carried it outside. She sat on the front porch swing and took a big drink of some ice cold garden tea. The atmosphere was one that created calmness in her soul. The butterflies fluttered around the flowers, and she smiled at the little kittens playing in the yard. She turned back the pages of the calendar to January and saw things her mom had written on the calendar. She glanced through February and all the way through August. She thought through each month and every event: the accident, the funeral, the sale, the move, the new job for Karl, and recently the protection during the tornados. Wow, God had been faithful in taking good care of them. She realized that He had seen them through a lot in such a short time, and she was convinced He would keep helping them.

She thought about all the big problems and tiny details God had worked out. Some of them were needs, but others were bonuses. The boys didn't need the gun safe in the barn, but it was awesome. She didn't need all the bells and whistles in the wash house, but the wash house sure was convenient. They didn't need the patio furniture from Dad or the quilt from Mom, but God gave them anyway. In a year of tremendous loss, they also had such blessings to help them as well. She shuddered to think about how different their circumstances could have turned out had her dad not been a saver and a planner.

It did her heart so much good to reflect how far they had come since the tragedy. She realized the good things outweighed the negatives. As she turned the calendar pages forward to September and October, she was surprised to see that her mom had written in the dates of the Covered Bridge Festival in Parke County, Indiana. Fall had been her mom's favorite season, and she had been planning on taking the whole family this year. Mom went almost every year and loved it. Elizabeth decided that she would contact a driver and plan on going. She thought to herself, *I need to go find out what Mom loved about it.*

The months that were the hardest to turn to were November and December. She was told that holidays like Thanksgiving and Christmas can be quite painful after losing loved ones. She contemplated what she could plan to make it easier for the boys. She assumed Mose and Carrie would have them over for Thanksgiving, which would be fun. At that moment, a thought popped into her head. *I should buy tickets to Florida for the three of us.* There were two bus lines that delivered Amish people to Sarasota from Shipshewana: the Pioneer Trails and Crossroads. Her Uncle Roger had a house in Pinecraft that he rented out, and he had told her if she ever wanted to go to let him know.

She was so excited she could hardly contain herself. She loved going to Sarasota, and so did the boys. The family had been down countless times over the years, so she knew a lot about what to expect.

The minute Karl got home, she asked if she could use his phone to call Susan. She left a message for Susan on the answering machine letting her know which day would work to get together. She hoped this day would work for Susan as well.

While she had Karl's phone, Elizabeth decided to make one more phone call. She took it into her bedroom so Karl couldn't hear her on the phone. She got the latest copy of *The Budget*, looked up the number for Pioneer Trails, and dialed it. She took out her calendar and asked if there would be any tickets available for the two weeks over Christmas. The woman took a bit to look and then confirmed only a few seats were left.

Oh no, Elizabeth thought. She was almost scared to ask but said, "Do you have three seats left?"

"Yes, we do," replied the woman on the phone, "but if you want them, you need to buy them as soon as possible because they won't be here long. These were actually cancellations."

"OK, I will buy three tickets right now." Elizabeth's hands were shaking with excitement and also nervousness because she had never done any vacation planning before. She put the tickets on her credit card, and the lady said she would send the tickets to her in the mail and that she should have them in a few days.

When Elizabeth got off the phone, she covered her mouth in astonishment at the courage that just rushed over her, the courage that allowed her to plan their first vacation as a family of three! She couldn't wait to tell the boys. She wasn't sure if she should tell them tonight or wrap the tickets up like a gift and give it to them. *They won't believe I did this*, she told herself.

All of the sudden, she realized that they had tickets taken care of but no confirmed place to stay. She quickly got her address book and dialed Uncle Roger. She was prepared to leave a message, but he answered the phone on the second ring, so she got to ask him right away. He told Elizabeth that those weeks would work. He went on to say, "We aren't going to be there, so help yourself, and you don't need to pay a dime."

Elizabeth thanked him repeatedly. Roger replied, "This will be good for the three of you to get away and have some fun. Your dad would approve of this plan. He always loved going down and soaking up the sunshine when it was snowing up North."

She hung up and started laughing. Yes, Dad would approve. He loved Siesta Key Beach and always looked forward to relaxing there. The whole family enjoyed biking around Pinecraft, eating at the restaurants, and socializing with other Northerners.

That evening for supper, Karl grilled some steak, and Elizabeth made baked potatoes and baked beans. It was a meal fit for a king. To top it off, she had cut fresh tomatoes from the garden and made a strawberry pie. The mood in the house was better than it had been in a while.

Karl and Willy couldn't help but notice her huge unrelenting smile. Finally, Karl asked, "What in the world is on your mind? You are acting like Little Miss Sunshine!"

"What do you mean?" Elizabeth asked. "I'm always like this." Her smile broadened even more.

"No, you aren't," Willy chimed in. "You've actually been kinda moody lately."

"OK, OK! I can't keep it inside." Elizabeth paused and then delivered the good news. "I bought us tickets to take the Pioneer Bus to Florida over Christmas for two weeks. Uncle Roger already said we could stay at his house. Everything is arranged. I was going to wait and wrap up the tickets to surprise you guys."

Both Karl and Willy jumped up. Karl grabbed Willy, and they both screamed in excitement and gave each other high fives. Then they came over to Elizabeth and grabbed her into a hug. They weren't normally boys who hugged, but this was a group hug that she wouldn't forget right away.

She didn't need to wonder if she had made the right choice. There was no doubt it would be a much-needed respite. The way the boys responded was confirmation that the getaway was a good idea.

Susan called later in the evening, confirming a day to get together. Elizabeth's first impression of Susan was that she sounded friendly. Elizabeth could hardly wait to spend time with someone who had walked this journey and would understand. They didn't get to talk very long because Susan was at a community phone shack, and someone else needed to use the phone. Amish people don't have landline phones into their houses but primarily use phone shacks. Some of them have cell phones for their business dealings.

Elizabeth was happy to get her calendar down again and write in the get-together with Susan and the two-week vacation to Florida in December. She also drew a big sun across the two weeks. Let the countdown begin. She made a mental note to herself to pray for warm weather for this vacation.

Elizabeth decided to re-read Susan's encouraging letter and was intrigued by the card that Susan had painted and signed. The painting was a bottle, and it had teardrops falling into the bottle. Below it, she had written a summary of Psalm 56:8: *God saves all our tears in a bottle.*

Susan also added her own thoughts on the card: *God does not waste anything. He will use your tears to water good things in your life and in other people's lives as well.*

This Susan must be quite the woman, mused Elizabeth.

As Susan walked in from the phone shack, she thought of the girl whom she had just spoken to. Elizabeth sounded very confident on the phone. She was relieved that she wasn't a fragile, whiny thing. She just hadn't known what to expect from a girl who had been through so much.

Susan Yoder was a 40-year-old Amish woman who knew grief all too well. Her husband, Lester, had lost a fierce battle with cancer four years ago. In their early twenties, Lester and Susan found out that they would never be able to have children, so they tried the adoption process. On two occasions, they had thought they were getting a baby, only to have the birth parents decide to keep the infant. Being burned twice was enough to sour Susan on trusting the system. She then decided to start a bed and breakfast to keep herself preoccupied. Lester and Susan poured their energy into making guests feel welcome in their home. They made many lifelong friends, many of whom were repeat visitors.

They often took the guests to Menno Hof to tour the informational building about Amish and Mennonite history. It was quite intriguing, and it helped a lot of people better understand their heritage.

Susan also loved to draw and paint. One of her guests encouraged her to send samples of her work to a studio in Chicago. It turned out that they loved her work, and even after Lester had passed away, she could earn a good living between the seasonal visitors in her home and the paintings.

She was the kind of person who had the gift of compassion. A lot of Amish women and girls talked to Susan because they knew they could trust her. She wasn't quick to give advice but rather listened well. She didn't just care about people. She also prayed a lot, and word got around that her prayers made a difference. Elizabeth was just one of many people who got a card and a letter. Susan had the gift of encouragement and exercised it regularly.

Her ears were in excellent shape because she would spend hours a day praying to God through journaling. She would write out her feelings and concerns to God, and then she would sit in quietness and listen for His answers and direction into her life. She also loved reading the Bible, her favorite books being the Psalms and Isaiah. She had discovered the Bible verse *My sheep hear my voice* in John 10:27 (KJV).

She realized it said *voice* instead of *My sheep know my words*. She knew that not only did she want to get God's word in her heart but also learn to know His voice, too. She knew that the Trinity had three parts: God, the Father; Jesus, the son who died for her sins; and the Holy Spirit, who guides and directs her daily. She would say this simple prayer every day: "Fill me up to overflowing with Your Holy Spirit."

She knew on her own that if she didn't ask Him to refill her, she would automatically fill up instead with worry, fear, and doubt, and she disliked how those made her feel. She wasn't sure how it worked, but it was kind of like having a tall pure glass of water when she'd ask Him to fill her to overflowing with His Holy Spirit. But allowing her thoughts to give in to fear seemed to put mud in the water.

When God had first started prompting her to pray for Elizabeth and the boys, she did it without thinking twice. That was as easy as breathing. But when God began prompting her to reach out to Elizabeth, she balked at the idea at first. She had gotten quite used to not having children of her own, and it didn't seem like something she wanted to do to open up an old wound of never having any to call her own. The timing seemed very inconvenient, and she even explained that to God in her journals. She wrote, *There was a time I desperately wanted children (in my twenties), but that door got shut. Why would you open that door now?*

The problem with being such a great listener is that if God prompted her to do something, she couldn't pretend He didn't say it. He had branded Isaiah 1:19 on her heart years ago, and it wasn't going away: *If you are willing and obedient, you will eat of the best of the land.* Eating of the best of the land simply meant God's best for her life. The second part of the verse was the part she didn't like: *But if you resist and rebel, you will be devoured by the sword.* That part was not a positive thought.

Sometimes it was easy to be willing and obey, though at times, she was obedient, yet the willingness dawdled behind. This was one of those times. She was reaching out to Elizabeth, but she sure was not very excited about it. She feared getting her heart involved and decided she would love from the top of her heart. She was not going to let herself care too much because after all, grief had finally lost its grip on her, and she didn't want to go back there. Four years was a long journey out of the deep pain of losing one person. She was concerned she would be overwhelmed by Elizabeth losing four people, and Susan did not want to be held onto like a drowning person in a pond. She was finally living again and had no time for death to pull her under. Not now. Not ever.

Somehow, because she had gotten to know God well over the years, she could almost read the writing on the wall. She sensed He was going to call her to get involved. She knew she could do it kicking and screaming or surrender to the plan.

Susan enjoyed being Amish but was not crazy about the Amish life of canning, cooking, and sewing. She knew how to do all three, but she always cringed whenever she saw the word *simple* associated with being Amish. She often wondered what was so simple about all the work. She felt like it was false advertising because *simple*, in her opinion, meant *easy*. It was not *easy* taking care of a house, a barn, and animals. *Simple*, to her, would be walking out of the house, turning a key in a car, and driving away. Catching the horse and having to hitch it up in the buggy was no small feat, especially in the winter months. She was thankful for a really reliable buggy horse. He was fast enough to get her places but calm enough to control.

The second meaning of *simple* among the Amish meant that someone was a few bricks shy of a full load. "See is bissel simple" (*She is a little simple* in Dutch) would be an insult, not a compliment. So that is the reason that the Amish rarely describe themselves as *simple*.

In the Amish setting, Susan never got a chance to go to college, but if she could have, she would have loved to learn more about the study of people, why they do the things they do. She loved reading and went to the library a lot. She enjoyed observing different personalities and how they interacted.

Later in the same evening, at both homes, two very different people were thinking about each other. Elizabeth felt a sense of anticipation and hope. She felt like she was thrown a lifeline. Susan felt like she was getting roped into a relationship with Elizabeth that she wasn't sure she wanted.

Normally, when Susan hesitated about something God called her to do, she ended up loving where He took her. She knew a few things right up front: God comforts us, so we can comfort others. She had often wished she would have had a "Susan" in her life when she had most needed one. She knew she could save people years of grief and heartache by helping them through their tragedies.

Susan knew that God had given His best when He gave His son, Jesus. She wondered why it was so hard for her to willingly give her life for others, even if she wanted to.

Chapter 19

The changing of the seasons in the Midwest are highly anticipated and seen as refreshing. September, which marks the beginning of fall, was still warm but not so muggy. Everyone seemed to be relieved that the tornado weather had stopped as quickly as it had begun. No one enjoyed that severe, threatening weather except maybe a few crazy storm chasers who lived for that adrenaline rush. While most people would take cover and run from the twisters, the storm chasers actually drove as close as possible into them to take videos of tornados up close and personal. Most people thought they were nuts because they risk their very lives to do it. They were famous on YouTube for their insane courage.

With autumn quickly approaching, all of the local die-hard hunters were living for deer hunting season. A few neighbors had cameras set up in their woods and had captured pictures of some trophy bucks. It made them talk all the more. The Amish man who leased the woods behind the farm told Karl and Willy to help themselves to using the land. His mom was failing in her health, so he was preoccupied and would not be able to get out much this year. He told them if they would bring him some deer jerky that he would count that as a good trade.

Willy and Karl were in on all the excitement and had both received their deer permits as soon as they possibly could. There were a limited amount of permits, so the boys followed the "if you snooze, you lose" mentality and hurried to get them. Both of the boys were chomping at the bit to tag a deer. The big thing was to go out spotting for deer before the season opened. They got their deer stands set up in the woods directly behind the farm, and Uncle Mose also helped them put a few in his woods. Many mornings before school and work, they woke up early in order to trudge back into the woods for a few hours to see what was going on. On some days, it was quiet, and they didn't see much, but on other days, they saw quite a few doe and also spotted a few average-sized buck.

Mose had set up a target practice shooting range about a mile from his farm, so on Saturdays; the boys always went there for the afternoon. Mose had a collection of deer decoys and also plenty of clay pigeon targets. He told both boys that they were shooting really well and were great marksmen. They became experts at hitting the targets, and he couldn't wait to take them. The boys were both required to have an adult over the age of 18 with them because they could only hunt on the youth hunt due to their ages. They were looking forward to having Mose go with them because he was a better woodsman than their dad had been. Dan used to go out for the boys' sake but never fully enjoyed it. He simply did it to spend time with his boys and because it interested them. Mose, on the other hand, lived and breathed it, too, so he taught them a lot. He would be very strict about the clothes being washed in scent free soap and stored properly. He taught them about wind patterns and cover-up scents to spray on the clothes so they wouldn't be noticed by the deer.

Elizabeth was fine with letting the boys wash the hunting clothes in unscented detergent. She totally left that task up to them because she didn't want to jeopardize the process. Once they had them sprayed with the cover scent, she made them keep them in the shack they called the hunting cabin. Karl would get after Willy if he even thought of touching the dogs before heading to the woods.

For Elizabeth, fall meant the canning season was almost wrapping up. It was such a good feeling to carry filled jars into the basement and add them to the shelves of canned food. She saw rows of peaches, red beets, pickles, and green beans and was so thankful for them. Her mom had canned a lot of it last year, and they still had food left from her hard labor. Elizabeth had a garden but not as big as the one they used to have at the Home Place.

The whole family loved to eat applesauce and ate it with almost every meal, except for breakfast, of course. The only time that applesauce was eaten at breakfast time was over mush and headcheese. It sounded disgusting but was actually quite delicious.

She had to guess at the amount of bushels of apples she would need to buy. Her mom had always put up at least six bushel, but there were four fewer people at the table, so Elizabeth thought three would be plenty. Elizabeth knew it was going to be a long day of putting up the apples because the boys weren't home to help her. Mose happened to find out she was doing them and told Carrie, who promptly offered to come help Elizabeth.

Carrie left her children at home with Mose so the two of them could get the work done faster. They also got a chance to really catch up on how things were going. Carrie was very impressed with how well-organized Elizabeth kept everything.

Carrie told Elizabeth, "You keep house just like your mom. She always had a place for everything and everything in place.

"That's funny! I guess I do," Elizabeth said. "I always like to keep things orderly so I can find them. This house is really easy to maintain, and it's a lot newer than the Home Place, so it's easy to clean."

"Well, you have done really well with having both jobs and still seeing after meals for the boys and all," Carrie complimented her.

"It hasn't been easy, but somehow it always works out," Elizabeth said. "I was having a tough week last week, and out of the blue, a woman named Susan Yoder sent me a letter and said she'd like to come over sometime. She said she knows you and Mose."

"Susan is a very kind woman," Carrie replied. "You two will dearly enjoy each other."

"Here's the card she painted for me," Elizabeth smiled at how thoughtful the card was.

"I believe she knows first-hand how God uses tears to grow things," Carrie said. "She has walked through a lot of trials and yet still remains a jewel. Some people get so bitter when life gets hard, but with her, it just made her more caring."

"I hope I can be like that," Elizabeth said.

Carrie wanted to know all about the Essenhaus and asked Elizabeth what it was like working for Cassandra.

It was great to have Carrie asking her questions, and Elizabeth talked non-stop for two hours. She told Carrie that the September days at the Essenhaus were still busy, but the customers weren't quite as hot and tired when they got seated. The weather being a bit cooler seemed to help and also the fact that children were back in school thinned the crowds out a bit. It didn't stop the long waits, but people seemed more pleasant. She also told Carrie that she was still receiving good tips.

"There's normally a bunch of food messes left for me at my tables," Carrie said laughing, "but I haven't found any tips on my tables lately. But I'm not complaining. I'm trying to enjoy this season with little ones because I know they grow up so quickly."

It was really refreshing for Carrie to be with Elizabeth, too. Her life was wrapped up with her little ones, and to hear about the local activities was a good change of scenery. Elizabeth was used to primarily talking about the boys' interests, so the two needed each other's company.

The conversation went from one thing to the next. After Carrie left, Elizabeth was pretty tired, so she curled up on the recliner in the living room and took a short nap. The chair used to be her dad's favorite seat in the house, so sitting in it made her feel close to him. He had such a demeanor about him. His demeanor always calmed Elizabeth, and when he was around, she felt taken care of. She could picture him sitting in it. Sitting in his seat brought back those feelings of comfort and safety, and soon she was sound asleep.

When Willy got off the bus, he got the mail and was walking toward house when the UPS truck dropped off a package. He was about beside himself with excitement because the box was from Cabela's. The boys had ordered a few things and were anxious to get their hands on this delivery. Willy, thoughtful boy that he was, decided to wait to open it until Karl was home.

Most of Willy's friends lived a few miles away but not too far to bike. He told Elizabeth that he was invited over to Ronnie's house to collect black walnuts. She told him he could go if he was home in time to eat supper. With that, he was out the door before she could change her mind.

The walnuts were plentiful this year, and it took buckets to get them all transported back to Ronnie's shed. This area had a lot of raccoon, muskrat and mink in the local ditches and ponds. The boys were working on saving money to buy traps to capture them.

True to his word, Willy was home in time to eat supper. All three children were home to eat together. They talked about school, work, and, of course, the Northridge football team. The boys thought it was cool that Elizabeth sometimes got to wait on the football team at the Essenhaus.

The high school was directly across from the Essenhaus, so it was a normal occurrence to see the players come in to eat. On Thursdays, the entire team would all come to eat together, though a few players here and there would come to the restaurant sporadically throughout the week. They could put down the food.

It was exciting to see how pumped they all were for all of their wins. The town of Middlebury put up banners all over town in support of their "Boys of Fall." A town of under 3,500 people sees it as a big deal when its team starts beating the teams of bigger schools.

Even the surrounding towns rallied with them, and a lot of Karl's friends would go to the Friday night football games.

That evening, when they opened the Cabela's package, it was like Christmas for Karl and Willy. They opened their new hunting equipment. They had ordered scopes for their shotguns and a Cuddeback trail camera.

The week leading up to opening day of deer season, the boys spent a lot of time getting their guns ready. They both were using 20-gauge shotguns.

Before they knew it, September 27 was finally here! The boys got to bed early the night before and planned to hunt on the land behind their own farm for the first day. Mose better not be late because they wanted to get into the tree stands before daylight.

It was a bit chilly, so they needed jackets. As they were putting them on, they saw Mose show up just in time, smiling from ear to ear. He was in his zone. He was created to hunt.

"Let's go get 'em, boys!" he said as they headed out. The walk down the long lane was quiet except for the tree leaves gently blowing in a slight breeze.

Karl was going to take the tree stand near the creek. They had placed it there because there is a big white oak that had started dropping acorns, and the deer were hitting the acorns like candy. Willy and Mose went on back to a deer blind set up on a bigger tree stand that they could both sit in. It was a picture perfect set-up on an inside corner of the field where someone had planted clover for a food plot.

Karl was sitting in his tree stand and was enjoying watching the woods begin to come to life. They had made it into the woods about a half hour before the sun came up. The birds were chirping, and the trees were blowing gently in the breeze. All of a sudden, he saw about six deer coming into the opening in the clearing. He knew there was a fork on the trail that they could either go farther into the woods or come right past his tree stand. His heart was thumping so loudly that he thought for sure the deer could hear him.

The deer stood for a long minute and then, one by one, turned and headed straight toward Karl.

He was calm and rattled all at the same time. He had been training for this moment, and now it was right in front of him. He saw a few doe, and then he saw antlers glistening in the light coming through the trees.

He thought to himself, *Easy, Karl, you got this.* He was slowly moving his shotgun getting it ready when the train whistle sounded about three miles out. The big buck was already at 50 yards and closing fast. The deer all paused, and the buck stopped. And in that brief moment of hesitation, Karl took advantage of the buck pausing. He pulled the trigger, and he hit the buck in the heart. The gun scared the other deer, and they took off running back into the woods. The buck was massive, and he staggered a bit but then dropped to the ground. The buck tried getting back up, and Karl thought, *Oh no, he's gonna run* and imagined a long day of trailing a blood trail. But he fell back down and this time stayed on the ground.

Karl was in hunter heaven. He could not believe his eyes. It had only taken 45 minutes of patience to harvest a big buck this morning, but he had waited for this one since he was 12 years old.

All hunters live for and dream about the "once in a lifetime" day. Karl was living that dream.

He knew immediately this one would be too big to move by himself, so he quickly texted his neighbor Mitch and asked him to bring his four-wheeler over to transport the buck out.

He told Mitch where he was in the woods and then quickly got down and tagged him. He made sure the deer had fully expired. He heard Willy and Mose talking and figured they had heard his shot and they were coming to help with the deer. Willy was so happy for Karl that he let out a huge whoop, did a little jig, and high-fived him.

Mose's mouth fell open in astonishment and exclaimed in Dutch, "Unfashtandeh! Sella ding is huge! (Unbelievable! That thing is huge!)"

It was a 13-point buck and appeared to be at least four years old. Mose was attempting to figure out how they were going to get this big beast out of the woods when he heard the four-wheeler and was thankful to see Mitch coming to help get it out.

Mitch had a pickup that he said he'd be glad to use to take the deer in to get processed.

Mose informed Karl that he needed to take this one to a taxidermist to get this buck mounted. There was no question that Mose was going to make this happen. He knew the kids had the cash to get it done, but even if they wouldn't have, he would have picked up the tab himself. There were some things that didn't need to be thought about. This was one of them.

Willy said, "I think we can call this a day, and I will try for my deer another day." He wanted Karl to get to enjoy this moment to the fullest. Willy was such a thoughtful soul. He was always thinking of others.

It took all four of them to get the buck onto the four-wheeler and then switched to the truck. Karl posted a few pictures of himself on his Facebook wall, and the likes and comments started pouring in. He was going to enjoy the attention and the victory of the day.

After Karl and Mitch left to take the deer to the check point and to get processed, Mose informed Willy, "We are just getting warmed up. Let's head back to my woods and get you one, too. There's no use burning daylight, and you can't kill a buck at the house."

"My dad used to say that, too," Willy replied. "I figured we'd be done for the day, but I will go if you want to."

"You better believe it! This was just the first inning!" Mose laughed. "You're up to bat next."

Mose knew it might be a long waiting game, but he was in it for the long haul. It wasn't until four in the afternoon that Willy spotted a doe within shooting range. He waited until he had a good angle on her, and then he also shot his deer for the day. Willy was thrilled. It was a great ending to a good day. Mose couldn't have felt happier if Karl and Willy would have been his own boys. He patted his heart and thought of how Dan would have felt.

Willy thanked Mose for spending the day with him. "My dad would have probably called it a day by 11 this morning," Willy remarked, and they both laughed because it was true.

Mitch helped them get Willy's deer in, too, and they all ended up at Mose's house to tell Carrie the whole story. Carrie fed them fried chicken and mashed potatoes and finished it up with homemade ice cream.

Karl and Willy thanked Mose and Mitch repeatedly for all of their help. This day would go down as one with some new favorite memories. They came home smelling like the woods. They had guns to clean and put away. They both had smiles that wouldn't quit. Life was good today.

Chapter 20

Susan was sitting in her normal spot doing her journaling. It was her morning routine. She made some coffee and opened her Bible to read a few chapters. She liked to have her notebook close by so she could jot down her thoughts as she read God's word. When she was finished, she always had a list of prayer requests she would pray over, but her favorite thing to do was to journal her thoughts to God. She would write down the questions she had for God and then sit and wait until the answers would flood into her mind, kind of like a journalist asking someone questions.

This morning was no different, as the sun creeped over the treetops she wrote...

Good Morning, God,
I'm wondering why you picked me to go see Elizabeth.

Instantly, she heard God reply with His own question for her – not out loud but just into her spirit and mind. She wrote down what she heard Him asking her.

Can you think of someone more qualified to talk to her?
Well, not really.
Can you imagine what kinds of things she's been told by people?
Probably that time will heal.
Does time heal? Is that true?
No, You have taught me that time is no healer. That is a lie. Bitterness can even grow with time. Only You, God, can heal. We can't rush healing, but we can lengthen it.

That is truth. She needs to have you in her life. Prepare for warfare. There's more than just grief going on in that home.

Now you have my attention. Now I realize why you need me here. Yes, God I am willing to be boots on the ground for them. *This will be no walk in the park or cake walk. It will not be easy, but it will be great. You are ready for this.* *I created you for this. You are up to bat.*

OK then. I am willing, and I will obey you, but I also want to want to do it. Can you put an excitement in me to want to? A desire to love helping them?

I will cause you to have a fire in your bones for this.
A fire in my bones?
Yes, look up that phrase.

Susan found the phrase in Jeremiah 20:9: *But if I say, I will not mention his word or speak anymore in his name. His word is in my heart like a fire. A fire shut up in my bones. I am weary of holding it in, indeed I cannot.*

Hmmm, that's funny! Yes, whenever I make myself be quiet about you, eventually, the fire in me just ignites, and I can't help myself. It will just come gushing out of me.

You are like a fire in my bones. I like that.

Susan had her marching orders from God. Today was the day she would be going to Elizabeth's house. The first thing she would do is ask God for His Holy Spirit to fill her up to overflowing. She also asked God to dress her with the full armor of God. On the way she spent time in prayer and enjoyed the pleasant October weather.

At the Miller house, Elizabeth enjoyed hearing the boys relive their big hunting day. She felt as if she had been in the woods with them because they spoke about it in such detail. She could almost see it like a video in her mind. The boys were also reading the *Goshen News* and looking at pictures of another Northridge win. The Raiders were on a roll like an unstoppable freight train.

Elizabeth had spent an entire day getting the house spotless for Susan's visit. She wasn't sure what to expect, but she hoped that the visit would be encouraging. She needed some hope and asked God to please let Susan bring her some.

The morning Susan was going to arrive, Elizabeth found herself pacing the house and straightening up pillows on the couch over and over. Finally, she heard the horse and buggy drive in the lane. Susan was here. Elizabeth looked out the window and was happy to see a very pleasant, young-looking woman walking toward the house.

God came through in a big way for both Susan and Elizabeth. Somehow, when Susan walked in the door, there was an instant bond without any awkwardness. This was God-ordained. She knew on her own, she would never be able to help Elizabeth walk through her grief, but with God, all things were possible.

The two sat and talked for hours. They laughed at times and other times filled Kleenexes with tears.

Elizabeth told Susan that she often has very vivid dreams and how Ridge, her most memorable customer at the Essenhaus, told her that dreams often have meanings.

Susan agreed with Ridge. "Yes, in the Bible, Daniel and Joseph had dreams with a lot of meanings in them."

"This morning, I woke up around 3, and I had been having an awful dream," Elizabeth stated. "I was here in our house, and all of the doors and windows in the entire house were open. I was running from window to window and door to door to close them. As I closed one, another opened up again, and I just could not keep them all closed. Then my dream switched to a fight between God and the devil. I was being pulled back and forth, and then I saw the lake of fire. As I was falling into it, I woke up. When I woke up, my heart was racing, and the fear was tangible in the room. It felt so real."

"That is awful! Do you have dreams like this a lot?" Susan asked.

"I've had dreams about Dad in heaven, but I haven't dreamt about hell before," Elizabeth replied.

"The reality is that there is a heaven and a hell, and all of us have a choice where we want to spend our eternities. Your parents both asked Jesus to be their Savior, so they get to be in heaven. If you would like to have the peace they had, all you need to do is to simply admit that you are a sinner and ask Jesus to forgive you of your sins and invite Him into your heart. Then He moves into your life, takes away every single one of your sins, and washes you completely clean. You get a clean slate and a brand new heart that the Bible says is as white as snow. Would you like to do that?"

"Yes, I would! I want to have peace instead of turmoil in my heart!" Elizabeth bowed her head and prayed.

"Jesus, that's what I want. I want you to come into my heart and wash away all my sins. I am sorry for all the things I've done to break Your heart, and I want to be forgiven. I'm sorry that I've been mad at You for not stopping the wreck. I want to live for You, and I want to go to Heaven someday with my dad and mom."

It was as if a heavy weight was lifted off Elizabeth. She started smiling and told Susan that she felt so light. Susan reached over, grabbed Elizabeth's hand, and added a short prayer for her, "God, thank you for sending Jesus to this Earth to die on the cross so that we could be forgiven and have new life. Thank you for forgiving Elizabeth and washing her pure. Fill her to overflowing with your precious Holy Spirit and help her to feel your love. I also ask you to please stop all tormenting dreams. In Jesus' name, Amen."

Elizabeth smiled at Susan after Susan's prayer. "Thank you so much. Ever since Dad and Mom were gone, I have wanted to do that and wasn't sure how. I feel like a brand new person."

"Well, the angels have a party in heaven when people on Earth do that," Susan replied.

Susan had been taught a lot about Jesus as a little Amish girl, but she had actually gotten to know Jesus through an unusual twist of events. After the devastation of the second failed adoption process, she struggled with deep depression and was tormented with oppression and didn't want to keep living.

She had gone to the doctor, and her doctor wanted to pump her full of anti-depressants.

She confided in some Amish friends about it, and they asked her if they could pray with her.

One of the wise, caring Amish women who prayed with her told Susan, "You could ask Jesus to show you where this oppression is coming from. He can reveal it to you."

So that's what Susan did. She prayed this simple prayer: "Jesus, can You show me where these thoughts are coming from and show me the source and the origin of where they started?"

Instantly, she saw a video going off in her mind. She saw herself as a baby being prayed over by a brauf doctor. Some call it pow-wowing.

Being braufed over, had also given Susan the ability to draw sicknesses from others. Mothers would bring their children to her, babies who were crying, and she would draw their stomachaches, toothaches, cold sores, and headaches from them. She would get their illnesses.

At first, she felt confused because Jesus was showing her that the oppression and depression was linked to the braufing, but she had always seen it as a gift she had received to help others. She had often wondered why she had to take all these sicknesses for God. She thought that was strange. Eventually, as she learned more about the life of Jesus by reading her Bible, she learned Jesus healed with the gift of healing, too. However, Jesus didn't take it onto himself, but rather God healed the sicknesses. For example, Jesus healed the blind man, but Jesus did not become blind. She learned that God still does miracles of healing, but now she would ask God to heal people in Jesus' name. She traded the brauf gift in exchange for His Holy Spirit power to heal.

People often asked Susan if their gifts to heal were from God or the devil. She said that through praying to God, He would clearly show them the answer. All they needed to do was to ask God to take the gift away from them if it was from the demons. They would need to confess it was sin if they had been using false powers. If it was a gift from God, He would not have them "take on" other people's sicknesses or illnesses because He did so by dying on the cross. The Bible says, *By His stripes we are healed*. It doesn't say, *By his stripes and a brauf doctor's body, we are healed.*

"We can pray to ask God to heal people in Jesus's name and ask Him to cover us with the blood of Jesus," Susan concluded. "The blood of Jesus is still powerful today. Because of the finished work of the cross, miracles still happen today when people pray for healing."

"This is all so interesting," Elizabeth told her. "Well, maybe God could tell us what my dreams with all the open doors meant."

"The concept of open doors and closed doors can mean good things and negative things. The reason I tend to think this dream was not a positive thing is how afraid the dream caused you to feel. In the spirit world, the phrase *open door* can mean there is something that is left open that can cause demonic oppression. For example, you wanted the doors and windows to your house closed to keep out wild animals and things that would harm. In the same way, we want our lives to be guarded from open doors that could allow evil to enter our lives or homes."

Susan suggested the two women pray again. "I will pray and ask God to show you."

Both women closed their eyes as Susan prayed: "Lord Jesus, we need your wisdom for Elizabeth, and we bring her dreams to you. Could you please bring to her mind anything that might be causing the night terrors and tormenting dreams?"

Almost immediately, Elizabeth said aloud, "I can see what it is. As soon as you asked God to show me, I saw the Ouija game that Cassandra gave us. Willy has it in his room. It always made me feel a bit uncomfortable, but I wasn't sure why."

"Now that makes a lot of sense," Susan explained. "That game is a subtle way to get people to dabble in witchcraft and occult games. It seems innocent, but it's really actually the opposite."

"I want to get rid of it as quickly as possible," Elizabeth said, and so they gathered the game and took it outside to burn in the dumpster.

Susan wasn't finished teaching, though. She explained, "I know it seems like it would be enough to just get rid of the game, but it's not. Whenever there are doors opened up in our life through things like the witchcraft games and the occult, then we need to pray and ask God to take back the ground we gave to the enemy through our involvement."

Susan wrote out a prayer for Elizabeth to use for Willy later when he got home. It said: "Dear God, I confess that I have opened up doors in my life to the enemy to cause me oppression through playing the

Ouija board. I recognize that it is not an innocent game, and I ask you to please take back the ground in my life that I gave the enemy access to. I renounce and reject all demonic involvement in my life and ask You to purify and cleanse me. I want You, God, to regain all the ground in my life. As for our house, I ask that You bring angels to come cleanse it of any and all demons that have been harassing us and causing oppression and depression in our home. You have no right here, and we ask God to station angels all around the property. Amen."

Susan anointed the windows and doors with oil and prayed through the house with Elizabeth.

It was a good day, and that night, Elizabeth had the most restful night of sleep she had in months.

The next day at the Essenhaus, Elizabeth and the other waitresses served a lot of pumpkin pie. Some people asked to have it heated a bit and then topped it with some whipped cream. Many diners loved having it heated because the whipped cream would melt down over the warm pie and literally melt in their mouths. Elizabeth had to have a piece of it after she got off work at 3.

She could hardly contain her excitement. It was a combination of what Jesus had changed in her heart and the fall weather that made her feel joy all the way to her bones. She simply radiated. She had never felt so free and so alive.

After work, five of the Essenhaus girls were going to ride their bikes from Middlebury to Shipshewana on the Pumpkinvine Nature Trail. They had asked Elizabeth to go with them a week before, and they didn't need to ask her twice. She loved autumn weather and especially enjoyed biking through Middlebury's Main Street during this time of the year. The houses along Main Street were primarily big, older homes with oversized porches. The swings and rocking chairs on the porches made the homes look so inviting. A lot of people had also decorated their front porches with hay bales and pumpkins. The American flags were waving in the breeze, and the scene was the picture-perfect postcard of a small Midwest town. As she pedaled her bike down the sidewalk, Elizabeth marveled at the magnificent maple trees hanging down over the road. They were full of spectacular shades of red, yellow and orange. They all had the perfect splashes of color by the Master Painter of all creation.

It was fun for the girls to ride through some leaves on the trail and hear them crunching under their tires. Amish farmers were out putting up corn shocks, and the girls stopped to watch them for a bit. They felt a bit like the nosey tourists who couldn't get enough of the Amish lifestyle.

Farther up the trail, they rode behind a house where a mom and her little children were out raking leaves. The smaller ones were making a mess jumping in the big piles, but their mom just patiently let them. They saw her taking pictures of the children having fun and knew that Mom realized the memories being made.

The best smell of all was at the farm they drove past. They could see a big pile of leaves burning but noticed the smell before they saw the pile. Elizabeth loved the smell because it was so intoxicating. Nothing said fall like burning leaves. She told the girls that she would love to create a candle with that exact scent.

The girls didn't realize what God was painting behind them until they emerged off the trail and looked into the western sky. The sky was on fire with shades of orange and reds. They all stopped and stared. One of the girls had her phone along and snapped a few pictures of the girls in front of the sunset. It was a day they had all enjoyed. Karen invited them to stop by for a drink and a snack before they headed for home.

Elizabeth thought to herself, *God, thank You for painting this sunset. This day was just what I needed. Who could ever see this and still doubt that there was a God?*

Chapter 21

The girls stopped at Karen's house for a snack after they finished their bike ride. Karen had made rice krispie treats, and together, the girls devoured the entire pan. Karen told the girls she was having a silent Tupperware party and got them all a new catalog. Elizabeth picked out a few things for herself and also ordered a few things to keep on hand for the weddings she suspected were coming up soon. Among the Amish, the wedding engagement is often kept a secret among family and close friends until the couple announces it in church.

As Elizabeth biked home, she couldn't help but sing, and her heart felt so full. It had been such a great week. She could have taken a few different roads home, but she decided to bike past John Hostetler's house. She hadn't seen him in a while. She thought about the stories of his coming home in the fall and remembered the leaf raking story.

When she got close to John Hostetler's house, she noticed that he was standing out near the road and that he was talking to someone. He had a weed eater in his hand, so it looked like he had been outside trimming. He had his back toward Elizabeth, so he didn't see her until she was almost in front of him.

He was talking to a girl whom Elizabeth didn't recognize, so Elizabeth wasn't planning on stopping to talk. But the minute John spotted Elizabeth, he immediately spoke up. "Hi there! What are you up to, Elizabeth?"

She slowed down and stopped her bike. "I just came from a long bike ride. A bunch of us Essenhaus girls rode our bikes from Middlebury to Shipshe on the Pumpkinvine, and I'm just on my way home."

"This is the best weather for that," John said. "I need to do that sometime. It looks like your tires are holding up OK today."

"Yes, I haven't had any trouble lately," Elizabeth replied.

"Hey, I heard Karl got that big buck everybody was hoping to get," John said with a big smile. "Good for him. Tell him I said I was happy to hear about it."

"OK, I will tell him," Elizabeth said. "Well, I'll see you later!" And with that, she rode away.

John watched Elizabeth until she was up the road a bit, and then John turned back to talk to his niece, Lisa. Lisa was his oldest niece and only a few years younger than he was. She had stopped in to tell him about the next family ice cream get-together.

Lisa was laughing and said, "Veah wah sell? (Who was that?) Du huschts schlim. (You have it bad.)"

"What are you talking about?" John asked laughing.

"It's obvious to me that you think a lot of her, whoever she is," Lisa said emphatically. "You watched her until she was clear down the road, and you didn't hear anything I asked you just now."

"I'm listening to you now," John said with a big grin on his face. "You have my undivided attention. What were you mumbling?"

"I wasn't mumbling!" Lisa gave it right back. "You were clearly distracted. By the way, whoever this Elizabeth is . . . she seemed really nice, and you need to make your move. It has to be boring here at this place all by yourself all the time!" Lisa gestured toward John's yard.

"Boring? Hey, it's fun here! I don't need to plan around anyone!" John insisted.

"Sure it is," Lisa said sarcastically. She wasn't convinced. "What are you having for supper tonight? Probably a cold peanut butter and jelly sandwich on some moldy bread?"

John thought Lisa was funny and laughed with her. He kidded her back, "Heck, I have ribeye steak every night!"

After Lisa left, John thought about Elizabeth and realized that every time he had ever been around her, she lit up any space she ever entered. Wherever she went, she carried an air of pleasantness, like a ray of sunshine and a breath of fresh air. Maybe Lisa was right about him making his move.

He decided that he was going to make more stops at the Essenhaus on the days Elizabeth worked.

As Elizabeth left from talking with John, her thoughts were a bit all over the place. On one hand, she was thinking how amazing she thought John was and that it was really good to see him. He was handsome, even in his everyday work clothes. His shirt was a bit dirty, and his sleeves were rolled up enough that she could see his toned arms. He had looked glad to see Elizabeth and was really friendly. But good grief, who was that girl in his lane? She had been friendly toward Elizabeth but had just politely listened to John's and her conversation. John hadn't introduced them, so she had no clue who she was.

Elizabeth realized that she was a bit disappointed and wondered who the lucky girl was. *That must be a girl he's dating*, Elizabeth incorrectly assumed. *She sure was pretty. I guess I'd rather know than not know. I just wish it would be me.*

Her thoughts turned back to the conversation she had with Susan. Her heart felt so clean, and she was thinking that she would really like to get baptized sometime soon. She would need to talk to the preachers and ask when the next baptismal would be so she could take the classes that are taught before the actual baptism.

When she arrived at home, the boys were both there. Karl had grilled some chicken breasts and made some potatoes. It was good to be home after the long bike ride.

She got a chance to talk to the boys about Susan coming over and how they had gotten rid of the Ouija board and why.

At first, Willy got kind of upset because he said he liked playing it, but Elizabeth explained to him about the oppression those kinds of games can bring into a house. She explained how it would be kind of like leaving a front door of a house open and allowing a skunk to meander in and stink the place up. She gave him the prayer that Susan had written out for him to pray. He read it and said he would put it in his room for later.

Elizabeth told Karl and Willy that she had asked Jesus into her heart and was going to get baptized. Karl said, "I'm not ready to do that because I'm not ready to join church yet."

"Asking Jesus into your heart has nothing to do with joining church," Elizabeth explained. "You remember that Dad always told us that. Dad taught us that a person can become a Christian before becoming a church member. People who become saved often want to get baptized and join a church, but they are two separate things. Dad also said you can be a church member and not be a Christian, too. The Bible teaches that it is by grace, through faith, we are saved."

"Think of it like this, Karl. Just because you want to be a hunter doesn't automatically make you a hunter. You had to get information on gun safety in order to get a hunting license. In the same way, in order to get into heaven, you need to become a Christian and ask Jesus for his free gift of forgiveness. We have to accept it, or we don't get it."

Willy understood what Elizabeth was saying and actually was more open to this type of conversation than Karl. Karl was having fun in his rumspringa years and didn't want to be inconvenienced in his fun. Willy had nothing to lose. He had felt the desire for something more, and that was why he had played the game. But it sounded like Susan told Elizabeth that God can speak even more directly to a person than the Ouija board ever could.

It sounded cool to interview God like Susan did. Elizabeth told the boys how Susan spoke to God. Willy decided he might try that. He had a lot of questions.

Before they went to bed, she reminded the boys about the upcoming trip to the Covered Bridge Festival.

Elizabeth had mentioned to a few friends that she and the boys were going to go to the Covered Bridge Festival in Mansfield, Indiana. Before they knew it, they had a van load going over there. They decided to go down on Friday after work and get a hotel to stay the night so they'd be there first thing in the morning. It was a much-anticipated trip because they had often heard about it from their parents. Mom's plan had been to take the whole family this year. The boys and Elizabeth couldn't wait to see what made Mom enjoy it so much. Mose and Carrie and another Amish couple, Ray and Katie Miller, were the only married people going. Elizabeth was taking three girlfriends, and Karl and Willy were taking Jerry and Joe Christner.

The day of the road trip finally came. The van ride was a blast. They all talked and laughed non-stop on the way to Parke County. When they arrived at the hotel, the boys were excited to see it had an indoor pool. Mose told them to wait to go swimming until after dinner. There was a Texas Roadhouse within walking distance of the hotel, so they all had dinner there.

Texas Roadhouse proved to have a fun atmosphere with country music, and every now and then, the waitresses would line up and dance together. Mose found out that it was Joe's birthday, so he told the waitress. Before they knew it, the whole wait staff was around the table and had Joe sitting on a saddle with a cowboy hat. Then the staff sang happy birthday to him. They also gave him a free dessert with ice cream. The Amish group laughed so hard because it was obvious that Joe was getting more attention than usual and that the waitresses enjoyed talking to them. Every now and then, they would come ask another question about the Amish lifestyle, but it really didn't bother this group.

The kids swam in the pool until it was closing down and then watched TV until midnight. They liked being at hotels for something different but knew they better get some sleep for the big day ahead.

They woke up around 7 and all met at Cracker Barrel by 8. It was a bit chilly, but the fire was lit in the fireplace in the middle of the restaurant. Soon they were all enjoying a great country breakfast. The two youngest boys got done first and meandered over to play checkers until the rest were done drinking coffee and visiting.

They had a half hour drive out to Mansfield, Indiana, where the Covered Bridge Festival had its main location. The surrounding towns also had activities, but the place Mom liked best was Mansfield, so that's where they were headed. They enjoyed driving through some Indiana back roads and passed several covered bridges on the way to Mansfield. The driver told them that Parke County is known as the "Covered Bridge Capital of the World" and that there are 31 covered bridges left standing out of the 52 the county used to have.

As they got closer to the town of Mansfield, the group had a bit of a wait in traffic trying to get in. Obviously, this was a popular place to be this time of year.

The weather was perfect. It had warmed up a bit, so they left their jackets in the van. They could see the booths and vendors, and all of the sudden, the covered bridge came into view. Elizabeth knew right then why her mom loved it here.

From the one end of the covered bridge, they could see the big old roller mill sitting right beside the Big Raccoon Creek. There were all kinds of colorful trees behind it, which made for a breathtaking scene. There were people strolling beside the creek to enjoy the sound of the running water.

They all walked together across the big covered bridge that separated the town from the vendors in the far fields. There were a lot of food vendors, and they knew they'd find plenty to eat later in the day.

The boys said they were going to go check out the mill, and off they went. Elizabeth made sure they had some money and a plan in case they got separated from each other. The boys were old enough to take care of themselves, but the youngest two didn't have phones, so she just wanted to make sure they were OK. Mose and Ray wanted to see the mill, too. The signs said it was built in the 1820s, so that made the mill all the more fascinating because it had stood the test of time. If its walls could talk, it would have been interesting to hear their stories.

The women and girls enjoyed the shops and booths with home décor and candles. It was fun to look through the different booths. Elizabeth realized that their home had many items her mom had collected over the years from her trips to this festival. It made her smile to think of her mom walking these very hills.

The men and boys explored the mill and, of course, had to purchase some food items. The boys ran off to go looking through the booths and shops, and the men walked over to their Amish friends who were selling the log cabins and the kettle corn. Mose thought the log cabins were awesome, and he would love to have one in his woods someday. He sat on the front porch of the display cabin and ate his kettle corn. He told Ray, "It costs nothing to dream."

At noon, the gang all met back at the bridge to get some lunch. They found a picnic table that overlooked the creek but still allowed them to people watch, too. The food choices were endless, it seemed, but a lot of them chose ribeye sandwiches. One of the girls got an onion blossom, and the rest of the girls helped her eat it.

Karl said, "Food eaten outside always tastes better," and the rest agreed.

The group noticed that a lot of people were snapping pictures of the scenery, but it was obvious that the Amish group was definitely getting photographed as well.

Some Amish people get mad if people take their pictures, but Mose joked about it. "Just think about it this way: next year, this good-looking bunch will probably be on all of their brochures." They all started laughing.

In the afternoon, they all went their own direction and decided to meet to leave around 3 so they could drive to see some more covered bridges.

Elizabeth found a bookstore and bought two new books to read. She also saw some cards in the bookstore. She found a card that had a poem about forgiveness. She instantly knew that she wanted to get it for Blake White. It said everything she had been thinking and wanting to say to him. She had written over 20 letters to him and always just threw them away because she had such a hard time writing exactly how she felt. She knew that eight months was a long time for him to carry his regret and also knew it was time to reach out to him. He had sent the children an apology months ago, and it was time to reply.

The boys met a local boy who told them about the four-wheeler fundraiser coming up in Parke County. It included four-wheeling the back Indiana roads. Karl thought it sounded like a lot of fun, so he got the information and dates to pass along to Mitch. It sounded like something Mitch would do.

The group decided to drive over toward Billie Creek Village and Rockville before heading for home. They enjoyed every minute and wished they could have stayed another day or two. On the way home, most of the kids sacked out and fell asleep. The autumn air had worn them out.

The next day, Elizabeth had the day off from the Essenhaus, and Cassandra had taken a month to go visit in New York City, so there was nothing pressing to be done.

Elizabeth looked at the card for Blake White and sat down to write a heartfelt letter to put in the card.

Blake,

Thank you for the apology. I choose to forgive you for the accident. It meant a lot to hear that you were sorry it happened. I think of you often and pray for you. I hope you can feel God's love and His grace every day. I know that my dad would have wanted us to forgive you, too. We do miss them, but it is comforting to know we will see them in Heaven one day.

I would encourage you to forgive yourself for this accident. It's what my dad would want for you. He always told us that in life, the person we need to give forgiveness and grace to the most is ourselves.

Praying for you,

Elizabeth Miller

She sat and cried as she thought of how terrible being locked up had to be. She wished the whole story wouldn't be the truth. Unfortunately, some choices we make aren't all that influential, but others like this choice are irrevocable and unchangeable. Blake's choices cost the Miller children an awful lot.

"Help us children make wise choices," she whispered to God.

Chapter 22

The prayer for wise choices came out of what had happened the night before. When the van load got back into LaGrange County, the van driver was going to drop the Miller children off at their house. Instead, Karl asked to be dropped off at Mitch's house to tell him about the four wheeler run.

Mitch was out back by his fire pit. He added more wood when he saw Karl had stopped by. These two could sit and talk for hours.

Karl was so excited and almost couldn't tell Mitch fast enough. "The area has a whole bunch of old covered bridges on these winding back country roads, and the four-wheel run goes right through the colorful trees. You're allowed to drive on the road that day, too."

"Sign me up," Mitch replied. "Karl, I know you don't have a four wheeler, but you are good at riding my dad's. I know he'd be glad to let you use it. Let's get this thing planned because it sounds like a blast."

They talked for hours about guns, girls and the fun weekend Karl just had. Mitch had gone to the Northridge-Concord football game, and he explained in detail the way the Raiders won again. They made plans to go to next Friday night's game and which girls they should take with them. They eliminated any girls not interested in football because the boys were going primarily for the game.

"A little arm candy that will let us fully engage in the game," Mitch explained, defining the stipulations. They both laughed hysterically.

Karl got home smelling like firewood and was obviously a bit tipsy but went straight to bed.

Elizabeth wasn't going to get into a fight with him and didn't say anything. She knew he had walked home and wasn't driving a vehicle endangering anyone, so she was thankful for that.

Susan had told Elizabeth that when conflict happens in the same family or on the same team, it can feel like a knife of betrayal, kind of like a knife in the front of one's heart because people tend to trust their family members or teammates. On other occasions, it may feel like a knife in the back when it seems like people we allowed close enough to hug us can also use a knife to stab our backside, too. It feels really cold when people on the same team work against each other. The Bible says quite plainly, a kingdom divided cannot stand.

Susan experienced it with some very close friends. She had confided in some women she had trusted immensely, and it had somehow backfired and turned into a deep wound of betrayal. She encouraged Elizabeth to love Karl no matter what and to not allow differences to drive a wedge between them.

The wedge at the moment was about how the two viewed God and alcohol. Susan encouraged Elizabeth to allow Karl to walk his own journey to know God. Karl had been taught everything Elizabeth was taught, but he also needed to find his own faith, not just hide behind his parents' faith in Jesus.

Elizabeth was enjoying the fact that the house smelled like life again. When Susan was at her house, she had taught Elizabeth how to pray and invite God to send angels to stand guard around the house and their property. She heard that some people actually see their angels, but she could just sense them.

It was really encouraging to have Susan visit every now and then. The last time Susan came, she got to come for supper and even met

Willy. Willy seemed to like Susan and opened up to her about some things.

Elizabeth knew it was time to get out of the house and let Susan speak with him alone. Elizabeth dawdled around the barn and watched the kittens play. She hadn't checked on the barn recently and was shocked at how neat and tidy Karl and Willy kept it. Karl's room wasn't this organized. Their dad would be happy to know his training paid off. He had always taught the children that anything worth doing is worth doing well. Two verses their dad used to quote quite often were *work as unto the Lord and not unto man* and *let me be a workman that needeth not to be ashamed*. It seemed Karl and Willy were listening and applied these verses to their work in the barn.

Inside the house, Susan asked Willy if he was still mad about them destroying his game.

"No, it was making me feel like I had to ask it things," Willy replied. "I was starting to feel sad and depressed a lot, and since I prayed that prayer, I feel a lot better. I want to have Jesus in my heart, too, because I know it is something Jesus wants for me. I'm just not sure I'm old enough yet."

Susan said, "Jesus was only 12 years old when he sat with the teachers in the synagogue, so if he was old enough, then I can't see why you wouldn't be old enough. Would you like to do that?"

"I really would. I feel like I really understand the concept. Some people think our age is under the age of accountability, but that doesn't make sense because at 12, a lot of us boys can do a man's work. And the 12-year-old Amish girls know how to do a lot of things that 18-year-old women know how to do, so I can't see why I can't do this, too."

"Why sure, Willy, I see that you totally understand it, and you have had a more serious side of life and death thrust on you at a very young age," Susan replied. "You are capable of choosing at your age."

Susan wrote out a prayer for Willy and told him to read it quietly to make sure this is what he wanted to do. She didn't want him to pray something he didn't mean or just put words in his mouth. She explained that the Bible says we get saved through grace and by faith, so it's nothing we can earn.

He read it quietly and then read it out loud.

"Dear God, I believe in your son, Jesus.

I want him to come into my heart and wash my sins away.

I admit I need a Savior to forgive my sins, and I want to be free of my past dabbling in the occult games. I need a power to guide my life, but I want it to be only God's power and not from the wrong source.

I confess that I _____".

Susan had allowed a space for Willy to just add anything he wanted. He started crying and telling God that he was sorry about how he had treated his sisters and that he wished he could take back all the teasing he did.

Susan wiped her eyes and couldn't hold in the tears. She sensed right away what she needed to tell Willy that would make him feel better.

"Willy, were you also a really nice brother to the girls?" Susan asked.

"Yes, I was really kind the majority of the time," Willy stated.

"OK, then think about those times and guess what you can do," Susan stated. "You can ask Jesus to give them a message from you saying that you are sorry. Then one day, you will see them again. While you are here on this Earth, you don't need to live with a load of guilt and shame. God is not the reminder of our faults and mistakes. That's the enemy, Satan, who wants to cause us guilt and shame and accuses us night and day. Just picture a tattle tale telling on your every wrong move. That's Satan. But Jesus sits right beside God, and he prays for you."

Susan continued to comfort and teach Willy. "The Holy Spirit is God's spirit that we get to have live in us if we ask Jesus to live in our hearts. The job of the Holy Spirit is to convict us of our sin and of our righteousness. (John 16:8) That means he wants to remind us that we are RIGHT with God because of Jesus forgiving us. Some people think that the Holy Spirit is like a cop trying to convict us of how bad we are. That's not what the Bible says. The Bible teaches that his job is to convict us that in God, through Jesus, we're righteous in his righteousness. Not because of ANYTHING we can do or we could boast. That means there is nothing good that you can ever do to be good enough on your own."

"You make it really easy to understand," Willy said.

"It is," Susan said. "But even though it is a free gift, a lot of people don't want it and actually misjudge Jesus as weak, and he is not. He chose to die for us; he wasn't forced on the cross. He wanted to die to take all your sins away. He can cause the worst criminals to be washed as white as snow, and he casts our sins as far as the east is to the west away from us. The amazing thing about Jesus dying on the cross is that he didn't stay there. He rose again, and he's alive. Some people focus on the cross only, and he's not on it, and other people focus on Jesus in the manger, too. The truth is that He's neither a baby in a manger nor dead on the cross. He is alive and well, and he will come back someday."

Susan was on a roll. She loved talking about Jesus. She said, "My favorite chapter in the Bible is Revelation 19, which says Jesus will ride on a white horse, and his eyes will be like flames of fire. He will wear His robe and many crowns. The words written on his thigh will say; KING OF KINGS and LORD OF LORDS. Then Revelation 21 says that God will wipe every tear from our eyes, and there will be no more death, nor sorrow, nor crying, no more pain because those things will all pass away. Willy, I know at your young age that you have seen a lot of these, but the Bible promises us that one day, all of this will be no more."

Susan reached for Willy, and he started crying.

He cried harder than he had ever cried in his life. He had kept all of his emotions, mostly his sadness, pent up, and finally, he was granted permission to let it out. Susan had never had a teenage boy and couldn't believe his tenderness to her.

He felt like he was talking to his mom. She had always let him be free to be himself, and this stranger was treating him the same.

Elizabeth came back in the house. Willy smiled at her and said, "I did it. I asked Jesus into my heart, too."

Elizabeth walked over and hugged Willy. She knew that he fully knew what he was doing and that there was no going back.

The three of them talked about how Karl might balk at the idea of Willy doing this, but it was okay. Susan reiterated to Elizabeth and Willy that Karl gets to have his journey in his own timetable. No two journeys are alike, and there is no judgment in that.

Elizabeth walked over to her dad's desk and got out his Bible. She told Willy that Dad would have wanted him to read it every day. There were markings and verses circled all through the worn Bible. Willy thanked Elizabeth and said he'd be careful with it.

Over the next few weeks, Elizabeth took her baptismal classes with the preachers. A total of six girls were getting baptized together. On the day of the baptism, the girls wore navy dresses. They got baptized by kneeling in front of the Amish church as the preachers poured water on them in three increments that symbolized the Father, Son, and the Holy Spirit.

Elizabeth would also now be a member of the Amish church. It wasn't a light commitment, and she was excited for the next step on the journey with God. As she got up from the kneeling position, she saw Karl and Willy both looking her way. Seeing her two brothers at that moment made her heart so glad.

Mose and Carrie had invited them over for lunch and to hang out at the farm for the rest of the day. They played bag games, and then at around 5, the neighbors came over to play volleyball. After a long day, Mose told Karl and Willy goodbye but lingered to talk to Elizabeth a bit more.

Mose told Elizabeth, "We got to see an answer to your dad and mom's prayers today by you choosing to publically get baptized to let people know you want to live for God. Your parents would have enjoyed being there today."

Even Karl nodded his head in agreement. Elizabeth replied, "Well, thanks for standing in the gap for them and making today a celebration. We all appreciate the support."

Karl wasn't against what Elizabeth chose to do, but he sure wasn't ready for that big of a commitment.

Mitch and Karl spent a lot of time gearing up for the four-wheeling weekend. It ended up growing into a camping adventure as well.

They used trailers to transport the two four wheelers over and met Pete, Bill, and two other friends at a campground. They brought tents and enough firewood for a week. The weather was a bit crisp, so they just put on a few more layers and sat a little closer to the crackling fire. They had bought brand new rakes along to roast hot dogs and marshmallows for s'mores. They had debated about bringing girls but decided they would be too much of a hassle.

As they were sitting around talking about the next day's ride, a guy walked by, and because he heard them speaking Dutch, asked, "Voh sin deh defun? (Where are you all from?)"

They started laughing because neither of them looked Amish in any way, shape, or form. "We're from Shipshewana. What about you?"

"I'm Darryl Gingerich from Illinois. My mom was from the Arthur area. I assume we are going to the same four-wheeler run in the morning. If you'd like to follow me over, you can. We've done this for the past five years, and I know some shortcuts to get you there ahead of the rush."

"Sounds good. We will be ready to roll first thing," Karl told him.

"By the way, they're doing karaoke over in the far cabin. It's a lot of fun if you guys wanna come," Darryl offered as he headed out.

The boys had a blast at the campground. They laughed at Mitch and Pete singing songs at the karaoke tent and formed real bonds of friendship at these campgrounds over hot dogs and campfires.

By 6 A.M., the boys were showered and were making bacon and eggs. The forecast was in the high 70s, and the sun was already peeking out.

The caravan of trailers and four wheelers arrived and saw a huge field packed full with hundreds of off-road toys. There were mostly four wheelers, but there were also some oversized ATVs that women were driving.

The cops stopped traffic so they could all cross the main road. They had maps to take with them so they could go different routes. It felt so amazing to be allowed to drive on the back roads. There were refreshment stops and lunch also served along the way. Karl hadn't known there were Amish farms in the area but saw a kid on a buggy in town. He yelled "hello" to him in Dutch. They explored around seven of the covered bridges and stopped to take pictures of themselves posing with each one.

They laughed at Karl because he suggested they take the pictures and make a calendar to sell. The one photo op that was by far the most hilarious was when Karl asked two grandmas if they wanted him in their picture. Karl's outgoing gesture made these older ladies' day, and he enjoyed talking to them, too. They told Karl they were going to tell their granddaughters all about him.

The last stop of the day was at the covered bridge in Mansfield. They went inside the little ice cream shop for a little dessert, and there sat Darryl, his wife Roberta, and all of their friends. Darryl asked them how they enjoyed their day, and they showed him a bunch of their pictures on Karl's phone. Darryl laughed. The boys thanked him for the campground hospitality. Darryl smiled and said, "Any time! Come on back."

Mitch leaned over, jabbed Karl and said, "Thanks for telling us about this event. How'd you find out about this place?"

"My mom. Before she died, she would talk about it," Karl answered. "This was her favorite place to come to every fall."

With that, Karl reached up, pulled down on his hat, and whispered, "Thanks, Mom."

They walked back to their four wheelers and sat on them while they listened to some music. No one was ready to leave. It made for the perfect fall outing, with the leaves falling from a slight breeze and the water gently running in the Big Raccoon Creek. Karl had hooked up his phone to the speakers on his four wheeler, and they all sat and sang "Flyover States" by Jason Aldean.

You'll understand why God made those flyover states.

Their favorite part of the song was, *Have you ever been through Indiana?*

Oh yeah, they'd been through Indiana. What a memory. What a weekend. They knew this weekend marked something that was bound to become a yearly tradition as they rode the winding back roads back to the starting point.

Chapter 23

On Sunday morning, Elizabeth and Willy hitched up the buggy and headed to church at her friend Marilyn's house. Marilyn's family belonged to a different church district, so her home was about seven miles away.

Karl and his friends decided to stop for the night at a hotel the evening before, and Elizabeth had no way of knowing exactly where they were. She had no phone, and she would have had to bike to the phone shack to call Karl. The Amish who don't have cell phones find it hard to stay in touch. Since the accident, times like these caused Elizabeth extra anxiety and fear. She asked God to watch over Karl and to please calm her down.

Willy could tell Elizabeth was worried, and he asked, "Do you want to stop at Mitch's house to ask his parents if they know where the boys are? I'm sure they could call them and find out."

"Willy, you are so thoughtful, and that's a great idea. If they aren't home by this afternoon, we could stop and ask." Elizabeth made sure she complimented him. "The boys might have decided to camp another night. I will try not to worry about it because I'm sure he's fine."

Before the tragedy, she had never been one to worry if people were dead or alive. February 15th had changed everything.

To get their minds on something else, Elizabeth and Willy talked about his classes at school, and she told him all about Cassandra. It was a great buggy ride, even though it was sprinkling. By the time they got to where the church was going to be held, it had started pouring. Elizabeth was not sure what she was going to do with the horse because Karl wasn't along. She was surprised at how Willy took charge and told her to go on inside, that he'd take care of the horse. She saw Monroe Yoder help Willy and was so thankful she wasn't alone this morning. In times like these, she missed Dad and also Karl. She wondered if Karl had felt like this when she had turned 16 and used to be gone for weekends at a time with her friends. He had never told her that it affected him, but looking back now, she thought it might have.

After church, she enjoyed visiting with Marilyn and her aunts. They asked Elizabeth if she had heard about Homer Zook's house fire.

"No! That's awful," Elizabeth immediately reached for her heart. "Did anyone get hurt?"

"Homer was the only one at home, and he got out with only minor injuries. But the house burned to the ground. They lost everything," Marilyn told her.

Elizabeth sat quietly listening to the women talking and knew what she needed to do. She was so much like her dad. He always found a way to help. She knew it was going to be hard, but she'd already made up her mind. She politely sat and talked for a bit more without telling anyone of her intentions. As soon as she could excuse herself without looking rude, she did.

She found Willy and told him it was time to go. On the way home, she told him about Homer's fire and said, "Willy, I think we are supposed to take them Barbara and Katie clothes. They might need Dad and Mom's clothes, too. It's going to be hard to give them up, but I think we need to."

"I do, too, that's a good idea," Willy replied. "But do you think we could keep one outfit from each of them? I just can't let them all go yet."

"Of course we can, Willy."

When they got home, they saw Karl unloading his things out of Pete's truck. It was good to see him arrive home safely.

Elizabeth told Karl about the fire and asked Pete if he could drive them to where Homer and his family were staying until their house was rebuilt.

Pete was happy to, and he took the three Millers over with a tote full of things. Elizabeth assumed she'd have to do all the talking, but she was very wrong. Karl took charge like Dad would have. She was impressed with her brother.

Homer and his family were surprised to see them. A lot of others had stepped in to help, but truthfully, out of the whole community, they didn't expect the Miller children to show up. It was understandable if they didn't reach out to help, as they were dealing with enough of their own issues.

Karl said, "We heard what happened and wanted to tell you all how sorry we are for your loss. I'm glad you all made it out OK, but we know you lost everything in the house. Our mom was pretty particular at her sewing, so these clothes we brought for you are in real good shape. We hope they help you two and a couple of your girls get some dresses back in their closet."

Homer's wife shed a few tears. "You have no idea what this means to us. I was overwhelmed with thinking of replacing all six of our wardrobes at the same time."

Karl and Willy went back to the truck, and Pete helped them carry in a few boxes full of jars of food.

"We just don't know what to say. This just . . . means so much." Homer and his wife were really touched.

Pete enjoyed helping take the family the food and clothes and wouldn't let the kids pay him for driving them around.

Pete said, "I oughta pay you guys for letting me. That was fun. Karl, not that your dad is an old block, but as the saying goes, I think you are a chip off the old block. You got some tenderness in that heart of yours. I never saw that side of you before."

"Oh, yeah, my heart is massive; I got more where this came from," Karl laughed.

The truth was, the children felt good about helping out. Their dad had taught them to be generous by quietly modeling it. He had explained to them that God prompts us with ideas and thoughts. He said that he learned to trust those promptings, especially when they didn't make 100 percent sense. He told them he sometimes felt kind of silly. One time, he felt like he was supposed to stop at the home of an older Amish couple whom he barely knew. When he got inside, he found out the daudy (Grandpa) had fallen, and the mommy (Grandma) couldn't get to phone shed. Their children weren't coming home until late that evening. The daudy ended up in the hospital with a broken hip. Dad had always said, *Listen to the promptings and go with them.*

Monday morning rolled around way too fast. Karl went to work, and Willy went to school. Cassandra had returned from New York City and needed help all day on Monday. This was also the week of Mildred's wedding. Mildred had invited all the cleaning girls and also Cassandra. This would be Cassandra's first Amish wedding. She asked Elizabeth if she could pick Elizabeth up so she could sit with her. *This ought to be interesting*, Elizabeth thought.

Weddings among the Amish were a big deal. When Amish couples get married, they celebrate with an all-day affair. Elizabeth told Cassandra to pick her up at 8:30 on Thursday morning. Cassandra picked her up, and the first question she had for Elizabeth was why the wedding was on a Thursday instead of a Saturday. Elizabeth immediately realized it was going to be a question-filled day.

Elizabeth explained, "The weddings are in our homes instead of in a church, so all of the work and cleanup is at our houses. If they would have the weddings on a Saturday, they would have to clean up on Sunday or leave it until Monday.

They arrived in time to shake hands with Mildred, her fiancé Fred, and the four witnesses. They all stood in a line and shook hands to greet the guests. They sat on backless benches, but the man seating them directed Cassandra and Elizabeth to a bench against a wall.

Cassandra noticed that the men all sat on one side of the room and the women on the opposite side.

At 9, the singing started. It was in High German, so Cassandra just listened. It was very different from any wedding she had ever been to. Several men got up and walked out with the bride and groom. Cassandra leaned over and said, "Now what's going on? Where did they go?"

Elizabeth realized she needed to give Cassandra play-by-play information. She whispered, "Those were the preachers, and they go talk with the bride and groom before they preach the service."

"ALL of those are going to preach?" Cassandra looked shocked. Her eyes were as big as saucers.

"Oh no, just some of them," Elizabeth almost giggled out loud.

About an hour later, the preachers and the couple returned as the singing was finishing up. The four witnesses joined the bride and groom as the six sat on chairs in front of the preacher and the guests.

All of the men sat on one side of the chairs, and the women sat on chairs facing the guys.

After the third preacher got up to preach in German, Cassandra whispered, "Are you sure they aren't all preaching?" She followed up her umpteenth question with a smile.

When it came time to say the vows, Fred and Mildred went up in front of the people. The witnesses watched from their seats. When were finished, the bride and groom sat back down. There was no kiss, no music, and no big formal announcement of Mr. and Mrs. It all ended with a prayer.

After the wedding church was over, Cassandra asked, "Why does Mildred have on a black cap instead of a white one?"

"You are very observant, Cassandra," Elizabeth complimented her. "Mildred wore a black one this morning because she is not married yet, but later today, she will get a brand new one to wear that is white to signify she is now married."

"Are you serious? How cool is that?!" Cassandra had really enjoyed the day so far but mentioned how she needed to walk around a bit because the bench was kind of hard to sit on for that long.

Cassandra was full of questions as they walked through the Amish house. She liked the bedrooms with the unique quilts. They could smell the food, and Cassandra said she was getting hungry. Elizabeth reassured her, "There will be plenty of food for you."

The food was delicious. The cooks had arrived early and had been preparing the food for a few days.

The wedding guests ate a meal that consisted of chicken, mashed potatoes, dressing, salad, sliced cheese, homemade bread, tapioca pudding, peanut butter spread, and a dessert to die for.

After the meal, Elizabeth took Cassandra outside to see the flower gardens. Cassandra couldn't stop talking about the food. She said, "I would gain so much weight if I'd go Amish."

Elizabeth laughed and said, "Look around at the women in the yard. You see a mixture of those who struggle to keep the weight off, but there are others who also work it off."

"You can't mean they go to a gym, right?"

"No, they work hard on their farms!" Elizabeth cracked up. "Some of them like to walk, but they don't need to go to a fitness center. They just walk down the road to get some fresh air."

"Well, my goodness, what a novel idea!" Cassandra replied, and the two started laughing.

It was fun to get to know each other's culture.

Later in the afternoon, they watched the bride and groom open all the wedding gifts. The crowd sang songs while they watched them. Mildred was gifted a lot of practical kitchen items. Fred seemed to be more excited when they opened up tools and other items he would enjoy.

By 3 in the afternoon, Cassandra was ready to call it a day and said goodbye to Mildred and Elizabeth.

She told Mildred, "I see you traded the black cap for your new white cap."

Mildred smiled. She was enjoying her big day. She thanked Cassandra for coming and for her gift.

Cassandra thanked Mildred for inviting her. She had really enjoyed it.

The Amish not only serve a wedding meal at noon; they also serve a dinner in the evening. The cooks and their husbands eat at 4:15. Then they finish preparing dinner and serve it.

Elizabeth had been asked to serve as a table waiter for the corner table for the wedding dinner. This was an honor because the corner table was where the bride and groom sat with their four witnesses.

When Elizabeth's parents were young, the evening wedding meals got interesting when some young Amish men who had not been invited to the wedding came, brought loud chainsaws, and made a bunch of racket right outside of where the couple sat. They intentionally interrupted the wedding celebration. They were called *bellers*. In order for them to stop all of the racket, they were normally invited into the house to come get something from the newlywed couple, like a candy bar. Bridal couples used to prepare for the bellers, but that tradition died out over the years.

Elizabeth had a great evening and enjoyed talking to the other table waiters. She thought it was wonderful to witness how happy Fred and Mildred were, and she wondered whom she would get married to one day. She had a lot of guy friends, but she couldn't picture a life with any of them.

Elizabeth got home pretty late after the wedding. She was pretty faithful at making the boys breakfast every day, but she had laid a note on the kitchen table telling them to not wake her. So on Friday morning, she slept in. It looked like they survived without her. She was scheduled to work from 3 to close at the Essenhaus, so she took it easy and read a book out on the front porch. This weather was the best weather, but she knew it would not last long. October weather was the kind that most wish they could keep around for four months, but all too soon, the cold winds of winter would be bringing snow. The swing was the best place to read because the smell of the flowers was so potent. Elizabeth was surprised to see so many monarch butterflies around. She wondered if they were migrating in a bunch because there were so many of them.

As Elizabeth was getting ready to go to work, she was oblivious to the fact that Ridge was heading to the restaurant in hopes of seeing her. He was riding his way out West, and he was trying to beat the cold weather. He had a great adventure, but he was missing California and his surfing friends. It was high time to get home.

Elizabeth was stocking up the waitress station and getting herself into waitress mode for the evening. For her, it was always a bit of an adrenaline rush whenever she began a new shift knowing it was going to be busy. The fear always pushed against her, mocking her, almost saying, *Can you do this*?

But somehow whenever that first table showed up, so did the ability to go out and be friendly. The fear would dissipate. The Essenhaus was always busy on flea market days and on the weekends.

It seemed funny to the hostess to have this Harley-riding dude ask for "Elizabeth's section, the Amish girl Elizabeth." But a lot of customers have their favorite waitresses, so she was used to it.

When Elizabeth came out to Ridge's table, she was shocked to see him. He stood up and laughed before giving her a hug.

"I had no idea if I'd ever see you again! How's it going?" Elizabeth asked.

She was so glad to see him, and they talked in between her serving the other tables. She told him that she had been dreaming more and that she gave her life to Jesus.

"I was praying you would do that," Ridge said. "He's my best friend, and he will be yours, too."

She told him they liked reading his blog about all of his stops. She gave Ridge Karl's cell number in case he ever came back to Indiana.

With that, he was ready to head out. He did ask if she would pose for a picture with him. She said, "Sure! Why not?"

As Ridge left, he said, "I will keep praying for you and the boys, and if you ever come to California, look me up."

Ridge admired the trees on Main Street and stopped to get an ice cream cone at the Dairy Queen. He uploaded four photos of his short time in Middlebury onto Facebook: one of the outside of the Essenhaus, one of Elizabeth, and two of the fall leaves along Main Street.

He punched in *Golden Gate Bridge* into Google Maps and saw he had 2,250 miles to go.

With that, Ridge was off.

Interstate 80 was packed with semis. Ridge knew to be cautious, but as he was passing the South Bend exit, a car sideswiped him. His motorcycle slid off the road, and he took a pretty hard hit to the head as he landed. He had his helmet on, which saved his life. The ambulance didn't take long to get there, and the medics transported him to the South Bend hospital. A local towing service took his motorcycle to a local shop to check it out. His phone wouldn't open without a password, and he was knocked unconscious. The medics searched his clothes, and all they found in his pocket was a phone number belonging to a Karl.

CORINA YODER

Chapter 24

Karl was sitting in the Northridge football game when he got the call. At first, he was confused as to why he was receiving a call about a guy named Ridge. Once it registered, he immediately left the game and went over to the Essenhaus to tell Elizabeth. She was in shock, as she had just seen Ridge an hour earlier. She confirmed that she had indeed written Karl's cell number on a placemat and had given it to Ridge not too long ago.

Elizabeth told Karl to step into the hallway, and they talked about what to do. Her eyes were filled with anxiety as Joel Miller came walking around the corner. Joel could see there was something terribly wrong. He knew that Elizabeth had lived through an incredible tragedy earlier in the year but that they had also seen her start laughing again and slowly turn back to her normal, calm self. When Joel found out what was going on, he immediately offered to take Elizabeth and Karl to the hospital.

On the way, Karl called Mose and asked him to take Willy for the evening. Elizabeth also called Cassandra and asked her to come to hospital. She also asked if she and Karl could sleep at her house for the night if they needed to.

The thing that touched Elizabeth the most was that Joel could have asked some of the van drivers to take them, but instead, he instantly helped out. He didn't even hesitate. The reason that the Essenhaus was successful was because the Miller family cared about the Essenhaus workers and their lives.

When they got to the hospital, Cassandra was already there. She was anxiously wringing her hands together. She looked relieved that the rest had made it. She reassured Joel that she could take the kids to her house when the time came to sleep, and they all thanked him a number of times for bringing them.

They immediately went to the nurses' station to request a visit with Ridge. One nurse told them that that he was awake. She warned them, though, that he was pretty groggy yet because he had been knocked unconscious, had a pretty bad concussion, but was lucky to be alive.

"Me being alive had nothing to do with luck," Ridge told Elizabeth, Karl, and Cassandra. "I pray all the time that God surrounds me with angels. It could have been a lot worse."

Elizabeth went over to his hospital bed and said, "Goodness, I'm glad you are going to be OK! Ridge, this is my brother Karl. They found Karl's number on you and called him. This is Cassandra, whom I work for. She lives close by."

Cassandra smiled at Ridge and said, "What a horrible way to meet someone, but I am glad you are alive."

Ridge lifted his fist to Karl, and they fist bumped. Karl said, "I hope your bike is OK, too. I've seen pictures of it, and it's pretty sweet."

The four sat and visited for the next few hours until the nurses came in and told Ridge that he would be released in the morning, as long as he kept improving.

Ridge smiled and said, "I'll be surfing before the week is over."

Cassandra heard this statement and vehemently disagreed. "Oh my gosh, Ridge, even if you are released in the morning, you can't get on your motorcycle yet. I am not letting you. You will need to stay with me until you get better." It was more of a demand than a suggestion.

Ridge had met his match. He was such a free spirit, and nothing was going to stop him from getting back on the road. He began to explain: "I gotta beat the cold weather, though. I was taking 80 out to Cheyenne, and I definitely wanna get back to the West Coast as soon as I can."

Cassandra quickly protested Ridge's plan. "Oh for Pete's sake, you younger kids think you know best. But this time, I'm not going to allow any other options on the table." She was quite emphatic in what she said and left no room for negotiating. "You will come to my place and rest up before I will let you have your keys back. I'm calling your mom, and she will agree with me."

"Good luck tracking her down," Ridge said. "I haven't seen her in five years. You sure you got room for me?"

Cassandra threw her head back and laughed, "Elizabeth what do you think? Do you think I have room for him?"

Elizabeth laughed and said, "Yeah, that's the least of your worries."

Cassandra added, "Well, then, you think of me as your mom while you are in South Bend. I've never had kids, but I can be bossy if I need to."

That settled it. Cassandra took Karl and Elizabeth back home, and in the morning, Cassandra came back to hospital bright and early. She explained to the doctors that she would take Ridge to her house, and they could send doctors and nurses there if they needed to check on Ridge.

Ridge thought it was quite humorous how excited she seemed to host him. She was a pistol. Taking care of Ridge, who was 30 years younger than herself, gave Cassandra a new lease on life. She felt like she was on a mission with a purpose.

Ridge was in utter shock when he walked into Cassandra's home. It was more like a mansion than a house. Now he understood why she laughed when he asked if she had room for him.

She made a list of his top ten favorite meals and asked what his favorite movies were.

He finally jokingly asked her for a bell to ring whenever he might need something, and they both laughed. They were both strong and a bit stubborn, so their interactions would have been hilarious to any bystander.

Ridge asked, "Why would I ever wanna get better if I can be waited on hand and foot? My recovery might get extended."

Ridge ended up staying for a week, and he and Cassandra became good friends. They laughed and talked a lot. He told her about his website chronicling his trip from California to the East Coast, so they pulled it up on her TV and watched video after video and read all of his blogs.

Cassandra asked Ridge, "Do you really believe in God? You talk about Him in every blog and on all your videos."

"Yes, I most definitely believe in Him. I can't do life without Him," Ridge replied confidently.

Cassandra finally came clean with Ridge on why she moved to South Bend. She was trying to escape demonic attacks. She said that she never heard of the power of Jesus before meeting Elizabeth. She had heard about Jesus but always thought he was just a prophet from long ago who died a gruesome death by crucifixion. She had never been told he resurrected in three days and that he was God's son.

When she had been introduced to Satan worship, she thought that would give her power. Instead, it brought a lot of torment and problems.

Ridge explained to her that there is nothing wrong with wanting a power greater than ourselves in our life, but we just need to make sure it's the right kind of power. He taught her how to ask God to "fill me up to overflowing with your Holy Spirit and to cover me with the blood of Jesus."

"What does blood have to do with it?" Cassandra asked.

"Well, Jesus died on the cross for us, and that blood still has power today. We can ask for things in his name and by the power of the shed blood to still be applied to things today. It's not literal but figurative."

Ridge explained to her in great detail about how there are lots of religions that believe in false gods and that Satan used to be an angel in heaven that wanted to be like God, so he got cast out of heaven. He formed a team of evil demons that fight against God and Jesus and good. He also explained that there are God's good angels and then Satan's evil angels. They both want us to give them our lives. God wants to bless us, but the opposite side wants to bring curses.

She was ecstatic to find out that she could have peace over her torment and fears. She prayed and asked Jesus to take charge of her messed-up life. Ridge helped her gather up items she had used for rituals, and they destroyed them. They walked through her house and prayed through every room and anointed every single door and window. Finally, they asked God to send angels to guard her home.

Cassandra was shocked because that night, she had the first night of peaceful sleep in years. She knew she had found something that was completely different from anything she had ever experienced before. She had spent lots of money on medications, doctors, psychologists, counselors, healers, and had tried mediation, yoga, crystals, hypnosis, and the list went on and on. In one day, Jesus had cleared the junk and brought his power to her life. She was a brand new person.

She felt different. She saw new colors she had never seen before in her life. She had always felt a cloud of something around her, but now the cloud was gone. Something had shifted to good because she could smell it. Her senses could smell the change. It was hard to put into words, but she could feel protection around her, and the smell was a scent of flowers, like springtime.

The house also had a better air about it. There was life and light back in places and spaces that had been dragging her down.

The Amish girls couldn't believe what a difference a week could make in the atmosphere of Cassandra's house. Ridge's stay had truly shifted the atmosphere for Cassandra.

Well, of course, it was God and Jesus and the angels, but Ridge had taught her how to pray for protection.

She didn't want Ridge to leave.

Elizabeth was very happy that Ridge was getting better and that Cassandra seemed to be completely set free of all depression. It truly was a miracle. Cassandra told Elizabeth how Jesus entering her life had changed her into a brand new person.

Elizabeth told Cassandra that she should meet her friend, Susan, because she believes in the same things. So it was arranged. Susan was invited to Cassandra's home in South Bend.

Elizabeth forewarned Susan that Cassandra lived in a mansion so that she would be prepared. Nothing could have prepared her because it was beyond anything Susan had ever seen in her life. A couple times, she had to stop her mouth from dropping open because it was beyond her comprehension. Elizabeth had almost grown accustomed to it because of the time she had spent working here.

Susan hid it well that she was walking into brand new territory. She appeared relaxed and calm, and it came from her deep relationship with God. She didn't see herself as less than Cassandra or that she didn't belong there. She knew God orchestrated this get-together, and she knew that He was going to do some brand new things. She realized God deeply loved Cassandra and that He wanted her to be free of all negative things. He sure picked a unique bunch of individuals to do it.

Susan had never met anyone as eccentric as Cassandra or as tattooed as Ridge. What bonded this group together was Jesus. He was the one thing they all had in common.

Susan had the chance to read Ridge's recent blogs and complimented him on his writings. She told him, "I also journal, but I just let God read my writings. I've never had the courage to share it with anyone like I do my artwork."

"The problem with keeping your journaling to yourself is that God could use you to encourage others," Ridge told her. "Most of the time, God doesn't tell us things to just keep it to ourselves."

"Yes, you are absolutely right," Susan replied. "It seems that every single time God gets ready to do a new thing in my life, He seems to put rocks into my comfortable nest, kind of like when a momma bird wants to teach her baby birds to fly. That's what she does so her babies take that leap of faith and learn how to spread their wings and fly."

"That makes perfect sense," Ridge said. "I think God wants to take the wisdom you have been stockpiling and give it away."

Susan smiled and laughed, "Huh, I never thought of it as stockpiling. That makes it sound like I'm hoarding." She added, "I've been thinking about writing up some things He has taught me so other people can be protected from making some of the mistakes I made. It would be worth my pain to keep others out of it, also, for those who need to be set free of things as well."

"I would read it," Cassandra said. "You would never believe the awful tormenting I went through in my life before Ridge showed up here."

"I would believe you," Susan said, "Unfortunately, I understand all too well. I believe that traumas in people's lives, like you had with losing your parents, can often create open doors for lies to be formed in our belief systems."

"That's interesting. Explain that to me, Susan," Cassandra said.

"Sure, I'd be glad to," Susan replied. "The truth is, the hurts in our past can no longer hurt us today; rather, the lies that Satan placed into those hurts can continue to wound us unless God shows us the truth and we are healed from them. For example, if a young girl endures physical abuse, is frequently told she wasn't planned, as in maybe her mom got pregnant and didn't want her, her belief systems could include *I'm a mistake, I have no value, no one will ever love me, I must be bad to deserve these beatings, it would be better if I would have never been born.* All of those statements are obviously lies. It hurts as a child to be hit, but as an adult, she is no longer in physical harm. But what can happen is that she could possibly still feel the sting of not being protected. She might be a successful grown adult but still get triggered by fear of being harmed. Jesus can show truth to souls that have been wounded and destroy false beliefs."

"I wonder if I believed any lies," Cassandra said with a puzzled look.

"Oh, that is easy to find out," Susan said. "All you need to do is ask Jesus. He can tell you. All people can hear from God, but we all hear Him differently. Some people see impressions or thoughts in their minds, some feel his guidance as a knowing in the gut, and some people hear his thoughts in words. It's similar to your learning style. A teacher I know once told me that all students learn differently. Some learn better by reading, and others learn better by seeing or experiencing something. Some even do better if they hear the teacher teaching out loud. Learning styles are all unique and different. There's not a right or wrong way. It's simply how God made each of us."

"OK, that's easy to understand," Cassandra replied.

Susan leaned forward, took Cassandra's hand into her own and simply asked with both of their eyes closed, "God, can you show Cassandra if there's anything she has believed that is a lie?"

Cassandra sat straight up and said, "Well, He showed me a picture of myself dressed for my Red Dress Gala, and I heard the thought *it's not your fault.*"

"But it *was* my fault," Cassandra said sadly. "I was selfish and begged my parents to come home early for my Red Dress Gala, and then their plane went down. My selfishness caused them to die."

Susan and Elizabeth knew Jesus was about to show Cassandra the truth, and his truth would also change her belief about this tragedy.

Susan asked very gently that Cassandra close her eyes and let God speak to her again. Susan said, "God, is it true that Cassandra's selfishness caused this accident?"

Like a video, memory after memory flashed into Cassandra's mind of Cassandra giving to homeless, to charities, to the poor, the hungry with her dad. It wasn't true that she was selfish at all. It was true that she had asked them to come early for the Red Dress fundraiser, but it was because her dad would be generous in helping the cause. All of the sudden, she realized that she had been blaming herself for all of these years. The depression had been anger pushing inward. No wonder she had a hard time liking herself.

She saw a picture of the airplane motor malfunctioning and said, "It wasn't my fault. It was a faulty motor."

She got up and danced around the room with tears streaming down her face. "It wasn't my fault! It wasn't my fault! It was not my fault!"

A weight was rolled off Cassandra right in the plain eyesight of Susan, Elizabeth, and Ridge. They realized she had been crushed for years by that false belief.

Susan explained, "The reason people live out of false beliefs is because when you are deceived, you don't know you are deceived. You think it's the truth, and then it sets up like concrete. God has the ability to break up concreted false beliefs about ourselves and give us the truth."

Jesus had set Cassandra free.

Chapter 25

Winter soon came and ushered autumn right out of Indiana. November was crisp and clear but pretty cold. It didn't stop the locals from turning out to the Raider games in full force. People just bundled up, brought blankets, and drank a lot of hot cocoa. The football team was on a roll, and the community was behind the team all the way. Signs were everywhere around Middlebury, cheering on the hometown heroes.

On the home front, Elizabeth was thankful for a warm wash house as the temperatures outside started dropping into the single digits. Most Amish people use wringer washers and normally have a room that is attached to the house (but not in the house, like the English) to wash the laundry. The wash house has concrete floors so water can splash out without ruining the flooring. Elizabeth had helped her mom do laundry since she was a young girl, so she understood how to use the wringer washer. She would wash the clothes and then feed each item of clothing through the rollers. The rollers would then wring the water out of the wet clothes. Whoever was operating the wringer washer had to pay close attention because it was easy to get fingers stuck in the rollers. Elizabeth had seen some injuries and never wanted to experience them herself.

Since most Amish go without electricity, they can't have electric dryers, so they would have to hang the clothes up to dry. In the summertime, the fresh air and cool breezes dried the clothes on the clotheslines in a hurry. However, in the winter time, if women hung clothes out to dry on the wash line, the clothes would literally freeze.

Elizabeth was glad she had the option of hanging up clothes to dry inside her wash house all winter long. Some women strung clotheslines in their basements as well. She always loved helping do the laundry at Cassandra's because the dryer would make the towels so soft and fluffy.

In the winter months, it was more work to go places in the buggy, so Elizabeth chose to stay home more. The house felt cozy and inviting, so she enjoyed it immensely. She had organized their home as soon as she moved in, and the upkeep was pretty easy. She had decorated the home with some pictures with some verses on them, and during the day, they would give her encouragement. One of them read, *Be still and know that I am God. Psalm 46:10.* She had read that one over and over. It calmed her on the inside. The picture she often got in her mind about stillness was of a crying baby who is quieted by his mother holding him.

The opposite of such a comforting visual would be if a frustrated or exasperated Amish parent would say to her little one, *"Huck duh anna and say do still!* (Sit down and be quiet!)" She never felt like God wanted to say that to her. She had enjoyed having two patient parents, and that's how she visualized God being to her. She had read somewhere that how parents treat their children often causes them to see God in a similar way. She wished everyone in the world would have had as good of examples as her parents had been. One thing she often wondered was why God took such good parents and let abusive parents live. It was something she couldn't understand. There were also all of the people whom her dad was helping and would have kept helping for another 20 years. That was a question that often burned a hole in her mind. Her dad had always talked about making hay when the sun shines. He would often sit and read the *Martyrs Mirror* and then repeat the stories to the family. He would quote verses like, *The harvest is plentiful but the workers are few* in his prayers. To Elizabeth, it seemed like he was taken out before his best days were up. She knew that he often lived out his faith and trust in God by doing good things that made a difference in people's lives. Why wouldn't God have wanted him to stay on Earth longer?

She thought about how some people are like manure spreaders but that dad was like a joy spreader. He was funny about it, too. He would say things like, *You can be a peacemaker or a pieces maker.*

She smiled to herself as she thought about all of his teachings. He was gifted in storytelling. He told the types of stories that would paint pictures in your mind. They would stick in her thoughts, and she would mull them over.

This morning, she told herself, *Regardless of the reason why and if I will ever know, I still am glad I had my dad and mom as my parents rather than anyone else's parents.* She realized that when she kept her focus on working at the restaurant or at Cassandra's, it kept her mind on other things. She made a choice to get off this mental treadmill since it was actually going nowhere.

She regrouped her thoughts and planned out her day. She was a list maker and loved to see things checked off. *Focus, Elizabeth,* she told herself.

She got out her recipe books to look for some new ideas. The cooking was pretty fun, but at times, she would get stuck in a rut of repeating the same meals. She would often ask the boys what they were hungry for. Meatloaf and lasagna were among the boys' favorites.

Karl had picked up the deer meat, and they were all enjoying the deer jerky and bologna with cheese from Yoder Meats. True to their word, the boys had stocked up Johnny's dad with some deer jerky in exchange for the use of the hunting ground.

Karl had also checked in with the taxidermist who was getting the buck head made into a deer mount. It was a work in process but looking great. Karl claimed he couldn't wait to hang it above his bed, but Elizabeth had a sneaking suspicion that he was secretly planning on hanging it in living room. Hunters tend to do things like that. They want to let everyone see what they conquered.

After she was done looking for new recipes, Elizabeth was finally getting to think of herself for a change. She was constantly serving others, whether at the Essenhaus or at Cassandra's or her brothers. Her gift was serving, so she enjoyed it. But sometimes people who like to serve also need to serve themselves, too.

She was getting ready to sew some new dresses for the trip to Florida. She had cut out three new dresses and was excited to see them take shape. Willy also needed a few more shirts, so she was going to sew those as well.

Karl primarily dressed in English clothes since he turned 16 , which, truth be told, made it easier for Elizabeth. There were things like Amish church or weddings that Karl would wear Amish clothes to. It wasn't being fake to do that but rather respectful to the Amish people to wear clothes the church required. Karl understood the regulations and didn't want to offend people.

His dad wasn't like some people who believed that the youth should sow their wild oats. His dad actually said that was hogwash and that no one needed to sow anything wild. You harvest what you plant, according to Dan. He told his children that there were plenty of good, clean, fun things to do that weren't illegal and/or sinful. Their father always said, *You don't need to sin to have fun. It's all in the attitude of the heart.*

Elizabeth got most of her sewing finished but put it all away in time to make some chicken pot pie for supper. It was nice to have all three at home together. They talked about how happy they were to get out of this cold weather in a few weeks.

Karl told Elizabeth and Willy all about how he was at the game at Norwell when the Raiders defeated Norwell on their own field. It was probably one of the most exciting games he had ever been at because it meant the Raiders would get to play for a chance to go to the state finals.

After they ate, Karl needed to take a letter over to Joe and Amanda's that had been sent to their old address. He hadn't been back to the Home Place in months, and as he got closer, he almost stopped in his tracks. An unexpected wave of emotions swept over his tough exterior. He slowly walked to the door and knocked. Amanda opened the door and welcomed him inside. Her two little girls were giggling and laughing just like Barbara and Katie used to do.

Karl tried to be polite to Amanda, but his eyes kept scanning the house. She was so friendly, but he quickly began to feel uncomfortable and extremely homesick. He gave her the mail and then told her he was going to check to see if Joe was in the barn.

She said, "Joe ran over to the neighbors' house, but he should be back soon."

Karl walked toward the barn, and it loomed high in the air. It was one massive building compared to the smaller barn he had to maintain. He opened the barn door, and memories avalanched into his mind. Like a tsunami, he got hit with the truth that he missed Dad, Mom, and the girls more than he would like to admit.

He sat on a hay bale and let himself melt from a man to a boy and be the one whom was taken care of instead of being the man of the house. He realized he had pushed his family out of his mind because he simply had no ability to process it all. The alcohol might take the edge off and numb some of it, but it sure didn't make anything better.

He sat and thought about a conversation he and his dad had on numbers of occasions.

His dad had always talked about how important it was for people to take inventory of their lives and if they need to adjust or tweak some stuff, then to do that. His dad had told him that so many people live in *coulda woulda shoulda land* and that living in regret is no way to live.

He taught Karl that people often need to ask themselves these questions: What could I do with what I have? What should I do? What would I do if I could?

Dad had told him that often all we need to do is a ten-degree shift of our thoughts to change them from negative to positive.

In his mind, Karl scanned over his life. He was happy as he thought of his job and the construction work. He loved the crew, was a great worker, and was pleased with what he brought to the table. *Dad would be pleased with me*, he thought.

He loved the new barn, and the animals were doing well. *Dad would be impressed and also surprised at what a good job I'm doing.*

He was willing to let Mose be the person in charge of the finances, and it took a load off him. Dad would be grateful that Karl let Mose do that.

He thought of his hunting season and wished Dad could have seen the buck. He knew what Dad would have done. He would have tilted his head back and laughed. His dad was not a jokester like Mose, but when he could not believe something, he would tilt his head back in almost unbelief and laugh.

Karl thought of his relationships with Elizabeth and Willy and realized they had improved a lot since he cut back on his drinking.

He knew where they stood in their faith in God. It wasn't that he didn't believe in God. He knew it was God who was helping the family get by.

As he sat thinking about God, he heard *I got your back, Karl* in his mind.

There was that small, still voice again. It felt good to know God loved to talk to him, even if he wasn't yet fully giving God his all. It really touched Karl pretty deeply to know God was covering his back. It was a thought he could understand because he'd been so intrigued with watching the Raiders cover each other's backs, especially their quarterback.

"Thanks, God," he whispered as he wiped a few tears out of his eyes.

He got up and walked through the rest of the barn. He saw a verse his dad had painted on the barn wall: *They that wait upon the Lord shall renew their strength, they shall mount up with wings as eagles; they shall run, and not be weary; and they shall walk, and not faint* (Isaiah 40:31).

He smiled as he thought about that verse. He could hear his dad saying, *If you want to fly like an eagle, you can't stay with the chickens on the ground.*

Joe never did show up, so Karl biked home deep in thought.

He knew that sometime he wanted a life with God in it. He realized the anger at Blake was gone and that he wasn't mad about not getting to have a truck. He was actually developing a good attitude, and out of his mouth came, "You are your dad's son."

Even though he was more of a jokester like Mose, Karl also had a serious side to him, too.

On November 21st, Karl was at the game when the Raiders lost their chance to go on to play at the state finals. It was a heartbreaking end for the players, but the community was really proud of the team's accomplishments and all the hurdles they had overcome. It would still be a season to be remembered for quite some time in this small town. Karl knew some of the players and afterward got to tell them he was sorry about their loss. One of his friends on the team said, "Karl, if anyone understands heartbreaking loss it would be you, so thanks for caring."

Elizabeth, Karl, and Willy spent Thanksgiving Day at Mose and Carrie's house with all of the Miller relatives. It was a loud house brimming to the full capacity of people. When the three children arrived, they smelled the food and knew it was going to be a feast. Elizabeth had made some taco rollups and some puppy chow for later in the day.

The cousins were already breaking out the games, and the laughter rang all through the house. The young children could be heard playing in the basement, and the men were sitting around talking in the living room. The women were in the kitchen working on the big meal. The children shook hands with the uncles and some married cousins, and then Elizabeth went to help the women in the kitchen. Karl and Willy both found their cousins who were closest to them in age and hung out with them until the women told everyone that dinner was ready.

Mose had to work to get everyone together for the meal. Once they all congregated in the kitchen and dining room, Mose said, "We're glad you could all make it today. We want to pray before we eat." Then the entire Miller family bowed their heads and silently prayed.

Because there were so many people, dinner was served buffet-style, and different family members sat at a few different areas of the house. For the Thanksgiving meal, they had turkey, ham, mashed potatoes, dressing, gravy, sweet potato casserole, applesauce, salad, homemade bread, strawberry jam, and apple butter. For dessert, the women had baked four kinds of pie: pumpkin pie, custard, and two cream pies (coconut and chocolate).

The children had a blast playing Dutch Blitz and Rook. Karl's age group played a ping pong tournament. The men sat around talking and laughing, and every now and then, one of them would take a short nap.

The songbooks were brought out in the early afternoon, and oh the singing that went on. . . The song that touched Elizabeth most was "When the Roll is Called up Yonder." She noticed she wasn't the only one grabbing for a Kleenex and thinking of her parents. They were all so glad for family because it felt so natural to be there. Of course, people missed Dan, Sarah, and the girls, but they were going to do all they could to make sure the children knew they were here for them.

In the early evening hours, the food started appearing again. This time, it was all kinds of finger foods: meatballs, White trash, fruit pizza, and the list went on and on. The children were stuffed with food by the time everyone started calling it a day and headed for home.

November was bitterly cold but had no snow. The week after Thanksgiving was hectic for Elizabeth, as she was scheduled for some banquets. She loved how the Essenhaus looked when it was decorated for Christmas. Everyone seemed more cheerful during this season. There were a lot of Christmas parties for businesses and church groups.

At home, she also decorated for Christmas but not with a Christmas tree, as Amish people don't have Christmas trees. She had set out some pretty candles with some greenery around them and opened the Bible to the Christmas story.

The Miller family normally drew names among themselves, and each person would get a gift for the person's name drawn but this would be the first year that the three would be alone to open gifts. Amish people do buy each other Christmas gifts, but they normally hide them in their closets until Christmas.

Elizabeth doubted that the boys would get her anything, but she got each of them some new hunting gloves and a few things to take along to Florida.

Chapter 26

December started with a blizzard that came from a lake effect snow. It looked like a winter wonderland. It was calm outside, so the snow piled straight up on everything. Every single tree branch had an inch or two of snow on it. Willy's school and Karl's work were cancelled for the day. Needless to say, the boys were ecstatic. The Miller children got out the Monopoly game and popped some Lady Finger popcorn to munch on while they played. The game lasted most of the day, and Karl won by a long shot. As if he wasn't big-headed enough, he rubbed it in, acting as if he could have won in his sleep. The others just laughed at him.

In the afternoon, they bundled up and went outside to enjoy the snow. The dogs loved it and ran around jumping in the snow. The boys built a snowman, and Willy and Elizabeth ganged up against Karl in a snowball fight. They tried to bring him down a notch.

The boys decided to do the chores earlier than usual and headed for the barn to check on all of the animals. Elizabeth walked toward the house and heard the wind chimes breaking the quiet with their soft tune. She noted that the wind must be picking up a bit because she hadn't heard the chimes all day. It reminded her of many cold winter evenings when she used to curl up on the couch at the Home Place to read her *Little House on the Prairie* books. She smiled at those memories. Today, she had made some new memories.

She saw the snowplow go by and was glad they could get out if they needed to, but it was also fun to be in hibernation. Life in Northern Indiana always sped by too fast, so the snowstorms were a way of putting the brakes on life and forcing everyone to slow down.

Later that evening, the wind began howling, and because it was a soft, light snow, it just blew like crazy. White-out conditions fell upon them in a hurry. The snow seemed to be drifting the road closed again, the road that the crews had worked hard to open. The region was now under a winter weather advisory, and only emergency vehicles were allowed out on the roads. Drivers caught on the roads could find themselves in trouble with the law. The storm was that dangerous.

By the next morning, the winds had died down, and Karl's crew was able to pick him up on time. However, Willy's school was delayed two hours. The only way they knew about the delay was because Karl had looked it up on his phone before he left. Elizabeth thought of a lot of other Amish kids who would have no way of knowing of the delay. They would probably think it was cancelled until the bus driver honked the horn. Hopefully they could get out to the bus in time.

She asked Willy to help her bake cookies until he left. He was excited to help and taste some for her, too. She was baking ten dozen cookies for the Gospel Echoes Ministry Prison Ministry Cookie Day and also wanted to bake some for the boys as well.

Gospel Echoes took cookies to prison inmates to hand out, and her heart was deeply invested in this cause because of all the prayers she had prayed for Blake. Elizabeth had written him a number of letters expressing the children's forgiveness. The boys weren't big letter writers, so they had never written him but wanted to meet him.

That day finally came. Karl, Willy and Elizabeth were finally getting to visit Blake in prison. They weren't sure what to expect. When they arrived at the prison, they were led into a waiting area where they sat down at a table. The door opened, and a cop stepped inside with a young-looking man. He immediately turned to Elizabeth and politely shook her hand and then Willy's. Last, he looked at Karl, and in just that instant, these two connected.

Elizabeth was stunned when she met Blake. She had imagined what he was going to look like. She had met his dad, who had looked like an unkempt mess. She had assumed that Blake would look exactly the same, but Blake looked quite the opposite – very clean-cut. His haircut showed he had style, and even though he was dressed in prison clothes, he walked with class and confidence.

Blake spoke first. "Thanks for coming to see me. I've wanted to meet all of you and apologize in person. Man, I hope you can forgive me. I wish I could rewind that day and rewrite it."

Karl said, "You can't beat yourself up over it. There's nothing you can change about the past. This sucks for all of us, but we don't hate you. We wish we'd have the power to get you out of here. If it was up to us, we'd get you out today."

Willy and Elizabeth nodded their heads in agreement.

"It means a lot that you apologized to us," Elizabeth said.

"Yeah, we forgive you," Willy added.

And with that, the conversation swiftly switched to hunting.

Blake told the boys, "I heard you two like to hunt." Karl got all excited and told Blake all about his big buck.

Blake said, "I love the woods; it's my favorite place on Earth. Sometimes I'm in my cell, and I just lie on the bunk, close my eyes, and imagine I'm walking the trails through the woods. It keeps me sane in here. Well, that and the basketball. I play a lot of hoops."

CORINA YODER

Karl found that interesting that the prisoners were allowed to play basketball. Elizabeth sat and politely listened to the guys talking. The guard eventually came over and told Blake he had ten minutes left in his visit. At that point, Blake's full attention quickly switched to all three children.

He looked directly at Elizabeth and said, "I know your parents were Christians, and I know they are in heaven, but if I could bring them back, I would. I want you to know that I pray every single day for all three of you. The prison chaplain is awesome, and he has helped me forgive myself. But I can't tell you what it means to me to see you three laugh and smile. I am glad God is helping you cope with the loss. You three are very strong, and the strength you have shows that you were brought up well."

As the visit came to a close, Elizabeth watched both brothers give Blake a hug. He then politely nodded his head at her. She told him it was good to meet him, and in turn, he replied that the pleasure was all his. Then he was escorted out, the doors locking behind him.

On the way home from prison, the children talked about how shocked they all were at the way he carried himself. Elizabeth said, "God must have helped him overcome his childhood."

Willy sat quietly thinking for a good while and finally said, "I wish I could go get his dad and stick him in there to trade places with Blake."

It made Karl and Elizabeth laugh because Willy normally saw the best in everyone. Then in all seriousness, he looked at Karl and said, "You'd better never *even think* of drinking and driving." Willy wasn't saying it in a condescending, judgmental way but rather out of love for his brother and the safety of his life. He loved Karl dearly from the bottom of his kind heart.

ELIZABETH

Karl heard it loud and clear. He didn't reply out loud but knew at that moment that he wanted to be a brother whom Willy could look up to. He knew he couldn't change, grow, and develop entirely on his own, but he remembered the words he had heard in the barn: *I got your back, Karl.*

He knew with God's help, he could be a dependable big brother.

Back at the prison, Blake got escorted back to his cell. It was a heartbreaking situation because before the tragedy, Blake had been working on staying sober and becoming a man of integrity. He was becoming the man God had created him to be when his bad choices had ended up costing him a lot more than just the cash he had spent on the alcohol and hard liquor.

Blake decided that he needed to blow off some steam and went to play basketball. He was normally pretty even-keeled, but today as he played, he even got irritated with his friends. One of his close friends got in his face, and Blake was about to physically retaliate. It was about to erupt into a big fight. People were going to get hurt. Blake felt himself getting to the place like he used to get to when his dad used to corner him and beat him. He felt backed in a corner, unable to escape, and today, he felt caged. In truth, he was.

A friend pulled him off the court and said, "Man, what's up with you?"

In frustration, Blake said, "The Amish kids came in to see me today. You know, the ones whose parents and sisters I hit and killed when I was drinking."

"Oh man. Come with me. We gotta find the chaplain before you get into a fight that is not worth getting hurt over. God forgave you. The kids forgave you. It sounds like you gotta forgive yourself again. Sometimes we are the toughest on ourselves."

"You're right," Blake replied somberly. "Thanks for getting me out of there because I was mad enough to flatten all of you. He then followed his friend to find the chaplain.

The second weekend in December marked the Christmas gift that Cassandra's Amish workers would never forget. Cassandra took them to Chicago for the weekend and paid for everything.

She hired a car service to drive them downtown. Cassandra, Ridge and the five Amish girls' first stop was Navy Pier. She took them to see all of the Christmas decorations and go ice skating in the big indoor ice arena. Cassandra wouldn't let Ridge skate due to the injuries he suffered in his accident. It irritated him, but he did listen to her. The irony of it all was that he was a California surfer who was not afraid to swim in the same water as sharks, but he was sitting off to the side in an ice skating rink guarding all of the Amish girls' purses, watching them get to have fun.

Cassandra told the girls that she wanted to buy them all a Chicago souvenir, so all of the girls picked out a snow globe from Chicago with the skyline inside of it. Then, she whisked them off to the Weber Grill for dinner. They enjoyed every bite.

She had booked rooms at the Embassy Suites Hotel, which was within walking distance of Michigan Avenue, so after dark, they walked downtown. The girls marveled at all of the lights. Cassandra showed the girls the two buildings where Nik Wallenda had walked blindfolded on a high wire between a mere month earlier. They ended their evening at Starbucks to get some hot chocolate to warm up before heading back to their hotel.

The girls loved the ice skating so much that Cassandra said they could go again the next day. They got to sleep in and then ate an early dinner at the Cheesecake Factory. True to her word, Cassandra took them ice skating again, but this time, they went to the outdoor ice skating rink on Michigan Avenue at the Millennium Park. They drew some attention as people marveled at their skating abilities while in dresses. The girls were used to skating on ponds wearing dresses, so this experience wasn't all that unusual for them.

It was the perfect evening for ice skating because snow fell softly on the rink as the girls skated. And the normal high winds of the Windy City were unusually calm tonight. The famous Chicago skyline lit up the darkness of a winter evening in the Midwest. Cassandra smiled as she fell asleep knowing she had pampered them with a fun, memorable weekend.

The next morning, she had the driver take them back to Shipshewana and the familiar land of horses and buggies. The last stop was taking the girls to the Glow bookstore and letting each girl pick out two books. Again, Cassandra picked up the tab for each purchase. The books would give them something to read over their Christmas break, she said. Elizabeth was so excited because she would take her books along to Florida to pass the time on the bus and to read on the beach.

A week later, as Elizabeth finished her last shift at the Essenhaus before the trip to Florida, she felt drawn outside to take a walk out to the Essenhaus Covered Bridge.

The snow had cloaked every piece of grass, and the wind was still. Someone had cleared the road going out to the bridge, but a new layer of fresh snow crunched under her shoes. As she walked, snow began to gently fall yet again. She smiled because it was almost magical. It was hard to believe that six months had passed since the day she had fallen apart on this bridge. A lot of water had gone under the bridge. So many places in her broken heart had been healed. She no longer felt like an orphan but rather that God was her dad. She could daily relate to Him and tell Him anything.

Her heart felt peaceful. She felt completely at rest within. Her mind thought of her dad, mom, and her sisters Barbara and Katie. She could imagine them smiling and happy.

Her life this year had been completely turned upside down, but God had steadied her heart. She had lots of hope for a good year ahead.

She had lost four amazing people this year, but God also gave her four amazing new friends: Blake, Cassandra, Ridge, and Susan. They would never replace her family, but they sure had helped to ease the trauma and heartbreak. They had been a big part of her healing journey.

Blake was thrust into Elizabeth's life in an awful way, but God still used it for good. Blake's life was spared from death, and he would be used by God to influence men to find true life and freedom, even behind prison walls.

Ridge turned out to be such a shocking and unexpected blessing. Elizabeth still marveled at the rerouting of his motorcycle road trip that caused Cassandra to find God.

Cassandra had hired a private detective to locate Ridge's mom and to rescue her out of a destructive lifestyle. Cassandra and Ridge were flying to Arizona over Christmas to see her. Cassandra felt like the Amish girls and Ridge were her new family and loved them deeply.

The one who really got to Elizabeth, as she reflected back, was Susan. Elizabeth reached up, touched her heart, and said aloud, "Oh, my dear Susan. What a gift from God."

Susan was so precious to her. She had taught Elizabeth how to journal and how to talk to God as her dad. She had taught her how to hear from God, too. She was a living, breathing example of a person living out the Spirit of Christ. Susan didn't only know about Jesus, but she knew Him. She had the Holy Spirit running out of her like the living water talked about in the Bible.

Elizabeth had tried to convince Susan to come to Florida with her for Christmas, but she had already agreed to host some guests in her bed and breakfast for Christmas. The guests were visiting from England, so she knew it would be an interesting group to host.

The last person Elizabeth thought about was herself. God had made beauty out of the ashes and had turned the tears in the night into joy in the morning. She realized how strong she actually was. She had often felt weak and unable to do it all, but God had given her a lot of perseverance and tenacity to get through a lot of adversity. She could see the wisdom and strength of her dad flowing out of her life as well as the kind gentleness of her mom. For anyone who knew her parents, it was easy to see that Elizabeth was a mixture of both of them.

Thinking of their marriage and love for each other reminded Elizabeth that her dad had always told her, *you'll know him when you see* him, referring to the man with whom she was supposed to share her life. Her mind instantly thought of John Hostetler. She had not seen him since the day she had biked past his house, but she thought of him quite often.

Her heart would be wide open to having John be a part of her life. He was exactly the kind of guy she wanted in her future. The problem was, she had incorrectly assumed the girl he was talking to on that day eliminated the chance of John and Elizabeth being together.

The truth was that John was very much single and had only been speaking to his niece. Elizabeth was still unaware of their relationship.

As she paused on the bridge to look out over the snow-covered landscape, she could feel the presence of God surrounding her, and in her thoughts, she heard His gentle voice saying, *Elizabeth, you are a crown in my hands.*

She knew that verse well. Susan had drawn a picture of God's hands holding a crown and had written the verse beneath the picture: *The Lord will hold you in His hands for all to see – a splendid crown in the hand of God* - Isaiah 62:3 (NLT). She felt precious and loved by God.

The wind picked up a bit and blew in her face as she headed down the lane. She thought of the upcoming trip and smiled at thoughts of warm weather, beaches and palm trees. She walked down the path back toward the restaurant, and lo and behold, she saw two cardinals perched against the white snow. The snow glistened like diamonds, and the birds brought out a lot of comfort. She knew who had placed the birds there.

Thank you, God, she whispered aloud in Dutch.

A Message and a Prayer from Corina Yoder

Hello, friend,

I hope you enjoyed reading the story of the Miller family. I have personally experienced the love of God in my life. I am forever grateful for what Jesus did for me on the cross by dying for my sins. John 3:16 says, "For God so loved the World that He gave His only begotten Son, that whoever believes in Him should not perish but have everlasting life."

If you would like to receive the free gift of forgiveness and the weight of sin lifted off your life, pray this prayer with me:

> *Dear God, I admit I've made a mess of trying to run my own life, and I admit that I have sinned and need Your grace and forgiveness. I understand that You sent Your son Jesus to give His life by dying on the cross for my sins, and it wipes my slate clean. Thank You for forgiving me of all of my sins. That kind of love is unfathomable, but I thank You for it. I choose to repent and turn from my old life and ask You to move into me and take over my life. Fill me up to overflowing with the Holy Spirit and the fruits of the Spirit, which are love, joy, peace, patience, kindness, goodness, faithfulness, gentleness and self-control. I ask all these things in Jesus' name, Amen.*

If you have ever been involved in pow-wowing or played games like the Ouija board, pray this prayer with me if you would like to be set free:

> *Father God, I would like to be fully and totally cleansed of involvement in witchcraft and games like the Ouija board. If I have ever used power other than Yours to heal or have been*

healed by power other than God's power, I ask You, God, to take back the ground in my life that I gave the enemy access to and ask that Jesus would set me free of the hold it has over my life. I renounce and reject all the curses, spells, and evil assignments over my life and ask You to create a new spirit within me. Thank you for that. Teach me to be wise.

If there are any areas of my life that I believe lies about myself (like Cassandra did in the book), please show me the lies and replace them with Your truth. Thank you, God. Amen.

Thanks for reading *Elizabeth*. If this book has encouraged you or helped you on your journey, I would love to hear from you.

Corina Yoder

PO Box 22092 Sarasota Florida, 34276

www.corinayoder.com

Coming soon...a book of Elizabeth's favorite recipes

John: Book 2 of the Set Free Series
Chapter 1

John was in a deep sleep when his nephew's phone started ringing. The ringtone was loud, and the hotel room was still pitch black. His nephew Jeremy answered, and by then, John and Jeremy were both wide awake. They were deep in the heart of Texas visiting John's old stomping grounds. John was enjoying watching Jeremy experience Texas for the very first time: He was seeing ranches and longhorns and eating some delicious barbecue. He couldn't believe all of the Texas state flags flying everywhere. It was true: everything *was* bigger in Texas.

By only hearing one side of the conversation, John could tell that Jeremy was being asked to come to play in the volleyball tournament in Pinecraft, a tiny village in Sarasota, Florida. Since John Hostetler had joined the Amish church, he often hired young Amish guys to drive him, and now he had a feeling where his driver was going to be heading. John knew he could hop a train or the bus to head back home to Indiana, but that choice included the snow. The other option would be to join Jeremy and head for the Sunshine State. If he picked that option, he would get to enjoy Christmas in warm weather.

John just shook his head and chuckled to himself, thinking, *Jeremy is a bit of an Amish Gypsy like me. We love to wander and explore new places.*

Sure enough, Jeremy wanted to get to Sarasota so he could play in the volleyball tournament. He punched in San Antonio to Sarasota on the GPS. "It's only 1,230 miles," Jeremy told John. "I think a good day's drive will get us there."

It didn't take them long to pack up and for John to decide to go South with Jeremy. It was good that John was flexible and loved adventure. He thought to himself, *why not*? Quite appropriately, the song "On the Road Again" played through the radio as they left San Antonio. The route was quite easy: they would take the 10 all the way to the 75.

For the Miller children in northern Indiana, the week before leaving for Florida was brutally cold. Not too much snow fell, but the arctic temperatures made it so miserable to be outside for any length of time. All of the nasty weather created even bigger excitement in them for their upcoming trip to a warmer climate. Karl felt like his fingers were going to be frozen, and whenever he got home from work, he took extra long hot showers. The house was normally pretty easy to heat, but the low wind chill factors were causing the furnace to work extra hard. Willy was not one to complain much about anything, but even he was getting tired of the miserable weather.

The bus they were taking ran back and forth into the Amish communities, and they left from the Yoders' parking lot in Shipshewana at 4 on Friday afternoon. They traveled all night.

By Saturday afternoon, the bus crossed the Georgia/Florida state line, and many of the passengers cheered. The bus stopped at the Welcome Center just inside of Florida, and they all enjoyed some free fresh orange juice. Then they were also given the choice between a free orange or grapefruit.

A few hours later, the bus slowed down and turned off at the Fruitville exit. The boys high fived each other, and all three children knew it meant they would be rolling into Pinecraft in the next 15 minutes. Many in the Amish and Mennonite communities visit or own winter homes in this community. Very few stay year-round.

The parking lot the bus pulled into was packed with people waiting for the bus to unload. Many were meeting friends and family, but many others were just curious to see who had arrived. It was the highlight of the day to watch who came to Florida. Elizabeth, Karl, and Willy unloaded all of their suitcases and rolled them the three blocks to Uncle Roger's house. The streets were packed with people. Little children were biking on tricycles up and down the streets, and the older Amish stood around visiting. Karl and Willy had brought along their basketball, so they dropped off their bags, quickly changed, and ran down to the famous Pinecraft Park. The park was full of people shuffling at the shuffleboard courts. Several others were sitting and visiting while they watched the shufflers. The Miller boys got there in time to join two teams and play a game of basketball.

Karl made plans to go to Siesta Key Village with some friends and then go play beach volleyball at Siesta Key Beach. The plans started with eight of them going, and by the time they met up, a group of 20 representing seven different states had formed. They all enjoyed the live music and open air dining. As they dined, a singer belted out Jimmy Buffet's beach-themed songs, creating quite the island atmosphere. For these Midwestern Amish kids, Florida was a different world. After they ate, they walked around the shops and bought some souvenirs before heading back to the beach. The sunset that God painted that evening was magnificent, and the kids played volleyball until dark.

Elizabeth and Willy met up with some cousins for dinner at the Der Dutchman Restaurant. There was a 45-minute wait for a table, so they meandered around in the gift shop. Elizabeth found a card to send Susan and some postcards to send Mose's kids.

The dinner was well worth the wait. They all got the buffet and enjoyed the fried chicken and mashed potatoes. The food was similar to the food she served at the Essenhaus back in Indiana. The two restaurants were owned by the same owners: Bob and Sue Miller. There was nothing like a good home-cooked meal. Willy wanted to get a pie to take home, but he couldn't seem to make up his mind. He didn't know whether to go with the strawberry pie or the pecan pie.

Their group walked to where John Schmid, a well-known singer and comedian from Ohio, was singing. He kept the crowd laughing and entertained. Willy and his male cousins biked all over Pinecraft, and their last stop of the night was to get some ice cream at Big Olaf's. Though there was a line well outside of the entrance, most of the customers, including Willy and his cousins, used the wait as an opportunity to catch up with each other and even make new friends.

On Monday, all three of the Millers went to the Siesta Key Beach to enjoy the number one beach in the entire state and, according to Trip Advisor, the number one beach in the entire country. Getting there was half the experience. The beach is located on an island, so they crossed bridges to get there. A driver dropped them off at 10, and the beach was already flooding with people. The sand was the finest, whitest sand. They all took off their sandals and walked in it as soon as they could. The beach had four lifeguard stations that were painted red, yellow, green and blue. The color coding helped people remember where they had been sunbathing and also helped them meet up with others.

It was a perfect day: the weather was in the low 80s without a cloud in the sky. They picked a spot near the yellow lifeguard station, and the boys immediately went to the water. It was a bit chilly at first, but they soon adjusted to the temperature. The colors of the water varied from blues to shades of aqua. In the horizon, the blue of the water met the blue sky, and it perfectly contrasted against the white sand on the beach. The scenery was perfectly designed by God.

Elizabeth sat and read a book for a bit and then enjoyed a long nap with the sounds of the waves putting her to a restful state of mind. It felt heavenly to feel the sun shining and to hear the boys laughing and having fun together.

She read a few chapters of Susan's writings. Susan was explaining how we can ask God for direction in our lives and also that we can ask Him for confirmation, too. Susan wrote out James 1: 5 (NASB): *But if any of you lacks wisdom, let him ask of God, who gives to all generously and without reproach, and it will be given to him.*

Susan also taught about God's promise in Jeremiah 29:11 (NLT): *For I know the plans I have for you,* says the Lord, *they are plans for good and not for disaster, to give you a future and a hope.*

Elizabeth decided to write to God:

> *Thank you, God, for this new memory with the boys. I'm so glad we are here over Christmas. Thank You for giving us direction so many times this year, and again, I ask for Your help and direction. I believe the verse that my future is for good and with hope. Give me wisdom from You. I know You will heal us because I can see You have done a lot of that already. I appreciate all You did for us and for me personally this year.*

Elizabeth told the boys she was going on a walk along the beach. As she was walking, a smile kept coming onto her face. This was paradise. God and salt water heal the soul.

The waves were washing up some seashells, and she picked up a few as she walked along. She was lost in deep thought and began watching a boat pulling some parasailers. On the beach ahead of her, she could see a young man walking toward her. She could tell he was Amish, but a few walkers got into her line of vision. All of the sudden, the young man was directly in front of her. They were both shocked and surprised that it was the other. Right here in front of her was John Hostetler, and at the same time, Elizabeth and John asked each other, "What are you doing here?"

ELIZABETH

Made in the USA
Charleston, SC
30 October 2015